BRIAN FLYNN

THE ORANGE AXE

With an introduction by
Steve Barge

DEAN STREET PRESS

Published by Dean Street Press 2019

Copyright © 1931 Brian Flynn

Introduction © 2019 Steve Barge

All Rights Reserved

The right of Brian Flynn to be identified as the Author of the Work has been asserted by his estate in accordance with the Copyright, Designs and Patents Act 1988.

First published in 1931 by John Long

Cover by DSP

ISBN 978 1 913054 51 9

www.deanstreetpress.co.uk

BRIAN FLYNN
THE ORANGE AXE

BRIAN FLYNN was born in 1885 in Leyton, Essex. He won a scholarship to the City Of London School, and from there went into the civil service. In World War I he served as Special Constable on the Home Front, also teaching "Accountancy, Languages, Maths and Elocution to men, women, boys and girls" in the evenings, and acting in his spare time.

It was a seaside family holiday that inspired Brian Flynn to turn his hand to writing in the mid-twenties. Finding most mystery novels of the time "mediocre in the extreme", he decided to compose his own. Edith, the author's wife, encouraged its completion, and after a protracted period finding a publisher, it was eventually released in 1927 by John Hamilton in the UK and Macrae Smith in the U.S. as *The Billiard-Room Mystery*.

The author died in 1958. In all, he wrote and published 57 mysteries, the vast majority featuring the super-sleuth Antony Bathurst.

INTRODUCTION

"I believe that the primary function of the mystery story is to entertain; to stimulate the imagination and even, at times, to supply humour. But it pleases the connoisseur most when it presents – and reveals – genuine mystery. To reach its full height, it has to offer an intellectual problem for the reader to consider, measure and solve."

THUS WROTE Brian Flynn in the *Crime Book Magazine* in 1948, setting out his ethos on writing detective fiction. At that point in his career, Flynn had published thirty-six mystery novels, beginning with *The Billiard-Room Mystery* in 1927 – he went on, before his death in 1958, to write twenty-one more, three under the pseudonym Charles Wogan. So how is it that the general reading populace – indeed, even some of the most ardent collectors of mystery fiction – were until recently unaware of his existence? The reputation of writers such as John Rhode survived their work being out of print, so what made Flynn and his books vanish so completely?

There are many factors that could have contributed to Flynn's disappearance. For reasons unknown, he was not a member of either The Detection Club or the Crime Writers' Association, two of the best ways for a writer to network with others. As such, his work never appeared in the various collaborations that those groups published. The occasional short story in such a collection can be a way of maintaining awareness of an author's name, but it seems that Brian Flynn wrote no short stories at all, something rare amongst crime writers.

There are a few mentions of him in various studies of the genre over the years. Sutherland Scott, in *Blood in Their Ink* (1953), states that Flynn, who was still writing at the time, "has long been popular". He goes on to praise *The Mystery of the Peacock's Eye* (1928) as containing "one of the ablest pieces of misdirection one could wish to meet". Anyone reading that particular review who feels like picking up the novel – out now from Dean Street Press – should stop reading at that point, as later in the book, Scott proceeds to casually spoil the ending, although as if he assumes that everyone will have read the novel already.

It is a later review, though, that may have done much to end – temporarily, I hope – Flynn's popularity.

> "Straight tripe and savorless. It is doubtful, on the evidence, if any of his others would be different."

Thus wrote Jacques Barzun and Wendell Hertig Taylor in their celebrated work, *A Catalog of Crime* (1971). The book was an ambitious attempt to collate and review every crime fiction author, past and present. They presented brief reviews of some titles, a bibliography of some authors and a short biography of others. It is by no means complete – E & M.A. Radford had written thirty-six novels at this point in time but garner no mention – but it might have helped Flynn's reputation if he too had been overlooked. Instead one of the contributors picked up *Conspiracy at Angel* (1947), the thirty-second Anthony Bathurst title. I believe that title has a number of things to enjoy about it, but as a mystery, it doesn't match the quality of the majority of Flynn's output. Dismissing a writer's entire work on the basis of a single volume is questionable, but with the amount of crime writers they were trying to catalogue, one can, just about, understand the decision. But that decision meant that they missed out on a large number of truly entertaining mysteries that fully embrace the spirit of the Golden Age of Detection, and, moreover, many readers using the book as a reference work may have missed out as well.

So who was Brian Flynn? Born in 1885 in Leyton, Essex, Flynn won a scholarship to the City Of London School, and while he went into the civil service (ranking fourth in the whole country on the entrance examination) rather than go to university, the classical education that he received there clearly stayed with him. Protracted bouts of rheumatic fever prevented him fighting in the Great War, but instead he served as a Special Constable on the Home Front – one particular job involved warning the populace about Zeppelin raids armed only with a bicycle, a whistle and a placard reading "TAKE COVER". Flynn worked for the local government while teaching "Accountancy, Languages, Maths and Elocution to men, women, boys and girls" in the evening, and acting as part of the Trevalyan Players in his spare time.

It was a seaside family holiday that inspired him to turn his hand to writing. He asked his librarian to supply him a collection of mystery novels for "deck-chair reading" only to find himself disappointed. In his own words, they were "mediocre in the extreme." There is no record of what those books were, unfortunately, but on arriving home, the following conversation, again in Brian's own words, occurred:

> "ME (unpacking the books): If I couldn't write better stuff than any of these, I'd eat my own hat.
>
> Mrs ME (after the manner of women and particularly after the manner of wives): It's a great pity you don't do a bit more and talk a bit less.
>
> The shaft struck home. I accepted the challenge, laboured like the mountain and produced *The Billiard-Room Mystery*."

"Mrs ME", or Edith as most people referred to her, deserves our gratitude. While there were some delays with that first book, including Edith finding the neglected half-finished manuscript in a drawer where it had been "resting" for six months, and a protracted period finding a publisher, it was eventually released in 1927 by John Hamilton in the UK and Macrae Smith in the U.S. According to Flynn, John Hamilton asked for five more, but in fact they only published five in total, all as part of the Sundial Mystery Library imprint. Starting with *The Five Red Fingers* (1929), Flynn was published by John Long, who would go on to publish all of his remaining novels, bar his single non-series title, *Tragedy At Trinket* (1934). About ten of his early books were reprinted in the US before the war, either by Macrae Smith, Grosset & Dunlap or Mill, and a few titles also appeared in France, Denmark, Germany and Sweden, but the majority of his output only saw print in the United Kingdom. Some titles were reprinted during his lifetime – the John Long Four-Square Thrillers paperback range featured some Flynn titles, for example – but John Long's primary focus was the library market, and some titles had relatively low print runs. Currently, the majority of Flynn's work, in particular that only published in the U.K., is extremely rare – not just expensive, but seemingly non-existent even in the second-hand book market.

In the aforementioned article, Flynn states that the tales of Sherlock Holmes were a primary inspiration for his writing, having read them at a young age. A conversation in *The Billiard-Room Mystery* hints at other influences on his writing style. A character, presumably voicing Flynn's own thoughts, states that he is a fan of "the pre-war Holmes". When pushed further, he states that:

> "Mason's M. Hanaud, Bentley's Trent, Milne's Mr Gillingham and to a lesser extent, Agatha Christie's M. Poirot are all excellent in their way, but oh! – the many dozens that aren't."

He goes on to acknowledge the strengths of Bernard Capes' "Baron" from *The Mystery of The Skeleton Key* and H.C. Bailey's Reggie Fortune, but refuses to accept Chesterton's Father Brown.

> "He's entirely too Chestertonian. He deduces that the dustman was the murderer because of the shape of the piece that had been cut from the apple-pie."

Perhaps this might be the reason that the invitation to join the Detection Club never arrived . . .

Flynn created a sleuth that shared a number of traits with Holmes, but was hardly a carbon-copy. Enter Anthony Bathurst, a polymath and gentleman sleuth, a man of contradictions whose background is never made clear to the reader. He clearly has money, as he has his own rooms in London with a pair of servants on call and went to public school (Uppingham) and university (Oxford). He is a follower of all things that fall under the banner of sport, in particular horse racing and cricket, the latter being a sport that he could, allegedly, have represented England at. He is also a bit of a show-off, littering his speech (at times) with classical quotes, the obscurer the better, provided by the copies of the *Oxford Dictionary of Quotations* and *Brewer's Dictionary of Phrase & Fable* that Flynn kept by his writing desk, although Bathurst generally restrains himself to only doing this with people who would appreciate it or to annoy the local constabulary. He is fond of amateur dramatics (as was Flynn, a well-regarded amateur thespian who appeared in at least one self-penned play, *Blue Murder*), having been a member of OUDS, the Oxford University Dramatic Society. Like Holmes, Bathurst isn't averse to the occasional disguise, and as with Watson and Holmes, sometimes even his close allies don't recognise him. General information about his background is light on the ground. His parents were Irish, but he doesn't have an accent – see *The Spiked Lion* (1933) – and his eyes are grey. We learn in *The Orange Axe* that he doesn't pursue romantic relationships due to a bad experience in his first romance. That doesn't remain the case throughout the series – he falls head over heels in love in *Fear and Trembling*, for example – but in this opening tranche of titles, we don't see Anthony distracted by the fairer sex, not even one who will only entertain gentlemen who can beat her at golf!

Unlike a number of the Holmes' stories, Flynn's Bathurst tales are all fairly clued mysteries, perhaps a nod to his admiration of Christie, but first and foremost, Flynn was out to entertain the reader. The problems posed to Bathurst have a flair about them – the simultaneous murders, miles apart, in *The Case of the Black Twenty-Two* (1928) for example, or the scheme to draw lots to commit masked murder in *The Orange Axe* – and there is a momentum to the narrative. Some mystery writers have trouble with the pace slowing between the reveal of the problem and the reveal of the murderer, but Flynn's books sidestep that, with Bathurst's investigations never seeming to sag. He writes with a wit and intellect that can make even the most prosaic of interviews with suspects enjoyable to read about, and usually provides an action-packed finale before the murderer is finally revealed. Some of those revelations, I think it is fair to say, are surprises that can rank with some of the best in crime fiction.

We are fortunate that we can finally reintroduce Brian Flynn and Anthony Lotherington Bathurst to the many fans of classic crime fiction out there.

The Orange Axe (1931)

"Gentlemen – I am going to kill André de Ravenac."

BRIAN FLYNN made an effort to do something original with each of his books. Most of these ideas cannot be discussed in any introduction without spoiling details of the plot. Some of these are subtle ideas as part of the solution, some of them more obvious, such as the murder in a house under siege in *Invisible Death*, or being strangled while alone on the top deck of a bus in *Murder En Route*. *The Orange Axe* is another example of the originality being in the set-up.

Major Daniel Wyatt gathers a group of six people together in the back room of Ricardo's restaurant in Soho – Wyatt himself, two sets of brothers and a journalist, all of whom are acquainted with André de Ravenac. De Ravenac is at best a blackmailer, but most probably a serial murderer, Le Loup de Poignard – the Dagger Wolf – who plagued Paris six years previously, and is currently threatening to destroy the life of a woman who all of the men care about. Hence a plan is hatched – De Ravenac is to be killed at a masked ball – but once all of the men agree to the plan, lots are drawn. Each is assigned a random role in the plan – as they are all of roughly the same build and will be wearing masks, nobody will know which of them is the man who carries out the fatal blow . . .

At the point, the pedantic reader may be questioning the logic of this plan. Surely there are easier methods of murder, and the idea that if one of the group is caught, they will not know who the murderer is . . . well, they could give the police a shortlist of five names and then it probably wouldn't be too hard to work out who did what. But this is the Golden Age of detective fiction and some suspension of disbelief when it comes to a criminal's plan is necessary. *The ABC Murders* by Agatha Christie is a classic of the genre, but if you think about it, the murderer's plan is ridiculously convoluted. A similar case could be made for a number of other books, usually, as in this case, to provide an alibi for the killer. A willing suspension of disbelief is required, but with that, *The Orange Axe* is a hugely enjoyable book, with one of Flynn's most exciting endings as Bathurst finds himself trapped alone with the murderer.

At this point in the series, one has to question the effectiveness of Scotland Yard. On discovering the dead body, Sir Austin Kemble, the head of New Scotland Yard, is told to summon "your finest English detective". Without a word of protest that the police force contains many fine detectives, he immediately summons Anthony Bathurst. This is by no means uncommon – in later books Kemble summons Bathurst to help before the problem is revealed to be a complicated one – but this is the first time that we see it occur quite so blatantly.

The Orange Axe was first published by John Long in 1931 and there was at least a second impression made of the original print run in 1934, but it remains an extremely rare title for collectors. It was not picked up by any overseas markets, in particular the US, so, having been out of print for eighty-five years, it is a delight to be able to reintroduce it to the current market.

Steve Barge

Chapter I
DE RAVENAC SNAPS HIS FINGERS

M. Ricardo, the portly, sycophantic and loquacious proprietor of the restaurant that bore his distinguished name, came bustling forward to meet his guest. Neither his volubility nor his obsequiousness suffered in any degree from the undoubted and incontestable fact that the tall man who advanced carelessly towards him seemed to be totally unconcerned at M. Ricardo's presence. It was accepted by the man in question as neither more nor less than part of the entourage. In exactly the same manner as the cruet and the wine-list were. Major Daniel Wyatt, D.S.O., M.C., never came to Ricardo's in Soho to inquire after the health of its proprietor or to flatter that same proprietor's sense of self-importance even infinitesimally. As a rule he was drawn there by the excellence of its cuisine, and, like a certain Anthony Lotherington Bathurst, he set Ricardo's *omelette espagnol* very high in its own championship class.

Nevertheless, on five counts he rated the establishment inferior to Murillo's, and perhaps on three of these five Mr. Bathurst would have agreed with him. But the fact that the opinions of these two gentlemen coincided so closely leaves very little room for argument. Ricardo's ranked high! Wyatt glanced impatiently at his wrist-watch, and his eyes indicated disapproval of something. He was expecting a company of five, and so far not one of them had put in an appearance. This fact was more surprising than appears from the bare recital, as the five did not number a woman among them.

"My people are confoundedly late, Ricardo," complained Wyatt. "Have you given us that special room I wanted?"

"But certainly, Monsieur Wyatt. Come with me. Everything is as you desired." Wyatt followed M. Ricardo into the selected apartment. "Also, everything is perfectly ready. When your guests arrive and you give the word, you will see that I have surpassed myself. Also, at your signal I have ordered that my waiters are to retire—*vite!* Just as Monsieur arranged.

Command me." Ricardo laid his fat hand across the region where his heart should have been, made appropriate obeisance, and bowed himself out.

Wyatt shrugged his broad shoulders and strolled across to the window of the brilliantly lighted room that looked on to the street. He had scarcely crossed the room when the sound of voices at the door behind him told him of the arrival of some at least of the people whom he awaited. They came in, Dick and Robin Blaker with Martin Pierpoint the journalist. Wyatt had scarcely greeted them when the door opened again and Gerald and Nick Twining entered. The gathering was complete.

"Sit down, you chaps," declared Wyatt; "I suppose you've all had a short one by this time. Or even two! I'll tell Ricardo to chivvy his chaps to get a move on."

The service was good and the quality of the courses beyond reproach, and the *pétoncles au champignons* for once approximated Murillo's. From the *hors d'oeuvres* to the sweet Wyatt summarily closured every remark that had the slightest indication of leading to a question of whys and wherefores.

"All in good time, Nick," he replied to the younger Twining. "This grub's far too good to spoil. Let's make the most of it while we may, for the love of Mike. I know there's a spot of courage in everyone here this evening. That's the primary reason, perhaps, why they're here, but I hope that there's a full-sized spot of patience as well." He raised his glass. "All the best, Martin."

Pierpoint returned the toast. "I heard what you said, Wyatt," he called down the length of table that separated them. "As a journalist merely on the fringe of success, I can assure you that I, at least, can claim to fill your bill."

"You'd be probably more popular if you paid it," returned Nick Twining. "That is to say, judging by most of the blokes that in the ordinary way float round me."

At length they reached the coffee, and Robin Blaker was just lifting his cup to his lips when Wyatt's raised voice arrested his attention.

"I'm fully aware that I owe you chaps an explanation," said the speaker. "When I invited you all to dine with me here to-night I told you at the time, in the letters that I sent you, that I had done so with a definite purpose. I told you that I should let you know what that purpose was some time during the evening. I am not going to waste time. I don't believe in that sort of thing. We have enjoyed our dinner, and the time has come for me to speak. Gentlemen, we are here in the matter of André de Ravenac." He spoke the name softly—almost caressingly—and as the words of the name left his lips Dick Blaker's eyes met those of his brother and their two mouths hardened perceptibly.

Wyatt went on.

"There is no need for me to mention here my own particular personal regard and affection for Josephine. I think everybody here knows of it. That is another story and belongs to another time and place. Count me in this business as just an ordinary decent fella—nothing more. I don't know that I would desire a better epitaph. The fact that Josephine needs help is enough. Her brothers know to what I refer, and they won't mind if I take the bull by the horns and put Gerald and Nick wise, because I imagine they already know something—but not all. Gerald and Nick are cousins to the other three, so that we can call it almost a family affair." He paused. "And Martin Pierpoint's my best friend."

"Perhaps," returned Pierpoint silkily, with a glitter in his dark eyes. "Put not your trust in princes or in any son of man. It's only the leopards whose labels are permanent, you know."

"I'll chance that," affirmed Wyatt unsmilingly, "and all you chaps listen to me. Then you'll realize how deadly serious I am. As De Ravenac is going to realize." The soft note crept into his voice again.

"I agree," said Dick Blaker quietly, "and I'm the senior man here. Tell them, Wyatt."

"Details won't matter two hoots," declared Wyatt, "so we'll skip most of 'em. But the main facts are these. De Ravenac has a bundle of letters written by Josephine to me in the old days. Three or four of them were written after she fixed things up with Pelham (because of my blood affinity with the proverbial ecclesiastical mouse), and she asked me to let her have them back. They represent all the letters of hers that I had kept. It appears now that she asked for them because she wanted to keep 'em herself—bless her heart. I returned 'em, and now this filthy swine has got hold of them. How, I don't know. Nor does she. But in some way that she can't yet fathom they've been stolen from her. She's parted with a couple of thousand already, as De Ravenac has been putting the screw on. Now he wants another cool thousand. Jo can't raise a bean, she says, and I, for one, believe her. He's given her a week before he calls on Sir Beverley. That's his devilish ultimatum. The long and short of it is that Jo's come to her brothers and to me. That's the position at present. Thanks, Robin." He took a cigarette from Robin's case, pulled his chair a little nearer to the table and continued. "Now, I don't propose to mince matters with De Ravenac for one moment. And the very last thing I purpose doing is paying him another penny-piece. Amongst other things, I wrote and told him so the day before yesterday. I will read you his reply." He took the letter in question from the breast pocket of his dinner-jacket.

"To M. Le Major Wyatt. My felicitations! But you pay me an honour that is too great—even for me. As for yourself, go to hell. 'Twill be but a little matter of antici- pation, but I was ever one to precipitate matters—both in love and war. André de Ravenac."

No sooner had he finished reading it than he brought his fist down heavily on to the table in front of him. Martin Pierpoint drew his breath through his teeth, and the slight hissing sound which resulted was the only audible recognition of Wyatt's action. The latter continued, and his habitual flippancy was now altogether absent. "M. de Ravenac's habits that lie outside the region of blackmail have no interest for me. In a very short time from now I hope that they will hold no interest for him. In a week—shall we say?" He gripped the edge of the table with his two hands. "Gentlemen—I am going to kill André de Ravenac."

Chapter II

THE NINE VICTIMS OF THE "WOLF"

Robin and Dick Blaker watched him intently and set their lips. The two Twinings—Gerald especially—seemed a trifle scared. He and Nick were about five and six years, respectively, junior to the elder of their cousins. The dark-eyed, sleek-headed, lithely graceful Pierpoint shrugged his shoulders.

"I think I understand. As you would a—"

Wyatt had no hesitation in completing his sentence. "As I would a dirty crawling beetle. Or, in fact, with even more abandon."

Pierpoint demurred. "Is a beetle worth hanging for?"

"Not on your life! I don't propose to hang for him, Martin— not I, not by the wildest stretch of imagination. When I announced my intention just now of removing this gentleman from the face of the earth I didn't altogether mean that my own hands were necessarily the pair that was going to do the job. That happens to be the other part of the reason why you chaps are here to-night."

Dick Blaker, habitually sparing of speech and matter-of-fact, looked at him with strong curiosity. "Get it off your chest, Wyatt. We're all of us ready and willing to help Jo—*ça va sans dire*—but the initial responsibility comes on Robin and me, and as you seem to be indicating a spot of murder—well—let's have the facts."

"I will," responded Wyatt immediately, and the grimness now in his tone was audible to all of them. "First of all, I am going to ask you a question. Who is De Ravenac?" He watched their faces as he awaited an answer. But they betrayed nothing, and the men themselves made no reply. Wyatt followed up his question with another. "What do any of you know about him? Anything?"

"Very little," admitted Dick.

"Very little, very little indeed. When did he first swim into your ken?"

Dick calculated for a moment. His brother answered for him. "Shortly after Sir Beverley Pelham and my sister arrived back from Santa Guardina."

"Quite true, Robin," corroborated Gerald Twining. "There's one more thing, too. He has a flat in Kensington. I can tell you that. Stanway Gardens. Don't know the number."

Wyatt nodded at the information. "I know that, Twining. No. 19. I found that out through putting a few discreet questions round. That was the address to which I sent the letter I mentioned. But does anybody know anything *else* about him? Anything definite? Anything particular?"

For a moment or so there was no reply.

"I've seen him at a crush or two," put in Dick Blaker guardedly, "particularly during the last week or so. He's been making himself so confoundedly attentive to Jo that I couldn't very well miss seeing him."

"Forgive me, Dick," remonstrated Wyatt, "but all of you are only telling me things about the man as he is now. As we all of us know him just at the moment, which aren't the facts for which I'm looking! What about before he attached himself to our present horizon? In other words, boiling it all down, *where* did he come from?" Wyatt flicked the ash from his cigarette as he waited for them. "As I thought," he declared eventually, "you've no idea. Not a glimmer! And what I'm going to tell you now must be absolutely 'four walls' and not a breath outside. If any part of what I think I know got out and reached De Ravenac's ears it's on the cards that the whole of my present plan might miscarry. But since I got Jo's S.O.S. I haven't let the grass grow under my feet, I assure you."

He threw his head back. He had always been a man of strong, compelling personality, and never had the fact been more in evidence. In a moment he took entire charge of his company. "I sent De Ravenac's photograph and general description to a pal of mine who 'digs' in Paris. Took it from the *Prattler*. He was in the foreground of a group taken at Lady Osmaston's reception a fortnight ago. Jo was next to him, by the way—don't know why—can't make that out at all. Well, to cut a long story short, the news I've had from Paris is rather staggering. I think it will astound you as it astounded me. I may have expected a parcel of whips, it is true. I hardly anticipated a cargo of scorpions." He turned towards Martin Pierpoint. "You were in France six years ago, Martin. I can recall you telling me so when I was introduced to you. Do you remember 'Le Loup de Poignard'?"

It was a moment or two before Pierpoint answered, and the savour of the reminiscence seemed to linger with him.

"Le Loup de Poignard," he repeated softly. "Very well indeed, Wyatt. For nearly a year Paris positively hummed with his exploits. It was believed at the Sureté Générale that at least nine victims suffered a horrible death at his hands. Or should I say claws? In each instance the murdered person was stabbed to the heart with terrific force. Hence the sobriquet."

"What happened to him—eventually?" Wyatt's question was eager and almost impatient.

Pierpoint's answer, however, was hesitant "Well I hardly know. He disappeared, and as far as was known, I fancy—his associates disappeared with him."

"He was never caught?"

"Bless your heart—no! I rather think that—"

Pierpoint bit his lip and stopped abruptly.

"What?"

"Well—it was pretty freely rumoured, I think, that, just as the authorities were confident of laying the philanthropic gentle-man by the heels, the 'Dagger Wolf' got wind of the move that they contemplated and cleared out of the country."

"Was he known to the Parisian police?"

Pierpoint grimaced. "Oh, Lord—how should I know that? I should think he must have been in the latter stages at any rate, if they were so—"

"H'm," muttered Wyatt. "Possibly! But it doesn't follow. Very often the police go after a man before they know the colour of his hair even. Anyhow, I strongly suspect that the man that we know as André de Ravenac, the man who is threatening Jo's life and happiness, the man whose existence has become intolerable to me, is no less a celebrity than 'Le Loup de Poignard'."

Martin Pierpoint's eyes mocked the statement, and for a moment there was dead silence round the table at Wyatt's announcement. Then Nick Twining gasped. There was derision almost in the dark depths of Pierpoint's eyes.

"Rather a sweeping statement, my dear Wyatt, after such a lapse of years," he declared. "May we inquire the facts on which you base this somewhat alarming opinion? I never heard it suggested even that he had made England his home. He was a sun-worshipper, you must understand. That he was a super-optimist also I never caught the slightest hint."

"How do you know he was a sun-worshipper?" asked Robin Blaker quickly.

Pierpoint turned and looked at him strangely. "It was a statement made entirely without knowledge," he conceded. "I'm a journalist, you see—with imagination. That's in extenuation. But pray proceed, my dear Wyatt! With unlimited trepidation, each one of us is hanging upon your words."

CHAPTER III

THE UNFOLDING OF THE PLAN

WYATT ACCEPTED, as it were, the challenge, and leant forward in his chair. "My statement was *not* made, as Martin here says his was—entirely without knowledge. On the contrary, rather."

"My dear Wyatt, I felt certain it wasn't." Again there was cynicism in Pierpoint's remark. Wyatt knew his man, however, and ignored it.

"My pal in Paris," he went on, "is pretty thick with the powers that be—particularly with a close friend of a certain Sergeant Perpignan. This sergeant happened to be closely connected with 'L'Affaire Loup', as I may call it, and my information may be said to come indirectly from him." Pierpoint smiled incredulously. Wyatt lowered his voice, and the company waited eagerly for his next words. "When this friend of Perpignan saw De Ravenac's photograph that I sent over to my pal, and which of course the same pal carted along to him, his eyes nearly dropped from his head. At least, that's the version that has reached me. Then he jerked himself from his condition of astonishment and spilled the beans. He swears that De Ravenac is either the man who was in imminent danger of arrest as 'Le Loup de Poignard' and whose sudden and mysterious disappearance saved him from the clutches of the police, or his twin brother."

"Just a minute, Wyatt," interposed Robin Blaker. "Did this man give your Johnny his grounds for that opinion?"

"He did, Blaker, and, better still, they have been passed on to me. I, in my turn, will pass them on to you."

A chair scraped as the occupant thereof slightly shifted its position. It was Gerald Twining's. Wyatt frowned at the hint of interruption—half unconsciously. All he saw now was his goal and the road that led to it. Everything else had paled into comparative insignificance.

"This is what happened according to the story that has reached me. 'The Wolf's' last two victims were men of some financial standing and stability, who were robbed of very large sums of money. One was found on the footpath at the end of the Rue Plâtrière just where it turns, and the body of the second man, a mere matter of five days later, was discovered by a gendarme who was passing, propped up against the doorway of a book-seller's shop in the Rue de Saint Merri. Each of the victims had been killed by a knife in the same manner—a swift and terrible blow to the heart. In the case of the outrage in the Rue de Saint Merri, the knife had been left in the murdered man's heart, and the gendarme remembered that a man had passed him hurriedly a few minutes previously at the other end of the Rue de Saint Merri. The description that he was able to give of this person eventually led the authorities to a man whom this friend of Sergeant Perpignan's now recognizes as our near and dear friend André de Ravenac. He was believed to have lodged in a somewhat obscure house in a street near the Pont du—"

"The old story—the police weren't quick enough," interrupted Pierpoint, with a quick laugh. "I well remember the sensation the affair caused at the time. Their failure to catch their man was very severely criticized. 'The Wolf' had taken unto himself the wings of a bird—and flown. *Le Matin* had a devastating article on the matter—asked pointedly, with fiery sarcasm, how many more victims would fall to 'Le Loup de Poignard.' If your friend had told you all the truth, he would have informed you that the knuckles of the Perpignan fool were very soundly rapped." The smoke of his cigarette was lazily exhaled. Confirmation of his latest piece of information came from (to him) an unexpected quarter.

"That's quite true," put in Robin. "I remember that particular article very well indeed. I too was in Paris at the time, as it happens. Just about then I had visions of embracing an artistic career—but like most visions they faded out under the stress of more human 'influences', and I've never had a 'close-up' since."

"Where does this get us, Wyatt?" demanded his brother. "Is Perpignan still moving in the matter, do you know? Is there any chance of laying De Ravenac by the heels through this channel, in time to—?"

"Help Jo?" Wyatt's question completed Dick Blaker's sentence for him, and the man who had interrupted to put it, took it upon himself to answer it immediately. "I think not, Dick. I, for one thing, doubt if there is anything like enough time for that to happen. Even if the case against him were all cut-and-dried, and as plain as a pikestaff, there would have to be authoritative communication established between the two countries. You all know how slowly the wheels of officialism revolve. No—that wasn't my idea. I told you the story of 'The Wolf' primarily to remove any false scruples any one of you might harbour against the manner of his elimination as suggested by me. If there were any, I'm pretty certain that I've removed them. If I haven't . . ." He shrugged his shoulders. There was silence in the room for an appreciable time. Dick Blaker broke it eventually, and his suggestion when it came drew an exclamation of impatience from Martin Pierpoint.

"Why not threaten him with what we know? Threaten to expose him! Don't suppose he'd be at all keen on an appointment with 'The Widow'."

Wyatt shook his head slowly. "I did—almost, that is! Don't you remember that sentence I read you in his letter of reply? My broad hint, identifying him as 'Le Loup de Poignard', was doubtless what provoked the expression—'an honour too great—even for me'." He drummed on the white cloth of the table with the points of his fingers. "That is the position, then. It has not changed one iota since I made the statement before. I am going to kill André de Ravenac. I have examined carefully the face of each one of you this evening. What I have seen in each satisfies me. With your general physique, too, I can find no fault. You all know, I presume, that Sir Beverley Pelham and Jo, his wife, are back from Santa Guardina in connection with the visit to this country of the President of the Republic of San Jonquilo—Sebastian Loredana. There is to be a carnival ball at Jo's town house next Tuesday in His Excellency's honour. I am arranging with Dick and Robin here to see Jo with regard to invitations being issued to all of us. That part will be easy. And we all know, except perhaps Pierpoint here, the geography of the house to a T. Now listen to the rest of it. Loredana is bringing his staff—including Da Costa, his Chancellor. . . ." His voice sank to a mere whisper, and the people round the table gathered closer to him as he unfolded his plan. "In the first place, we are all of a height. . . ."

* * * * *

For a moment or so after he had finished, nobody spoke. The first expression of opinion came from Nick Twining. "I certainly see your last point, Wyatt. At the very worst—providing we are careful—it would be extremely difficult to prove."

"Yet it has weakness," urged Pierpoint—critical as ever. "One glaring weakness."

"All plans have," retaliated Wyatt, "that are born of humanity. After all—'to err is human'. But this one has strength besides, and if the chosen man is swift and sure we are almost certain to succeed. Still, it is for us to decide. Time is getting on. I take it the majority governs—eh, and the minority, if any, falls into line?" He surveyed the company, dominated them—commanded them. "For the plan! Show of hands—please. Four?

Against. One? What's the matter with you, Martin? Cold feet? Well—that's settled." He turned to Dick Blaker with a peremptory gesture. "Six slips of paper, Blaker, please, and write the names down that were agreed amongst us just now."

There was a wait and a silence as Blaker tore the paper and did his bidding.

"Right? I will add to each name the work he is to do and the role he is to play." He did so. "Put them in this glass—I'll empty it first." He poured the contents of his glass into a bowl of flowers that stood at hand on the table. "It is understood," he proceeded, "that the result of the ballot will be and will remain an absolute secret of every one of us. Everybody has given his word of honour to that effect. The man who draws the slip of paper that means 'direct' action may be any one of us. And only one of us will ever do more than suspect who it actually is. That fact alone will ensure that none of us is placed in an entirely false position, for that man who suspects must forget immediately. Before we draw I will recapitulate the more essential points of our programme, omitting only the final touches themselves, which will be known only to the two directly concerned." He repeated his instructions. "Is that clear? Good! I'll draw first and you others can follow me. You first after me, Dick." Wyatt drew. Blaker, Josephine's elder brother, took a slip of paper from the glass that the masterful Wyatt held out to him. He was followed in order by Robin, Gerald, and Nick. Pierpoint took the last remaining slip. There was a deathly silence as the six men unfolded the six slips. Each read what was written on his own. Still nobody spoke. Gerald Twining went deathly white. He pushed back his chair.

As he passed out of Ricardo's that evening, Martin Pierpoint laughed softly to himself. "After all," he muttered, "matters couldn't have turned out more appropriately. I wonder who's drawn the—"

He stopped in his musings to hail a passing taxi and jumped into it as it slowed down by the kerb at his side. On the journey home he considered again the events of the evening. On the whole, he concluded, *"pêches flambées"*, to be at their best, needed Perrier Jouet '17.

Chapter IV
SIR BEVERLEY PELHAM ENTERTAINS

JOSEPHINE PELHAM caught her husband's sleeve and impulsively pulled him towards her. Sir Beverley, looking down from his height, regarded her indulgently. He had been twice her age at the time of their marriage, and was secretly overjoyed that the relentless passage of time was always reducing this proportion of difference. It was the one point of view that reconciled him to the condition of advancing years. He patted his wife's hand with an odd sense of proprietorship and slightly inclined his tall spare form to hear the better whatever it was that she had to say to him.

"Isn't it a nuisance," she told him with a little flare of temper that showed in her eyes and added to her attractiveness, "the President himself cannot be here until close on ten o'clock. Gerald Twining has just 'phoned me. Señor Loredana has an appointment or something with somebody from the Embassy that is frightfully important, and which will keep him till ten or thereabouts. He hopes that the Chancellor, Da Costa, will be able to represent him until his arrival. Isn't it the very limit of annoyance—after all the trouble we've taken?" She almost shook her husband's arm in her disappointment.

The lines of Pelham's hard mouth curved into the semblance of a smile. "Don't worry, Jo! That will be all right. Ten o'clock's early for some of these blighters. Suppose, for example, we were in Santa Guardina now—why—you wouldn't expect to start out for a show of this kind till about then. Now, would you? Ask yourself! Your four years out there should have been sufficient to tell you that. What time is Gerald coming?"

Josephine returned his smile. "Fairly early, I believe. I suppose you're right, Beverley, about His Excellency, but it was rather short notice, and I was annoyed for the minute, because I'm desperately anxious for everything to go off just so."

Pelham chuckled. "Loredana's noted for his supreme indifference towards social conventions. You mustn't expect all the canons of etiquette from him. Remember the affair of the Duke's yacht in the harbour of Santa Guardina and how thoroughly stuffy Grant was over it?" Josephine nodded, and her husband looked at his watch. "Better go and dress, Jo—time's getting on, you know, and no doubt there are dozens of things that need your personal attention. What time do your guests unmask?"

"At midnight," she returned, with a strange lack of enthusiasm that he was quick to notice, although he refrained from comment. "At midnight," repeated Josephine. "To the tick—as is the custom at these affairs in the Republic of San Jonquilo— abominable, appalling, and yet attractive place." With a moue in her husband's direction which he playfully acknowledged, she turned and ascended the broad staircase that led to her room.

*　*　*　*　*

The big black clock with the ivory hands which, stood at the far end of Sir Beverley Pelham's ballroom chimed nine, and although the evening was as yet but an infant in arms, his four hundred and more guests threw themselves with even greater ecstasy into the spirit of carnival. Sebastian Loredana's visit to England, accompanied as he was by the British Minister at his capital of Santa Guardina, was being worthily recognized by the latter gentleman. The fancy dresses and quaint costumes affected by the great majority of the guests were as striking and as original as London had perhaps ever seen.

Sir Beverley Pelham himself had, however, been somewhat easily distinguishable, for he wore on his breast the Grand Order of the Red Star of San Jonquilo and the Orange and Black Ribbon of the Republic.

Almost as the last chime of the ninth hour sounded, André de Ravenac, in his guise of an Arab sheikh, crushed a piece of paper in the palm of his hand with a dramatic gesture and turned to leave the ballroom. Had anybody been close enough to him to look into his eyes beneath his mask, that intimate person would have been amazed at the dark fire that smouldered within them. Optimistic excitement held him in its thrall.

He reached the head of the staircase that led to the rooms below, and as he did so, four young men, boisterously exuberant, mockingly but resolutely barred his further way, and with a somewhat exaggerated exhilaration demanded from him the "countersign". When they realized the strength of his determination to descend, and his entire failure to appreciate their particular form of humour, no matter how attractive their argument, Barbary Turk, Moor of Venice, Franciscan Friar and Knight of the White Cross, dropped back with ready and graceful apologies and bowed him with grandiloquent courtesy on his way below.

As they straightened themselves from this operation, a thin, bent figure in ordinary evening dress, with monocle and pointed grey beard, slipped quietly through their self-imposed cordon and followed unostentatiously down the staircase in the wake of De Ravenac. Save, perhaps, for the four men at the head of the stairs who had failed in their attempt to hinder his descent, this incident passed unnoticed by all. In the first reception-room on the floor below stood several of the guests, talking and exchanging wishes over glasses that held a rich variety of beverage. The room had been turned into a general refreshment buffet by Josephine's planning, and seemingly ancient historical characters mingled with more modern costumes and even conventional dress in a fantastic pageant that at any other time, in any other place, would have seemed an incongruity and the highest absurdity of confusion.

At one end of the cocktail bar, the end nearest the door, stood a tall figure enjoying a dry Martini. He had been there, and in that same position, for some little time, and was one of the most arresting figures of the ball for his costume was that of the "Headsman" of tradition. He was in black, true in every detail to history. Black doublet, black hose and shoes, and black skullcap, but on the black of the back of his doublet was patterned an orange axe, out of compliment, no doubt, to the national colours of the Republic of San Jonquilo. When the thin, bent figure of the man with the monocle entered, this man that has just been described looked up as though surprised at the sight of him, but then turned away imperturbably to drain the last drops of his refreshment and replace his glass upon the table. As he turned, his eyes again met those of the slim old man. Why had—?

The cry that rang out so suddenly seemed for a period to paralyse everybody that heard it into a condition of masterly inactivity. It held distress, pain and an infinity of fear. Senses were bereft temporarily of their natural attributes. The guests partaking of refreshment in the apartment that has already been mentioned looked at each other for the few stupefying seconds that followed the cry with amazement, wonder and anxiety written very legibly upon their faces. The man dressed as the "Headsman", however, was eventually stung into action and at the door of the refreshment-room in a flash. Two marble steps led from it to the tiled passage that ran below. For a moment the people behind him saw him linger on the second of these steps, sway undecidedly, and then call out to somebody coming from the direction of his right hand. Then they heard this second person, whoever it might be, call shrilly, "Through those two doors, I think. Straight ahead."

The "Headsman" nodded hurriedly as though in acceptance of this theory of direction, and hesitated for a second. Then the others, now treading almost on his heels, at the door of the refreshment apartment, saw him swing abruptly to the left, jump the last step, and dash away towards the two panelled doors a dozen yards or so down the passage. Beyond these two doors lay the room that had been reserved by Sir Beverley Pelham and his wife Josephine for refreshments for Loredana himself, his personal entourage, and a few other guests of special distinction. It was from this apartment, evidently, that the cry of distress had come, for the company from the first refreshment-room saw the "Headsman", preceded by another figure, hurl himself through the panelled doors. Within a space of five seconds or so the group of pursuers (if seekers of the cause of a cry can be so described) had struggled and straggled, one by one, through the two doors and come in their motley costumes to the open door of the room that had been specially reserved for His Excellency the President of San Jonquilo. The "Headsman" and a man dressed as a footman who had first understood from where the cry had come and given the direction, were bending over the body of a man masked and costumed as an Arab, that lay helpless just outside the room but almost across the threshold. The burnous that he wore was partly open, and it was plain to all of them as they looked that the cry they had heard had heralded death.

As the "Headsman" turned the body over on to its face the cause of death became just as obvious to everybody. A long knife with an ivory handle had penetrated the heart of the dead man, and his death to all appearances must have been almost instantaneous.

"The police and a doctor," muttered the "Headsman"; "will someone get them here, please, as quickly as possible? There's a 'phone at the foot of the main staircase."

The footman turned and ran swiftly up the corridor followed by a short, stout young man garbed as a matador of Spain.

"Don't touch a thing, please," ordered a tall, thin, middle-aged, but well-preserved man in regulation evening dress who had advanced to the forefront of the pursuers. "This is murder, unless I'm very much mistaken, and a very remarkable murder at that." He turned to the "Headsman". "I was in the refreshment buffet when the dead man screamed. I saw you there. You spotted nobody, I suppose, as you and that other man, the footman chap, ran towards here?"

The "Headsman" shook his head. "Nobody at all. That's what positively amazes me. You remember how I ran to the door of the room where we all were, when the cry came? You remember how we dashed along here—well, we never saw a soul. When we got to the door of this room, this chap was lying just outside the doorway, exactly as you see him now. Who is he, I wonder? Do you think we should take off his mask or leave it—?"

"Take my advice and leave it to the police," said the tall man firmly; "touch nothing whatever. They're bound to be here in a moment or so. But I'd better introduce myself. My name is

Grant—Sir John Grant. I was British Minister at Santa Guardina before Pelham was appointed." As he spoke, an interested look entered his eyes, and he suddenly pointed to the dead man's left hand. "What's that?" he asked, and four or five of the curious crowd behind surged forward to see better what it was that Grant had indicated.

The "Headsman" frowned as he saw what Grant had seen. In the dead man's left hand there was clutched a torn fragment of what looked like black silk splashed with orange. The "Headsman" looked up, to find Sir John Grant's eyes fixed on him and on the costume he wore, in an excess of curiosity. Down the tiled corridor the panelled doors opened again to admit an Inspector of Police, an ordinary constable, and a Divisional Surgeon. They were followed by the two men who had sped to the telephone for them. They approached the body—very rapidly, very silently, and yet with an overwhelming suggestion to the whispering onlookers of admirable efficiency. Dr. Sugden, wasting no time, knelt by the body on one knee.

*　*　*　*　*

At that precise moment Fate ordained that from the floor above there came the crashing notes of the opening bars of "Crescent Moon and Star-strewn Sky", the National Anthem of the Republic of San Jonquilo. Its President, His Excellency Sebastian Loredana, having no more business to detain him at the San Jonquilese Embassy, had just arrived, and his reception was in every way worthy of the guest of the evening. It would, however, have annoyed him excessively to know that coincidentally as he bent over the finger-tips of Josephine Pelham's altogether delightful hand an Inspector of Police was investigating a case of murder on the floor below. A man murdered? "Sweep up the body and on with the dance!" So would have argued Sebastian. Sebastian who loved cats and canaries more than anything on earth—excepting, of course, himself!

Chapter V
The Murder of André de Ravenac

Dr. Sugden pushed aside the soft silk of the burnous that the dead man had worn and drew the ivory-handled knife from the wound by the blade. He performed the operation very deliberately, partly from show and partly from force of circumstance. For the blade had bitten hungrily into the wound and scarcely an inch of it was visible.

"Well, Doctor?" asked the Inspector somewhat impatiently. It is only fair to him to remark that he endeavoured to keep the impatience out of his voice and only failed because of his fretting anxiety for immediate action.

"Stabbed through the heart, Hargreaves, with much more than ordinary force. Not been dead very long either. Put it at about twenty minutes and you won't be very far out. Perhaps that knife-handle may tell you something."

Inspector Hargreaves nodded meaningly. "I'll have it attended to. Now, gentlemen"—he turned to the clustered knot of men that crowded round the prone body—"who is in charge here? Which of you is Sir Beverley—?"

Sir John Grant did not wait for him to finish his question. "My name is Grant—Sir John Grant. Sir Beverley Pelham is not here amongst us at the moment. I should say that he knows nothing of what has occurred. Unless—" His eyes sought those of the footman, who at once understood his unspoken question.

"No, Sir John. All we did after we left you was to 'phone for the police and the doctor."

"I see. Will one of you gentlemen be good enough to bring Sir Beverley down here at once, then? In the meantime, Challis, get along up there and guard those connecting-doors. Let nobody through either way with the exception of Sir Beverley Pelham and whichever one of these gentlemen goes to fetch him. Understand?"

"Very good, Inspector." Constable Challis walked quietly to the panelled doors and stationed himself by them as the messenger garbed as a Franciscan Friar passed between.

Hargreaves turned again to the men that stood round. "And I'll ask all you gentlemen to take your masks off, if you please. It's my unpleasant job this evening to investigate a case of murder, and I must know where I am and who all of you are." The impatience of his tone had now given way to something akin to contempt. Surely all the smirking wraiths of Pleasure and Indulgence should hide their heads when Death the Admiral stalked abroad. The traditions of Inspector John Hargreaves had never impinged on carnival. Shrove Tuesday was Pancake Day to him—by no means *Mardi Gras*. "Take off the dead man's mask, will you, Doctor, please."

Dr. Sugden knelt by the body again and obeyed. At the same time the company unmasked themselves, and, each identifiable, looked on the dead face of the man known as André de Ravenac.

Inspector Hargreaves sought help in what he considered was the most likely direction. "Can you tell me anything about this, Sir John? Who the dead man is and how you came to find him here dead, murdered—if you like?" Hargreaves looked at Sir John Grant as he spoke and produced his notebook for the record of results.

Before Grant could reply, however, Doctor Sugden broke in again. "Look here, Hargreaves. Your pardon, Sir John. What do you make of this—here in the man s left hand?"

"That piece of black silk?" asked the Inspector imperturbably. "Leave it for a while, if you don't mind, Doctor, please. I saw it directly I looked at the body. I have a particular reason for not wanting it disturbed. Now, Sir John."

"I'm afraid I can't help you at all, Inspector, much as I should like to. The dead man is an absolute stranger to me. And as to how I, in common with others, came to find him here, I think this gentleman can assist you very much more ably than I." He indicated the man habited as the "Headsman".

Martin Pierpoint, unmasked, bowed to the Inspector.

"I will tell you all I know, Inspector, with the greatest pleasure, but I'm afraid it isn't very much."

As he was speaking, the panelled doors opened for that monument of stolidity, Constable Challis, to admit Sir Beverley Pelham and Robin Blaker, the Franciscan Friar who at Inspector Hargreaves' request had taken it upon himself to produce his brother-in-law.

The British Minister's thin, clean-shaven face betrayed the indignation that he was feeling. Indignation that he considered was eminently justifiable. Robin had spoken to him very quietly in the ballroom when he had conveyed Inspector Hargreaves' message. Sir Beverley had just disentangled himself from the President.

"It's Robin speaking," Blaker had said to him; "you're wanted downstairs at once. There's been an accident of some kind, near the special refreshment buffet. The police and a doctor are there."

"Good God, Robin!" he had replied. "Whatever do you mean? Who's hurt?"

"Don't know," Robin had returned laconically.

"Who sent for them—the police, I mean?"

"Don't even know that. I wasn't there when it happened. Grant very probably, I should think—he's down there. I saw him. But come along down with me at once."

After protesting his excuses to Sebastian Loredana, Sir Beverley had allowed himself to be led away. When he arrived, with Robin at his side, Hargreaves introduced himself sturdily. He told Pelham the manner in which he had been summoned to the scene of the tragedy.

"Do you know this man, sir?"

Sir Beverley looked at the dead face, and although he paled at what he saw, his lip curled very slightly. "I do, Inspector. As it happens, I can identify him as a man whom I knew under the name of André de Ravenac."

Hargreaves regarded him with some curiosity. "I don't quite get you, sir. Why do you put it like that exactly, may I ask? Have you any reason to believe that De Ravenac wasn't his name?"

Sir Beverley hesitated for a moment before he answered. "No—Inspector. Although I shouldn't be tremendously surprised if I heard that it wasn't. But I know of nothing—really. I'm sorry if I conveyed a wrong impression."

"Very good. Now—you, sir—proceed from where you started, if you don't mind."

Martin Pierpoint's dark, emotional face was alive with the racing impulses of deep feeling. His words came quickly and heatedly. "I said I'd tell you all I knew, Inspector. I was in the refreshment buffet the other side of those doors when I heard a scream. It sounded so horrible and so—intensely tragic—that I dashed to the door to see what was doing. As I did so this gentleman, who had no doubt heard it too and better than I had, I expect, came running past." He motioned towards the man habited as a footman—Major Daniel Wyatt, D.S.O., M.C. The latter nodded immediate corroboration. Martin went on. "This gentleman had evidently sensed the direction from whence the cry had come, and I could see that he was running towards it. I followed him. We dashed through the doors as hard as we could pelt. When we got abreast of this doorway—we found this. He will confirm all that I have said if you ask him."

Wyatt nodded his head again. "What Mr. Pierpoint has told you is quite true. I was on my way from the direction of the ball-room to the other refreshment room when I heard the scream that has just been described."

Inspector Hargreaves frowned before biting the stump-end of his pencil. "What did you gentlemen do when you found the dead man?"

Wyatt replied first. "I ran into this room to see if there were any sign of the murderer. The idea came to me that he might be hiding in there somewhere." He indicated the room at the door of which they stood. "The room was empty—absolutely empty."

"And you, sir?" Hargreaves came back to Pierpoint.

"I tried to lift up the dead man—to see if I could help him if he weren't absolutely dead. But he was past help, Inspector. He was dead. I could see that at once. Directly I touched him."

"H'm," muttered Hargreaves. He tacked back again to the personal. "What is your full name, sir?"

"Martin Pierpoint. I am a journalist."

"What paper, sir?"

Pierpoint shook his head. "Free lance."

"Really!" Hargreaves turned to Wyatt. "And your name, sir, if you don't mind?"

"I am Major Wyatt."

"I see." Hargreaves noted the facts.

He then went back to the body before addressing Pierpoint again. "Do I understand that you were alone when you heard this cry, sir?"

"Lord—no! I told you I was in the general buffet. There were at least half a dozen to a dozen of us in there. Including Sir John Grant here."

"That is so, Inspector," said Grant. "I and several others can testify to that. We were in the buffet, as Mr. Pierpoint has stated, and we all, I think, heard the dead man cry out. Mr. Pierpoint rushed to the door, as I think I made clear before, and we heard—or at least I did; I can only vouch for myself, naturally—Major Wyatt speak to him and call out something."

Hargreaves considered the reply. "Without, of course, at that moment knowing who it was that called?"

"Of course, I and the others followed these two gentlemen. You can see for yourselves what we found."

"I understand. Now for another question to you, Mr. Pierpoint." Hargreaves ran his eye up and down the "Headsman's" costume mercilessly. He took in every detail. Nothing escaped him. "What is that stain on the palm of your right hand?"

Pierpoint frowned at the question, but coolly turned his palm upwards for inspection. There was a vivid splash of blood that ran from the base of the fourth finger to the wrist. Sir Beverley shuddered. But the man that was so marked remained entirely unperturbed.

"Looks like blood, Inspector. The blood of André de Ravenac—no doubt. But surely the explanation is simplicity itself. I think I told you that I lifted the dead man up to see if I could help him." He fluttered his dark eyes almost insolently at Inspector Hargreaves.

Hargreaves made no reply. Then Sir Beverley had a brain-wave.

"By Jove!" he cried, slapping his thigh. "Where have my wits been all this time? One of my guests upstairs who came along with President Loredana is the Commissioner of Police, Sir Austin Kemble himself. We must get him down here at once, Inspector."

"As you wish, sir," bowed Hargreaves, in submissive acceptance of the inevitable. "I'm in your hands."

CHAPTER VI

THE COMMISSIONER AND MR. BATHURST

SIR AUSTIN Kemble was with Loredana and Lionel Pelham when Sir Beverley approached him. All three were unmasked, but the President wore the national orders of San Jonquilo. The Commissioner was in conventional evening dress. Nothing of the tragedy below had as yet been allowed to reach the ballroom from an official source, and the riot of festivity was proceeding slowly but surely to its height. Josephine was dancing with a huge tawny-bearded Viking who handled her in the manner of a steam crane dealing with a frolicsome cork.

Sir Beverley motioned to his younger brother to bring the Commissioner of Police and the President to a comparatively quiet corner of the room.

"I'm awfully sorry to worry you, Sir Austin," commenced the British Minister in subdued tones, "and I must crave your Excellency's pardon, but we've run into trouble downstairs."

"Trouble?" echoed Sir Austin importantly. "How do you mean?"

"A guest of—er—mine has been found dead in the doorway of the reception-room that had been reserved for His Excellency here. As far as we can see, he has been stabbed through the heart with a long-bladed knife. The police are here, an Inspector named Hargreaves, and also the Divisional Surgeon. The whole affair seems most mysterious—so mysterious, in fact, that, knowing you were here, I determined to come to you."

Sir Austin looked even more important as he listened attentively to his host's story. Naturally Pelham would desire him to straighten things out.

Loredana frowned heavily and offered Sir Beverley his condolences. "It is an affair that is disconcerting," he contributed. "Have you any knowledge of this man who has been murdered?"

"Yes," supplemented Sir Austin. "Do you know the man, Pelham?"

"I know his name—but little beyond that. It is André de Ravenac—a Frenchman undoubtedly."

"How is it, then, that he comes as your guest?" Even his most implacable enemies admitted that Sebastian Loredana missed little. Lionel Pelham could see that his brother found the question distasteful, but before he could temporize Sir Austin was quick to follow it up.

"Yes—why is he here, Pelham? Surely you take some precautions to—"

"As it happens, my wife was responsible for his invitation. That was sufficient for me. I don't ask her to justify to me all that she—"

"Quite so, Pelham, quite so; very natural. I understand perfectly." Sir Austin beamed sympathetic approval, and Loredana smirked maliciously at Sir Beverley's temporary discomfiture, for he admired Jo Pelham himself. More than once he had whispered her name to his canaries, and there had been an occasion when he had eulogized her to his cat.

"Will you come down, Sir Austin?" Sir Beverley clinched matters.

"Why, yes—with pleasure. Anything that will help you."

"Good, then. Stay here, Lionel, with His Excellency, and keep things going. After all, it isn't as though the murdered man had been one of our most important guests. I don't mean to exhibit a lack of taste, or feeling, but you know what I mean."

He turned to conduct the Commissioner to the rooms below. But Loredana disengaged himself from Lionel Pelham and stepped forward with an air.

"One moment. You will pardon me—I am sure. But is it permitted that I accompany you? I should indeed like to witness one so famous as Sir Austin at his work. In my country, my beloved Republic of San Jonquilo, we look upon the famous Scotland Yard as a pattern of all the virtues, that pounces like lightning upon all the vices." His white teeth gleamed with the compliment.

"Come readily, your Excellency," assented Sir Austin, swelling visibly; "the honour is mine."

When they had passed Constable Challis and reached the spot where the body still lay, Hargreaves was at work examining the room itself, and the various members of the gathering who had followed Wyatt and Pierpoint to the discovery of De Ravenac's body, were still congregated on that same side of the communicating-doors. Dr. Sugden was at the end of the line and in earnest conversation with Sir John Grant. Upon Sir Austin's somewhat ostentatious arrival, Inspector Hargreaves came to the salute, but under the influence of distinctly mixed feelings. To work under the direct supervision of the Commissioner of Police himself was an honour that had every appearance at the moment of being double-edged. Success might make him—there was certainly the possibility. But failure would equally certainly be counted severely against him—a condition very much more than a mere possibility.

"Well, Hargreaves," opened Sir Austin, with more than a suggestion of his well-known pomposity, "this is a bad business. How are things shaping?"

"Not at all well, sir," returned the Inspector, with profound despondency, "and that's a solemn fact."

"Give me the full details, will you?"

Sir Austin handled the reins. He made that fact glaringly apparent to everybody. Hargreaves complied. He quoted Pierpoint, Wyatt and Sir John Grant and showed how their stories were supported by others to be beyond any doubt. The Commissioner listened, with, for him, exemplary patience.

"Nobody in the room, you say, and they passed nobody on their way here? Extraordinary, to say the least of it. Most extraordinary. How about the murderer escaping in the other direction? Isn't that the probable explanation?"

Hargreaves shook his head with strong emphasis. "Not a room or window either side, sir—and the passage ends in a blank wall. A rat couldn't have got away that way, sir."

Sir Austin veered. "Examined this refreshment-room thoroughly?" he inquired.

"I was doing that when you came, sir. You see, there's something very puzzling indeed that I can't fathom at all. Leastways—yet awhile. Take a look at the murdered man's left hand, sir. Inside it, I mean." Sir Austin bent over the body. Loredana joined him. The President's eyes glinted at what he saw.

"I haven't moved it yet," explained Hargreaves to the head of New Scotland Yard. "I'm waiting for the photographer, but it's a piece of black silk with an orange stripe that's been torn from somewhere—perhaps from the murderer or from what the murderer wore—perhaps not. Now come and look inside the room, sir, then you'll see my point." Hargreaves took them across and pointed with very deliberate suggestion round the apartment. "Black and orange everywhere, sir. Look at the decorations! The cushions on the chairs are black and orange—the settee too—these four big cushions on the floor—the curtains—everything! Just like the piece of silk in this De Ravenac's hand."

"But I can explain the room side of the question, Inspector," broke in Sir Beverley. "There's absolutely nothing in that, because the colour design is deliberate. My wife arranged it out of compliment to this gentleman here—His Excellency Sebastian Loredana, the President of San Jonquilo. This other gentleman had doubtless much the same idea when he decided upon his costume." He indicated Martin Pierpoint.

"Orange and black are the colours of my Republic," growled Sebastian aggressively, "and orange and black are in the dead man's hand. Why? Why? I am intrigued. My curiosity was always inflammable, and I, for one, would probe this mystery to the bottom. It is possible that there may be some black treachery here aimed against San Jonquilo—against *me*, its President." He paused, and his dark eyes smouldered with a mixture of what looked like anger and fear. "Count me as your lieutenant, Sir Austin, in this matter, but certainly! After all, the man was murdered at a ball given in my honour. I will therefore take it upon myself to avenge him. I desire that you bring here at once your finest English detective—I will see that he is paid handsomely for his trouble—I, Sebastian Loredana." As he almost purred the words the smoulder changed to a flash, and the onlookers caught a glimpse of a man of infinite purpose. Like Hargreaves before him, Sir Austin accepted the inevitable.

"In that case, your Excellency, if that is really your desire—I shall send for Anthony Bathurst. I will 'phone to him immediately."

Chapter VII
THE ABSENCE OF THE WAITER

A CLOSE friend of Anthony Lotherington Bathurst, who had known him from his earliest days at Uppingham, was once heard to advance the opinion that the main reason for Bathurst's exceptional powers as an investigator of crime problems was his complete indifference to women. He argues that Bathurst's powers of memory, observation and intellect were free from the inevitable strain that accompanies the fretting propinquity of femininity. With regard to this point, it is quite true that the so-called gentler sex was almost non-existent from the point of view of presenting Bathurst with anything like an attraction, but it would be an exaggeration of the actual conditions to assert that Bathurst was a confirmed misogynist.

It would be very much nearer to the truth to say that he regarded women from an altitude that was built in the main of a quality that can be better described as tolerant cynicism than as intellectual arrogance. There was, of course, as is almost invariably the case, an excellent reason for this outlook. Bathurst had Irish blood from both his father and mother and the usual idealism that accompanies it. As a result, he had learnt an early lesson that had violently attacked and almost undermined his natural chivalry, and the lady who had acted in the capacity of instructress had performed her self-appointed task with the highest degree of efficiency. The full story of this affair may one day be told. Let it be said that her faithlessness went hand in hand with her beauty. When he had assimilated the unpalatable truth that there were no rules in games when women played—that their personal code differed in every essential particular from his own and from that of all the men he honoured and respected, and that the courts of love were marked out with many base-lines—Anthony Bathurst closed the leaves of the affair with a steady hand, shrugged his shoulders, and climbed to that eminence of tolerant cynicism that he was henceforward determined to occupy for the remainder of his time.

And because of this perhaps it may be argued that the opinion of the friend quoted at the beginning of this chapter was not altogether without reason. We will at any rate grant to it a soupçon of veracity.

When he answered Sir Austin's 'phone message, put through from the house of Sir Beverley Pelham, Anthony Bathurst had pushed away the fifteenth chapter of the Pauline epistle to the people of Corinth with a movement of supreme annoyance at the interruption. For the Levantine's mighty mentality had always captivated his understanding. The Commissioner's recital of events, however, spurred him into moderately satisfied acceptance. Within twenty-two minutes he was examining the dead body of André de Ravenac. Hargreaves had now placed a barrier across the panelled doors which Challis translated into actual effect.

Bathurst listened in turn to Sir Austin, Sir Beverley, Sir John Grant, Hargreaves, Wyatt, Robin Blaker, and Martin Pierpoint. The story of the last-named interested him intensely, and to the unconcealed pleasure of Sebastian Loredana he asked Pierpoint to repeat it so that he might be able to understand it thoroughly in every meticulous detail. Bathurst heard it through attentively for the second time and then turned to Sir Austin.

"You weren't called down here in the first place, I understand, Sir Austin. Why was that?"

"For the best of reasons, my boy. The Commissioner's reply bordered on the peevish. I wasn't here when the man was killed. I called upon President Loredana at his hotel on my way here as I had arranged and came along with him. The murder took place some time before we arrived."

"It is true," corroborated Loredana banteringly, "quite true. You cannot arrest Sir Austin. He has what you call the perfect alibi."

Bathurst acknowledged the quip with the suggestion of a smile. He turned his attention to Major Wyatt. "You examined the room, you say, directly after you ran into the dead body of De Ravenac?"

"I did. Directly after. In fact, as my companion went to his assistance I ran straight into the room, thinking of course that there might be somebody still in there. It was absolutely empty and the only exit is through the one door."

"Strange," observed Bathurst, "very strange. Where was the waiter?"

The question was of course put directly to Wyatt. But no sooner had it left Bathurst's lips than everybody in the company found himself wondering why it hadn't been asked or even suggested by anybody before. For it was such an obvious question, and one that ought certainly to have occurred to every one of them. In Sir Beverley Pelham's case it produced an additional effect, for he at once saw the position very clearly. After all, the occasion was his as host of the evening and he must take the primary burden of responsibility.

"There is just this point, Mr. Bathurst," he urged, as though putting forward an atmosphere of extenuating circumstances, "this room—we intended to reserve it for President Loredana and special guests who were with him. It was by no means to be used in any sense as a general refreshment-room. I feel that I must make that clear to you. And as His Excellency was not arriving until about ten o clock there had been no call for use, by the time the murder was committed, upon the room at all."

"I understand that perfectly," admitted Bathurst, "but it doesn't dispose of my question, does it? I asked, 'Where was the waiter?' Your reply to my question was, in effect, 'The waiter had done no work,' or better still, perhaps, 'The time had not arrived for him to do any work,' which, I respectfully submit, is no answer at all to the point that I put forward."

Sir Beverley Pelham looked exceedingly uncomfortable. "You're quite right, of course," he conceded. "I see your point very clearly. As a matter of fact, the waiter who was in charge of this special buffet had come upstairs to me with a special message. The incident had passed entirely from my mind until you recalled it by mentioning him. When my brother-in-law, Robin Blaker, first acquainted me with what had happened down here, the fact that the waiter in charge of this room had been in recent conversation with me in the ballroom itself slipped me completely. I never thought of associating the two events at all. It simply didn't occur to me. I suppose it was wrong of me and I should have done." As he made this admission Sir Beverley wiped the perspiration from his forehead with his handkerchief. Had it been a confession of the murder itself it could scarcely have occasioned him more distress. Why the dickens had Josephine placed him in such an awkward position? He felt himself to be occupying, temporarily at least, the very centre of an area of suspicion, for he was astute enough to anticipate accurately the line of country that Bathurst's next questions would take.

Matters were made definitely worse for him by the proximity of Sir John Grant, his predecessor at Santa Guardina. Sebastian Loredana was alone, perhaps, in extracting some amusement from the British Minister's present position. It was his habit to extract either a thrill or a laugh from most things, and it was a new departure for him to be able to survey this exalted representative of the conquering race in a set of circumstances that fringed upon a condition of social discomfiture. It reconciled Loredana to more than one incident that had occurred in San Jonquilo after Sir Beverley had taken up his position there. André de Ravenac had not died in vain. Bathurst returned to the attack exactly as Sir Beverley had anticipated that he would.

"What you have told me about this waiter is most interesting, Sir Beverley. May I be permitted to inquire what the message was that took the man away from the room in which in ordinary circumstances he would naturally have been expected to remain? A room, too, mark you, in which, or close to which, a murder was very soon subsequently to be staged?"

Sir Beverley did not find the question as disconcerting as he had, in the first stages of his mental disturbance, expected.

"Quite a trifling matter, Mr. Bathurst, I assure you. Powell— that was the name of the waiter, by the way—came to me with a question that concerned the quality of the claret cup that was to be prepared for His Excellency."

Loredana rubbed his hands with an air. "With the superb excellence of that question I can find no fault, and I take Sir Beverley Pelham seriously to task for dismissing it as in any way 'trifling'. I would that my hosts and hostesses—all of them—cherished for me such pleasing and eminently gratifying consideration. Has it not been said, with perfect justification, by one of your countrymen, too, I believe, that only a gentleman can drink and enjoy claret? Sir Beverley, and Mr. Bathurst, I thank you from the bottom of my heart."

Bathurst disregarded Loredana's interruption. He had another question to put to Sir Beverley, and one which was perhaps of even greater importance than the preceding one. "Who was it sent this waiter, Powell, upstairs to you with this message? Were you informed?"

Sir Beverley bit his lips, but the grey eyes of Anthony Bathurst allowed no compromise and drew the truth from him.

"Yes. My wife," he answered curtly.

"Did Powell tell you that in so many words," cut in Bathurst again, "or are you deducing it as a kind of general assumption from what he asked you?"

Sir Beverley's next reply came almost sullenly, and held a distinct tinge of impatience. "He told me so in so many words. He informed me definitely that Lady Pelham had ordered him to come upstairs, to ask me what he had asked."

Sir Austin Kemble took a hand here. "But where the devil is this man Powell now?" he expostulated. "Why hasn't he shown up here since? Looks to me extremely suspicious."

Inspector Hargreaves was ready and able to answer the Commissioner's question. "Probably still the other side of those two doors, sir—no doubt Challis has seen to that." He spoke with deference.

"Go and find the man, then, at once," ordered Sir Austin peremptorily. Hargreaves left the group and made his way towards Constable Challis.

"I can put my hand on him, sir, almost at once," replied the latter to the Inspector's question. "When I refused him admittance through these doors in accordance with your instructions he just shrugged his shoulders and walked away. He went into the other refreshment-room. I watched him, and as far as I know he's in there now. I haven't seen him come out."

"Go and get him," returned the Inspector. "The Commissioner wants him at once. If he isn't in that room come back and report to me here immediately."

Challis made off, and Hargreaves saw him ascend the two marble steps that led to the room to which he had stated Powell had gone.

"Bolted, I expect," he mused, "but how was I to know that—"

But his fears were short-lived. The door which he was watching opened even as he looked at it, and to his own no small satisfaction Challis reappeared with a tall cadaverous man attired as a waiter. Certainly, part of Hargreaves' depression vanished as the two men came towards him.

"Stay here, Challis, as before," he instructed, "and you, Powell, come with me. You're wanted along here, by the Commissioner of Police."

A look of something very much like fear took possession of the lean, hungry-looking face of the waiter, but he made no attempt to dispute the Inspector's command, and silently fell in at his side. Within a matter of half a minute Hargreaves had delivered up his charge to the Commissioner.

Sir Austin with a quick nod of meaning indicated to Sir Beverley to explain to the man the entire position. The British Minister understood what was required of him and complacently accepted the situation.

"Oh, Powell," he said, turning to his servant, "I regret to say that during your absence from the room where you were placed for this evening a tragedy has taken place—a murder has been committed—that is to say, as far as can be seen at the moment. Now, these gentlemen here—among whom I may tell you is Sir Austin Kemble, the Commissioner of Police—desire to know what caused you to leave the bar. I know, of course, that you came to see me, but please tell Sir Austin the full circumstances that made you do so."

When he realized the gravity of his employer's statement, Powell looked more scared than ever.

"I was sent up to you, sir, by Lady Pelham herself. Lady Pelham came down here and asked me to find you and deliver to you the message that she gave me."

Anthony Bathurst intervened. "Did Lady Pelham come down here *to this room* to give you that message?"

"Yes, sir," replied Powell.

Bathurst considered for a moment. "How was it, then," he asked, "that you didn't return here as soon as your message had been delivered?"

Sebastian Loredana nodded his quick agreement with the fact that Bathurst had raised this point, almost immediately.

Powell looked around the knot of men, and his glance flickered unsteadily and uncertainly from one to the other. Ultimately it came to rest on Sir Beverley Pelham. "I was unable to find Sir Beverley," he explained, "for quite a considerable time, sir, through no fault of my own. When I did succeed in finding him and came downstairs again I was prevented from passing through the panelled doors by a uniformed and very discourteous policeman who was stationed there."

It was the explanation that Hargreaves had foreshadowed.

"H'm," said Bathurst, "I see." He swung round towards the Commissioner, but before he could speak, Doctor Sugden, who had been re-examining the body of André de Ravenac, came forward with Inspector Hargreaves and addressed the Commissioner.

"If it's any interest to you, sir," he stated, "the dead man has a long white scar at the back of his neck Nothing, of course, to do with the present case—it's years old I should say—but nevertheless important from the point of view of definite identification. My experience has taught me that all these matters assist in the long run."

"I quite agree, Doctor," Bathurst concurred. "But I think our next step will have to be a short interview with Lady Pelham. It is certainly indicated. For one thing, it is imperative that we should be able to substantiate this man Powell's story, and secondly, Lady Pelham herself, when she was down here, may have noticed something that it was impossible for anybody else to notice afterwards. I take it that you agree with me, Sir Beverley?"

The British Minister to Santa Guardina lifted his shoulder with a movement that denoted annoyance and reluctant acquiescence.

"I suppose that we had better speak to my wife," he conceded, "although I am perfectly certain that she will be able to tell you no more than I have told you. Robin," he said, turning to his brother-in-law, "go upstairs and bring Jo down here, will you?"

"Don't trouble, Mr. Blaker," interfered Mr. Bathurst sweetly; "let Powell go. Let us employ a man experienced in the delivery of messages of importance."

Sir Beverley Pelham glared at the speaker, and Sir Austin in his capacity of that gentleman's guest looked at Bathurst somewhat critically. The latter, however, was the personification of imperturbability and showed no signs of yielding. The Commissioner looked and understood, and when Anthony Bathurst desired a thing very strongly, it was Sir Austin's wont to grant it to him, for Bathurst neither did nor said anything purposelessly.

"Yes, Sir Beverley," Sir Austin declared, "let Powell go. It will be just as well. For one thing, his appearance in the ballroom as a messenger will excite no particular comment, and another man's might: he has been up there before."

Powell bowed and departed, and as Constable Challis allowed him, at a nod from Hargreaves, the freedom of the connecting-doors, Wyatt and Martin Pierpoint exchanged significant glances. Sir John Grant took a cigarette from his silver case, at the same time offering the latter to Robin Blaker; but the last-named, still chafing at Bathurst's handling of the message to his sister, refused Grant's offer with a quick shake of the head, and out of it all there came to Loredana's quick perception the idea that more than one member of the company was not too pleased at the turn that the investigation had suddenly taken.

CHAPTER VIII
THE SPILLING OF THE CLARET CUP

PILOTED BY the cadaverous Powell, Josephine Pelham came through the two doors and joined the group of men on the threshold of the room that should have been reserved for President Loredana. The body of De Ravenac had been carefully lifted by Doctor Sugden and Inspector Hargreaves and laid by them on the settee that was positioned in the corner. The orange and black colours of the Republic of San Jonquilo in which the settee had been specially decorated, harmonized exactly with the piece of orange and black silk that was still clutched in the left hand of the dead man. Sir Beverley Pelham went anxiously towards his wife as she reached the company of men and ranged himself, with a somewhat plaintive gesture of protection, at her side; Josephine thanked him with her eyes.

"Tell Lady Pelham, Sir Beverley," said Bathurst gently, "what has occurred, and that I should like, when you have finished, to ask her one or two questions that concern her very directly."

Josephine Pelham listened to her husband's narrative with admirable self-possession. On her way down to the scene of the crime in the wake of Powell she had summoned all the resources of her self-composure (which were by no means meagre) and felt herself ready and efficient to face the ordeal which she knew lay inevitably in front of her. When Sir Beverley Pelham had finished his recital of the circumstances she was sufficiently self-controlled to murmur in her low-pitched voice, "André de Ravenac—killed—how terrible! But what does this gentleman want to ask me? In what way can I—?"

Anthony Bathurst bowed courteously. He was quite appreciative of the combination of Lady Pelham's unusual beauty and undeniable charm, but unhappily for her, situated as she was, it made no difference to the depth or the character of his investigation.

"Lady Pelham," he opened, "my name is Anthony Bathurst. I am here at the invitation of your guest, Sir Austin Kemble, the Commissioner of Police, to see whether I am able to throw any light upon this extraordinary murder. Your waiter, Powell, who was evidently at service in this room, has made a statement to us that, in a way, affects you yourself. He states that he was instructed by you to leave this room where he was and convey a message to your husband. Will you confirm that statement?"

Josephine Pelham was the embodiment of coolness as she answered, but there was an almost involuntary squaring of her shoulders.

"That is quite true, Mr. Bathurst. I sent Powell upstairs to my husband. What of it?"

"Upon what pretext?" asked Bathurst nonchalantly.

"Pretext?" It was apparent to all from the tone that she used that the choice of the word displeased her.

Bathurst smiled. "Reason, then, if you prefer the word," he said courteously.

Josephine Pelham became an epitome of disdain. "The words you use are quite immaterial to me, Mr. Bathurst," she countered frigidly. "I can't say that I find your conversation sufficiently interesting to criticize such a matter as word-selection.

My reason"—the last word was heavily stressed—"for sending Powell upstairs is perhaps insignificant to you as you hear it now, but was important enough to me then. It concerned the claret cup that Powell had prepared for President Loredana."

It has been said already in this history that Sebastian Loredana missed little. He grasped this opportunity with both hands.

"Although the time is late, Lady Pelham," he declared, "and possibly the occasion a little inopportune, I thank you from the bottom of my heart. Ingratitude is a vice which the Loredanas have deplored for many generations."

"Thank you, Lady Pelham," acknowledged Bathurst, ignoring the interruption. "You have told me what I wanted to know." His eyes lazily explored the members of the party, and almost before it came more minds than Josephine's dreaded his next question.

"When you gave these orders to Powell, where were you?"

"In this room."

"Were you alone?"

"No, of course not! Powell was with me."

Loredana sniggered audibly at Josephine's rejoinder, but there was neither laugh nor semblance of humour on the face of Wyatt, Pierpoint, or Robin Blaker.

"Naturally," smiled Bathurst imperturbably, "but was there anybody with you besides Powell?"

Josephine's eyes sought those of Powell. "Not in the room," she answered.

"Where, then?" continued Bathurst relentlessly.

"It's awfully silly," proceeded Josephine, "and there's really no point in it at all that I can see, but I will tell you exactly what took place from the time I came downstairs to the time when I went up again." She paused for a moment as though making an effort to gather together all her faculties, and then looked fearlessly round the group of men that confronted her.

Sir Beverley patted her arm with what was intended by him to be a gesture of courage and reassurance.

"That is just what I should like you to do." The tone of Bathurst's reply to her was almost as encouraging as her husband's caress.

"I came downstairs," she commenced to explain, "entirely in my capacity as hostess, in order to put the finishing touches to His Excellency's room. The question of the claret cup arose simply and solely out of that idea. Another thing that I had to do was to finish the decorations that my husband and I had decided should be used in the room. There were several cushions which I had to bring down from upstairs—orange and black—the colours of the Republic, and I asked the gentleman who happened at that moment to be nearest to me in the ballroom upstairs if he would help me by carrying them down for me. He gallantly responded. I can see now that that gentleman was Major Wyatt." Josephine gave a half-smile in Wyatt's direction, paused for a moment, and then almost immediately proceeded with her story. "You can see the cushions to which I have referred, in the room now. Just where Major Wyatt placed them for me, in fact."

"Was that when you sent Powell upstairs?" inquired Bathurst.

"Yes," replied Josephine.

"What did you do then yourself, Lady Pelham?" Josephine considered. "I went upstairs again."

"Straightway?"

"Almost. I just called in at the other refreshment-room on my way—to see that everything was all right in there. I don't think I could have been there more than a couple of minutes. Since then I've been upstairs all the time until I was sent for just now. Do I have to answer any more questions?"

Bathurst seemed lost in thought for a moment.

Eventually he replied to Lady Pelham's last question by launching a query of another kind.

"Try to assist me as much as you can, Lady Pelham, by giving me the very best of your memory. About what time would you say it was when you came downstairs with Major Wyatt and the cushions?"

Lady Pelham smiled prettily. "I was very busy, you know, Mr. Bathurst, and I had been all day, and I wasn't thinking particularly about such things as time, so that I couldn't swear to it to a minute—or anything like that. But I should say that I came downstairs with Major Wyatt and—er—the cushions about eight minutes to nine."

Bathurst noted the terms of her reply and made a rapid calculation mentally.

"So that," he said slowly, "allowing a matter of five minutes or so for the arrangement of the room and your instructions to Powell concerning the claret cup for President Loredana, we may assume that you entered the other refreshment-room somewhere about nine o'clock. Would you accept that assessment?"

Josephine inclined her head to one side non-committally. "I'm hopelessly futile at mental arithmetic, Mr. Bathurst, of the simplest possible description even, but I should think that from the way in which you've worked it out, you're very nearly right."

Sir John Grant stepped forward.

"May I intervene here?" he asked with his customary urbanity. "Merely from a genuine desire to assist the investigation."

"Certainly," said Bathurst in invitation.

"Well, if it's any use to you on the point that you're discussing," contributed Sir John, "I am in a position, as it happens, to confirm absolutely what Lady Pelham has just stated. Almost *in toto*. She entered the general refreshment-room at nine o'clock exactly. I was in the room at the time. I heard a clock outside somewhere strike nine, and as luck has it, I looked at my own watch also."

"What do you make the time now?" said Mr. Bathurst quickly, consulting his own watch.

"Ten-seventeen," said Sir John Grant.

"Thank you, Sir John," replied Mr. Bathurst; "my own watch appears to be a minute slow. I shall have to see that it receives attention."

Sir Austin Kemble immediately and hastily consulted his watch, but discovered, apparently, a satisfactory state of affairs, for no comment on the matter escaped him.

Anthony Bathurst once again turned his attention to Major Wyatt. "I'm sure you also will do your best to help me," he opined, "because you will understand that I am forced at this period of the case to consider the vital question as to how the murdered man arrived down here. I may ask you on that account to amplify what you have already told me."

Wyatt nodded—evidently in cordial agreement. "Of course, I understand. Ask me anything you like."

"You accompanied Lady Pelham down here carrying some cushions?"

"Quite true," returned Wyatt coolly, flicking the ash from his cigarette. "I happened to be handy for the job and naturally was only too pleased to help."

"And then Lady Pelham returned upstairs, after giving the instructions to Powell about which we have heard so much?"

"She did," admitted Wyatt. "Exactly as she informed you."

"Leaving you alone in the room?" questioned Bathurst.

"For a moment or two—that's all," returned Wyatt imperturbably. "I arranged the cushions as Lady Pelham had requested me to do, and then started to make my way upstairs again. There was nothing to keep me in here. I went through the panelled doors to the end of the tiled passage that brings you to the main staircase leading to the ballroom and then changed my mind. For an excellent reason, Bathurst, which I am sure you, as a man of the world, will thoroughly appreciate." A smile of banter played round his lips.

"Let's have it," said Bathurst, "then I shall be in a position to judge better."

"I turned back for a drink. I had just passed the refreshment buffet on my way upstairs, and I suppose that put the idea into my mind. It doesn't take much. Just as I was retracing my steps, I heard a terrible cry which seemed to come from somewhere in front of me. As I think I told you before, there was no mistaking the fact that the person who had cried out was in either intense pain or grave peril, so I put on a spurt and ran in the direction from which I fancied the cry had come. This gentleman"—he motioned to Martin Pierpoint—"was standing on the first or second step outside the general refreshment-room, having heard, no doubt, the same cry that I had heard. He fell in behind me and we ran together through the doors and found the body of the dead man as has already been described to you."

Bathurst pondered deeply upon the information with which Wyatt had furnished him. He turned to the Commissioner. "We appear to be confronted, Sir Austin, with a condition of circumstances that seems impenetrable."

"You mean—"

"I mean just this, sir—how did the dead man, De Ravenac, get here? The circumstances as we have them are inexplicable. Major Wyatt didn't see him, Lady Pelham didn't see him, and as far as I can understand Powell didn't see him—a most extraordinary affair. Moreover, not one of them seems to have seen anybody else, the suggested murderer, for instance, either coming or going. Is it possible that he could have been in the general refreshment-room?" He turned rapidly to Sir John Grant. "Can you remember, Sir John, if the dead man were one of the company in the room with you about nine o'clock, shall we say?"

Sir John Grant thought carefully over the question, and all that it might eventually come to mean.

"I shouldn't like to say definitely," he ventured at length, "as there were several people in the room at the time. But I don't think that he was. That is to say, I have no recollection of anybody being in there dressed in that burnous affair—jibbeh, or whatever you call it. I feel pretty certain that I should have spotted that particular rig-out."

"What about you, Mr. Pierpoint?" continued Bathurst, casting in another direction. "You were in the same room as Sir John at that time. Have you any recollection of this man De Ravenac being in there?"

"Haven't an earthly," responded Pierpoint. "He may have been, but I was at one end of the room all the time, so perhaps my testimony isn't worth very much."

"Thank you," acknowledged Bathurst dryly. He went across and conferred with Sir Austin Kemble, President Loredana, and Inspector Hargreaves. The conversation was of but a few moments' duration. Sir Austin bustled forward to the group of people. Here at least was something that he could do.

"For the moment," he declared impressively, "we do not think it necessary to detain any of you people here any longer, and we consider it best to permit the affair upstairs to proceed as though nothing of this kind had happened. There is no reason, as far as I can see, to do otherwise. Inspector Hargreaves, under my instructions, will take a certain course of action later on in the evening, before the guests disperse. His Excellency will accompany you and his presence will help to preserve the normal atmosphere. Besides that, it will help to stifle rumours should any be rife."

"I shall be delighted," returned Sebastian Loredana. "*A moi!* Lady Pelham and gentlemen! To the ball-room."

The various members of the group walked slowly away, and Constable Challis passed them through. Bathurst, Sir Austin and Doctor Sugden entered the room wherein lay the body of De Ravenac. Hargreaves, after listening attentively to the Commissioner, followed upstairs.

Sir Austin surveyed the corpse with a critical appreciation of externals. "What do you make of this piece of silk in the left hand, Bathurst?" he asked curtly.

"No idea at the moment, sir. Haven't been able to place it at all. You observe, however, that it's in the colours of San Jonquilo, matches beautifully the costume worn by our friend Martin Pierpoint, and is also all of a piece with the general decorations of this room. Orange and black. But why? I confess that the feature puzzles me."

"A struggle with the man or woman that killed him?" suggested Sir Austin with elementary straight-forwardness.

Bathurst shrugged his shoulders. "No part of Pierpoint's costume was torn in any way," he asserted. "I took particular care to notice that, and nothing that I can see appears to be torn, or out of place, in here. What do you think yourself?"

Sir Austin looked around him and examined the orange-and-black curtains, cushions and coverings that the room held. "Nothing at all," he corroborated.

Bathurst followed up his point. "I am therefore reluctantly forced to the conclusion, Sir Austin, that the piece of silk was *deliberately placed* in the dead man's hand for a definite purpose. What that purpose actually was, I eventually hope to discover. But the case at the moment is black, Sir Austin." He pushed his right fist against the palm of his left hand. "As dark and as baffling as any which I have ever yet been called upon to investigate."

Doctor Sugden nodded in agreement. "That's how it struck me," he concurred, "directly I came across and got to grips with it. It occurs to me that the various stories that have been retailed to us to-night don't altogether fit. What do you think yourself?"

Bathurst turned and looked at him curiously. What Doctor Sugden had said afforded him interest. "I don't know that I altogether agree with you there, Doctor," he submitted; "it seemed to me that they fitted excellently, almost too excellently, if such a condition be possible—save for the astounding fact that nobody set eyes on De Ravenac till after he was murdered. We have incontestably corroborated evidence from independent sources that Lady Pelham, Pierpoint, Wyatt and Powell, whom I may term the four main actors of the periods most nearly preceding and most nearly subsequent to the murder, were all definitely elsewhere when De Ravenac was killed."

"That statement is only partly true, I think," urged Doctor Sugden in correction. "I'm thinking of the case of Lady Pelham herself. We have Sir John Grant's evidence that she entered the general buffet at nine o'clock or about that, but it seems to me that it's quite on the cards that she could have slipped out again, and instead of going upstairs as she stated, quietly slipped back."

"I see your point, Doctor, and I thank you for the idea. For the moment, the possibility that you suggest had eluded me." Bathurst walked towards the improvised counter upon which stood the various foods and drinks that had been destined to titillate the gastronomic activities of His Excellency the President of San Jonquilo and those of his personal *entourage*. The great cut-glass bowl filled with claret cup occupied a prominent place almost in the middle of the table. Bathurst looked at it intently for a moment or so, a curiously puzzled expression on his face. Suddenly he turned and beckoned to the others to come nearer.

"We have not yet heard," he said, "that any guest has so far been privileged to participate in His Excellency's claret cup, have we?"

"What on earth do you mean, Bathurst?" Sir Austin frowned at what he considered the irrelevant nature of the question. He thought also that it was ill-timed and a little out of place. But Anthony Bathurst showed his first manifestation of successful progress. He rubbed his hands, a sign of old that the Commissioner of Police knew well.

Ignoring the frown that was levelled at him, Bathurst proceeded to develop his idea. "And yet the claret cup that you agree should be untouched has sunk almost half an inch in the bowl! What do you make of that, sir?"

Sir Austin demurred in attempted demolition of Bathurst's theory. "Nothing—it is quite feasible that the bowl may never have been full," he declared oracularly.

"I disagree, sir. It may have been full enough to flow over the sides and to spill. Look for yourself." Bathurst pointed to the reddish liquid that had obviously been spilled from the bowl and which had stained the white cloth on the table all round it. Sir Austin stared at the red stain. "There are more possibilities than the one that suggests itself to me, but just to test my theory, sir," persisted Bathurst, "come and put your hand to the bottom of the bowl, will you? I've a strong suspicion that you may discover something interesting."

Sir Austin, with a show of reluctance, pulled up his coat and shirt sleeves with some fastidiousness, and obeyed. He plunged in his hand, and his fingers closed on something that lay at the bottom of the bowl, hidden from careless and casual glance by the floating portions of fruit at the top. He withdrew his hand with an exclamation of amazement.

"Good God, Bathurst! A revolver! Fitted with a silencer too!"

Mr. Bathurst rubbed his hands for the second time that evening. "We progress, Sir Austin," he said quietly. "Although I will admit that a revolver was not what I expected you would find."

CHAPTER IX
THE GUESTS UNMASK

"H'M! GLAD you're so sure of our progress," growled the Commissioner of Police. "Well—it's your find—I shall be interested to know what you make of it."

Anthony Bathurst held out his hand, and Sir Austin passed the revolver over to him. "An ordinary six-chambered automatic," declared Bathurst. He examined it carefully. "Fully loaded," he added, "and with a silencer attached, mark you. Of course." The last two words were uttered softly, as though indicative of an after-thought.

"Why 'of course'?" inquired Sugden.

"It was very necessary that it should be a silent crime, Doctor."

Sir Austin partly disagreed. "That's all very well, Bathurst, as far as it goes. But why on earth use a knife when the first intention was to use a revolver? I don't see how you—"

"Hold on a bit, Sir Austin. You're asking me too much," intervened Bathurst. "Give me a little more time and I may be able to answer you. But even now there are more hypotheses than one. For instance, the murderer may have *prepared* two strings for his bow. Alternatively, some condition may have arisen, or unforeseen incident occurred, that caused him to change his plan suddenly. All I am asserting for the time being is that each of the weapons that we have discovered in connection with the crime ensured that it was to be committed in comparative silence, which is a point worth considering. As I am placed at present I am unable to go beyond that."

Doctor Sugden furrowed his brows. "I appreciate what you say," he stated slowly, "but the fact remains, doesn't it, that the actual murder did not turn out in accordance with what you say were the murderer's desires. That's so, isn't it?"

Bathurst put the revolver down on the table by the great bowl of claret cup, and regarded him curiously. "Go on, Doctor," he urged encouragingly; "let me hear exactly what you mean."

"Well," replied Doctor Sugden, "this condition of silence was broken, despite all the murderer's precautions, by the cry of the murdered man. It seems to me, too, that any murderer of even ordinary intelligence would have to reckon with that possibility and thoroughly consider it. Don't you yourself agree with me, Bathurst?"

Anthony Bathurst caressed his chin and considered the point that Doctor Sugden had made very carefully. "With such a thing as a revolver-shot, do you think, Doctor?" he asked at length. "Do you think that a man shot vitally, say, through the brain or through the heart, would have time to cry out, as we know from all the evidence that has been brought to us, that this man cried out? Surely, Doctor Sugden, death from either of the revolver-shots that I have just instanced would be to all intents and purposes instantaneous?"

Doctor Sugden nodded, with perhaps some little reluctance. "I suppose it would," he agreed, with a movement of the head. "Certainly I don't think that any man shot vitally as you suggest, would be able to cry out as the evidence says this man did."

"Then that brings us back to my original position," interpolated the Commissioner. "As I said before, why use the knife and risk the cry that the murderer, if he had any sense at all, knew would be almost bound to follow?"

Mr. Bathurst smiled at Sir Austin's vehemence. "The whole case is excessively puzzling, Sir Austin. Consider again for a moment the point that bewildered me before. This man De Ravenac is murdered in this room, or on the threshold of it, at least. Lady Pelham, Major Wyatt, Pierpoint and the waiter Powell have all either come down the tiled passage leading from the ballroom, or gone up it, in some cases just before the murder and in other cases very soon after it. Yet, not one of these four, according to their respective stories, sees either De Ravenac or anybody else between the ballroom, the general refreshment-room and the room in or near to which the murder took place. And the evidence doesn't altogether rest there either. In addition to these four people whom I have already mentioned, we have Sir John Grant, Robin Blaker and several other people, guests of Sir Beverley Pelham, whose names I don't know, who were also close at hand. The same story again. Not one of them appears to have seen anybody. My problem is not only to find the murderer, but also how he escaped observation, and in what manner was De Ravenac enticed to his death." He paced the room and suddenly picked up one of the orange-and-black cushions that Major Wyatt had brought downstairs for Lady Pelham. Tossing it absent-mindedly into the air, he caught it and replaced it on the settee from which he had that moment taken it. Sir Austin Kemble and Doctor Sugden watched his actions but remained silent as they thought over the points that he had presented. "Nevertheless, Sir Austin," he continued, "our difficulties are perhaps less than they were. We have found a fully loaded revolver, which proves that this room was the centre of the murderer's operations. He or she, at least, or a confederate, seems likely to have been in the room either just before or just after the murder. Perhaps both. I think we may regard that fact as established." He went silently across the room to where the dead man lay, and looked at the body with the most careful scrutiny. "It would be interesting to know, Sir Austin, if this man De Ravenac were left-handed. If you come here you will observe that the piece of silk is clutched in his left hand."

Sir Austin joined him at the dead man's side. "You mean," he declared hopefully, "that he has used his left hand to clutch, say— at his assailant in preference to his right, from force of habit."

"Perhaps," returned Bathurst.

Sir Austin looked doubtful and sensed Bathurst's disagreement. "I forgot for the moment that you decried the likelihood of a struggle."

"I did and I still do," replied Bathurst. "As I view the case I don't think a struggle on the part of De Ravenac at all probable. I'm thinking, you see, of the question of time. Though all the same, I suppose I am bound to consider it as a possibility. That is why it would assist me to know if he were left-handed. Without, of course, it being anything like a conclusive factor." He looked at his wrist-watch. "I think that Hargreaves should have been able to get the information that he wanted by now. I propose, then, that we go upstairs, Sir Austin, in order that we may be 'in at the death', shall we say?"

"Not another one, I hope," rejoined the Commissioner cynically.

"Merely a *façon de parler*, sir. Are you coming too Doctor?"

The Commissioner of Police and Doctor Sugden followed Anthony Bathurst past Constable Challis through the connecting-doors, along the tiled passage and up the magnificent staircase, to the fringe of the ballroom itself.

Sir Austin found Inspector Hargreaves without much difficulty. The Inspector, who had been prosecuting his inquiries unobtrusively, listened carefully to the Commissioner's instructions. Hargreaves expressed his understanding.

"I have made full arrangements for everything, sir," he confided—"the usual photographs, fingerprints and a general comb-out all round. Your friend Mr. Bathurst can have the word he wants with the flunkey fellows as soon as the little twelve o'clock ceremony is over. That suit you all right, Mr. Bathurst?"

Bathurst gestured his agreement.

*   *   *   *   *

It may be observed at this stage that when the masked guests revealed their respective identities, it was seen that Dick Blaker had been present as Othello, the Moor of Venice, Gerald Twining as a Barbary Turk, and Nick Twining, his brother, as a Knight of the White Cross. They were, it may be said, the last three people upon whom the living eyes of De Ravenac had rested. For Robin Blaker, the remaining member of the quartette, had stood a little apart from his three companions when De Ravenac had forced his way through the cordon at the top of the staircase and gone to his death.

CHAPTER X
THE MAN WITH THE MONOCLE

As Bathurst stood in the vestibule and watched the array of costumes, one of the first things that he noticed was the size of the masks that had been worn by Wyatt and his five companions. Suddenly a man emerged from the company and a hand touched Bathurst lightly on the shoulder. He turned quickly, to find Sir John Grant at his side.

"I should like a word with you, Bathurst, if it's not troubling you unduly. *Now*—if you can spare the time."

Bathurst, assenting courteously, looked with some curiosity at the man who had accosted him. The glance gave him the same impressions that he had obtained before, that Grant was the possessor of no mean intellectual powers. More than that, even, that his powers in that direction were not only far beyond the average, but also in the habit of sustaining frequent and regular usage.

"Where's Sir Austin Kemble?" inquired Sir John.

"With Inspector Hargreaves for a few moments. Not very far away. He'll be back here before very long. Do you particularly want to speak to him?"

"No—I'll tell you what I want to say. It'll keep for Sir Austin—that is, if you consider it worth while passing along to him."

This time Bathurst did not answer him immediately. To Sir John Grant it seemed that this tall, grey-eyed man was summing up, not only the situation, but him as well. When Bathurst's reply did eventually come, it was not as Grant had anticipated.

"Thought of something you didn't think of before?" queried Bathurst.

Grant smiled. "Well, in a way, I suppose I have. But it isn't something that I actually forgot. It happens to be something which I've had the opportunity of considering more carefully in the meantime, and perhaps it's taken on a different aspect." He paused as though unable to proceed with words that pleased him. At length, however, he seemed to find them, for he turned again to Bathurst and launched himself upon his story. "It's just this, Bathurst. Quite a trifling sort of incident, perhaps, but yet one the more that I think of it and dwell on it, seems to puzzle me just a little and make me curious. But I don't know why, exactly, and you, when you've heard it from me, may form the opinion that there's absolutely nothing in it. At any rate, listen to what I've got to say, and then you can let me know what you think." He stopped again in an obvious attempt to marshal facts and incidents in their proper sequence and order. "You will remember, Bathurst, that at the actual moment of the murder I was in the refreshment-room, the ordinary room that is on this side of the panelled doors. In the room at the time there was a man who attracted my attention by reason of his somewhat unusual appearance. I will attempt to describe it to you. He was a thin, spare man with a rather bent figure. He wore a grey pointed beard and affected a monocle. He wore it in his left eye.

"Pierpoint, the chap dressed as the headsman, was, as you've heard, in the room with us, and I'm certain that he spotted this feller too. In fact, I think that I saw them look at each other. I may as well tell you that they gave me the strong impression of being none too pleased to meet, but of course I realize that's neither here nor there, and merely conjecture on my part. Well, when we heard De Ravenac cry out, we dashed to the door, and then when we got the hang of things a bit better we rushed after Wyatt and Pierpoint and, as you've already been told, came to the body of the dead man lying just outside the farther room." He paused, and yet again hesitated, as though uncertain of his ground. "I'm afraid I'm telling this very badly," he recommenced, "and failing to give you the right impression or the real idea that I desired to convey, but to compress my whole meaning into a nutshell—the bearded man with the monocle *disappeared*. It was as though he had vanished into thin air."

"How do you mean?" questioned the interested Bathurst.

"Well," returned Grant, "I know he came to the door with us when he heard the cry, because I have a distinct recollection of seeing him there, and I'm also moderately certain that he was on the fringe of the crowd as it flowed into the corridor. Yet I never saw him again anywhere, and that's the point that strikes me as rather remarkable."

"He could have returned to the ballroom," suggested Bathurst as a solution.

"He could have done, certainly," responded Sir John Grant in a tone that suggested some measure of disappointment at Bathurst's reception of his story, "but do you—?"

"I see your point," conceded Bathurst. "Your contention, of course, would be that this mysterious man seemed to avoid, very deliberately, coming face to face with the tragedy. That if he turned in the opposite direction and came upstairs when all you others, actuated by a common purpose, were intent on discovering the cause of the trouble, he did so from—well, what reasons shall we say, Sir John?"

"Reasons?" retorted Grant interrogatively, and intentionally stressing the plural. "I can only think of one."

"Which is—?"

"That he had definite knowledge of what had happened," returned Grant.

"Yet there is also the possibility of another," argued Bathurst.
"What?"

"Personal cowardice! That quality of shrinking from the contemplation of, or the encounter with, something horrible or unpleasant. For instance, he may have read tragedy in the cry that all of you heard, and revolted from what he thought he might be called upon to visualize. Remember how many people there are, for instance, who shrink from the sight of blood. Under the influence of this fear, it is quite feasible that he went upstairs while all you others were rushing to the murdered man's assistance, and has remained quietly up here ever since."

Grant's disappointment increased. He had not expected that Bathurst would analyse motives in the way that he had.

"You attach little importance to it, then?" said Grant somewhat coldly.

Bathurst shook his head. "By no means, Sir John. Don't think that for a moment. It may prove in the end to be of tremendous importance and I shall docket it carefully away for future reference."

"Look here," persisted Sir John, "if you aren't satisfied with my version, try Pierpoint about it and see whether he registered any similar impressions to mine."

"That's an idea, certainly," acknowledged Bathurst. "I will. I'll do something else besides, Sir John. I'll raise the point with Sir Beverley Pelham's servants, who were on duty at the entrance door. I had already formed the intention to interview them with regard to the guests generally. I'll kill two birds with one stone and settle this point at the same time. Come with me, Sir John, will you? Here's Sir Austin Kemble with the Inspector. I promised him that I'd wait till he returned before I made another move in the investigation."

As Hargreaves made his way towards Sir Beverley Pelham, who was also approaching the vestibule from the other side of the ballroom, Sir Austin joined Bathurst and Grant. After Bathurst had formulated the next step that he proposed to take, the three men set out. They discovered, with very little trouble, that the four footmen who had had charge of the entrance to Sir Beverley Pelham's house, had information for them that was replete with interest. Bathurst and Sir Austin Kemble learned, in the first place, what Inspector Hargreaves had already made it his business to glean.

"I can assure you, sir," said the man who was obviously in charge of the arrangements, "that everything to-night has been above-board and beyond suspicion. Not a single guest has been admitted by us to this house without presenting his or her card of invitation. Lady Pelham issued a ticket of invitation to every single individual. Husbands and wives, for instance, had two tickets. I've already informed Inspector Hargreaves to that effect, and he has checked the information that I gave him. He has counted the invitation cards and he has also counted the guests who are present in the ballroom now. There are four hundred and seventy-four cards and I understand that the Inspector is able to account for four hundred and seventy-three people." He had hardly completed his sentence when Hargreaves came up and joined the group. In fact, the Inspector had overheard the last remark.

"That is quite true, Sir Austin," he said; "cards and guests tally, allowing, of course, for the dead man downstairs. I had hoped that we might possibly discover that the guests were one short."

Bathurst looked at Sir John Grant, and, calling the footman towards him, put the question that the Baronet had been anticipating and of which he thoroughly approved.

"Tell me," said Bathurst, "have you been on duty at the front door for the whole of the evening?"

"I have, sir." The man spoke confidently and without the slightest hesitation.

"I want you to understand my question thoroughly," persisted Bathurst; "have you been away from the doors for any part of the time? For *any* part, mind you. I don't care of how short a duration it may have been—a matter of minutes even."

But again the man replied with definite emphasis. "I haven't moved, sir. I've been the last man of us four chaps to pass every guest that's come along to Mr. Smithson-Day."

At the name Bathurst raised his eyebrows in interrogation. "Smithson-Day," he repeated.

"That's right, sir, the famous toastmaster," explained Sir Beverley Pelham's footman. "Lady Pelham had arranged for him to be here to announce her guests."

Sebastian Loredana, who had, with Sir Beverley, joined the conference, proceeded to amplify the footman's last statement.

"Lady Pelham, as always, chose and acted with the greatest possible discretion. The announcer was grand—more than that, he was magnificent! What a voice! And elocution superb! Never before have I heard the name 'Loredana' rolled across a room to the accompaniment of such majestic thunder."

Bathurst allowed this unsolicited tribute to the distinguished toastmaster to pass without comment. He returned immediately to the man whom he was questioning.

"Could you swear," he asked, "that no one guest has left the house since the ball started?"

The reply was possibly somewhat surprising.

"No, sir. One of the guests certainly did leave during the evening, but only temporarily. He told us that when he went. He came back again."

Bathurst regarded him with intense interest, and all the others pushed forward to hear fuller details.

"Is that really so?" Bathurst spoke very quietly. "Can you remember that particular gentleman's name?" The footman nodded quickly and with a sense of self-importance to show that he was able to furnish Bathurst with the information he desired.

"I can, sir! The gentleman in question was Señor Miguel Da Costa, the Chancellor of San Jonquilo. He left the house soon after nine o'clock, and told me when he went out that he would be returning before the evening was over."

Loredana considered this statement to be so serious that he broke in before Bathurst could put his next question.

"I do not suggest that you do not tell the truth, my man, but I strongly suggest that you are mistaken. What you have just said is flagrantly impossible. For Da Costa, my Chancellor, was at the Hotel Florizel with me until we came together to this house. He was to have preceded me, but found himself unable. You have been deceived, my good fellow, into thinking as you do."

The man addressed began to shake his head in denial of the President's interruption.

Loredana smiled and imitated the man's action.

"I can support the President's statement, Bathurst." Sir Austin Kemble was emphatic. "I called at the Florizel and came along with His Excellency and Señor Da Costa."

"One moment, Sir Austen and your Excellency, if you don't mind," contributed Bathurst. "Before we dismiss the story, let me see what else this man has to tell us."

Loredana shrugged his shoulders. "As you will," he consented, "but what I have just said is true. The matter is beyond argument. Da Costa could not have been here when this man says he was."

Bathurst returned to the footman, and Sir John Grant listened curiously to what the man had to say in answer to Bathurst's next question.

"Could you describe this man who called himself Da Costa?" queried Bathurst.

"Quite well, sir. He was a slim, spare man, a bit bent over, as you might say. Had a pointed grey beard and an eye-glass in his eye."

Sir John Grant, for one, found the answer eminently satisfactory, and his eyes sought Bathurst.

"How was he dressed?" asked the latter.

"Not in costume, sir, just ordinary evening dress. No mask or anything like that."

Loredana continued to shake his head. Bathurst turned to him. "Does the description fit the Chancellor?"

"In every way. I must admit that. All the same, he was not here."

Bathurst considered the situation and resumed with Sir Beverley's footman. "You stated that this man came back When did he come back?"

"I can answer that," assisted Loredana. "It is as Sir Austin said. He came here with me, as my Chancellor should. Assuming, that is, that we still speak of Da Costa. We entered together."

Sir John Grant could control his eagerness no longer. "If that's so," he cried, "the man's here now."

"Of course he is," assented the President; "he is in the ball-room, where he has been ever since we arrived. There is no mystery about him. He is where I should have been if a man had not been foolish enough to get himself murdered. Ask Da Costa to come along. There are moments when he touches intelligence. Not many, perhaps, but some. You will find that he was not here at nine o'clock—he will tell you so himself, and the man who came in his name was somebody up to no good."

"We will certainly ask him what you suggest, your Excellency," concurred Bathurst, "for the question of this mysterious man's identity had presented itself to me before I obtained the footman's evidence. Sir John Grant here had informed me that he had seen a man of the description concerned in the general refreshment-room, and had mentioned the fact to me. Also there is another issue to which I find myself giving consideration."

Loredana screwed his face into a grimace. "It is certainly all very extraordinary," he declared, "but see Da Costa and hear what he has to say. It is your best plan. He mumbles a little and may even repeat himself. But your perseverance impresses me."

Bathurst turned towards Sir Austin Kemble, and the latter caught his look.

"Inspector Hargreaves," said the Commissioner, "go and find the Chancellor of San Jonquilo, Señor Da Costa. He's over there talking to Sir Beverley Pelham's brother. Bring him here to us, will you, please? Or rather into the ante-room on the left there. Tell him that Sir Austin Kemble, the Commissioner of Police, desires to speak with him."

Chapter XI
THE CHANCELLOR'S STORY

When Hargreaves returned and ushered Da Costa into the ante-room that Sir Austin Kemble had suggested as a suitable one for the interview, Bathurst found him easily recognizable. For Sir John Grant's description fitted him well. His thin, spare frame was bent in the way that Grant had described. His trim, pointed grey beard served to distinguish him very clearly from almost the entire company, and he wore his monocle with the ease and sang-froid of the *habitué*. The Chancellor of San Jonquilo accepted the chair that his President indicated to him, with a somewhat perplexed expression on his countenance. Loredana and Sir Austin exchanged glances. It was as though each was waiting upon the other to begin. Sir Austin decided to concede the right of examination and question to Anthony Bathurst. Quinton, the footman who had told the story of the Chancellor's exit and re-entrance, stood respectfully between Bathurst and Sir Beverley Pelham. Bathurst opened with his usual courtesy.

"Señor Da Costa," he commenced, "His Excellency suggests that you may be able to clear up a matter which is troubling the

Commissioner of Police here, Sir Austin Kemble." He gestured towards Sir Austin, and the latter bowed his acknowledgment. Loredana, not to be outdone, returned Da Costa's bow of reciprocation and then bowed to the Commissioner. Bathurst continued.

"A statement has been made by the footman in charge of the admittance arrangements here this evening to the effect that you came to the ball in advance of President Loredana, that you left somewhere in the region of nine o'clock, and that you then returned with the President when he himself arrived later. Is there any truth in that statement?"

Amazement was plainly written on Da Costa's features. "Certainly not," he replied, in his slow, halting English; "there is no truth whatever in such a statement. No truth whatever. Bring the man here that makes it."

Despite Sir Beverley Pelham's intervention, Quinton made a half-step forward, seemingly undecided as to the best course for him to pursue. Bathurst motioned him to be silent.

"In that case, Señor Da Costa," he said, "we of course accept your assurance that Quinton, Sir Beverley's footman, must be mistaken in what he says. Strange to say, however, his story receives a certain amount of corroboration from an unexpected quarter."

Da Costa made a quick movement with his shoulders. "I am sorry," he returned, "but I was not here, as is suggested. That is all there is to it. I cannot say any more, can I?"

"Nobody appreciates that fact more than I, Señor Da Costa. But oblige me for the moment, if you please, by listening to the story that Sir John Grant has to tell you." Bathurst turned to the ex-Minister at Santa Guardina and invited him to take up the narrative.

Grant told the company in general and Señor Da Costa in particular what he had just previously told Bathurst. Da Costa listened attentively, and at the finish of Sir John's story it was apparent to all the onlookers that Da Costa was now in a state of astonishment that was even greater than before. "I have no doubt," concluded Sir John, "that Quinton, the footman, was deceived in the same way as I was. But in appearance, the man whom we saw was your double, Señor Da Costa, and anybody must be excused for imagining in the first place, not having heard your story, that you were here."

Da Costa became almost querulous in his denial. "It is impossible for me to have been here. Quite impossible. Indeed, Sir Austin Kemble himself will tell you that he called at our hotel, the Hotel Florizel, and brought us along here, the President and I and the various other persons of His Excellency's staff that were invited by Lady Pelham."

Sir Austin Kemble, in his very best manner, handsomely confirmed the Chancellor's statement. "Quite true, Señor Da Costa," he declared; "in fact, I as good as told these gentlemen so before they sent for you. Rest assured that I know your statement to be true."

Sir John Grant approached Bathurst and spoke to him very quietly. Bathurst heard what he had to say and put it in turn before the Commissioner. Sir Austin nodded in vigorous acceptance of the proposition.

"Certainly, Bathurst," he affirmed, "do as Sir John suggests, by all means. Tell Hargreaves at once."

The Inspector listened attentively to his instructions, left the apartment, and within the space of a few moments returned there with Martin Pierpoint. During the absence of the Inspector, Sir Austin took the opportunity to inform Da Costa of the tragedy that had occurred downstairs that evening. When he learned the more important details the Chancellor of San Jonquilo seemed thoroughly taken aback and turned to Loredana as though for sympathy.

Pierpoint, upon his entrance, surveyed the ring of people that confronted him with a frown. Bathurst temporarily surrendered the attack to Sir John Grant. "Oh, Pierpoint," said the latter, "we're rather up against something that seems to require a deuce of a lot of explanation, and I'd like you to confirm, if you would, a piece of evidence that I've put forward. I ask you because I know you're the best man to do it."

Martin Pierpoint subsided easily into a chair. "Which is?" he said interrogatively.

"I told Bathurst here of the man with the pointed grey beard and monocle, and there seems to be a grave doubt concerning his identity. You remember the man well, don't you?"

Bathurst watched closely Pierpoint's reception of this question, and the look he saw flit across the man's face as Sir John Grant put it was extremely difficult for him to diagnose accurately. For Pierpoint hesitated and it seemed as though he was at a distinct loss to answer. "There's something here," thought Bathurst, "that most certainly, plagiarizing Sir John Grant, requires a good deal of explanation."

The answer came at last. "I'm sorry, Sir John, if I don't seem able to help you, but I really don't remember the man that you mention."

Apparent as Da Costa's amazement had been before, that of Sir John Grant now was infinitely more so. "You don't remember him?" he questioned incredulously; "why, man, he looked straight at you, and you at him."

Pierpoint shifted uneasily in his chair. "I'm sorry to let you down, Sir John, if you've been calculating upon my evidence to support your own, but my excuse must be that the events afterwards must have driven the incident from my mind."

Grant looked hopelessly at the company generally. Then he glanced specially at Bathurst. Pierpoint, evidently sympathetic, threw out a suggestion very much on the same lines as Grant himself had done a quarter of an hour previously, and once again Inspector Hargreaves, prompted by Sir Austin Kemble, made his departure from the ante-room. When he returned on this occasion, he was accompanied by Major Wyatt. In the same manner as he had done with Pierpoint, Grant told the newcomer, put forward Pierpoint's suggestion that he might be able to help, and invited his corroboration. Anthony Bathurst leant forward, wondering eagerly in what form the answer would come this time. Strangely enough, Wyatt hesitated as Pierpoint, his predecessor, had done, and Bathurst felt moderately positive that he found the question at least disconcerting and very possibly distinctly annoying. Certainly neither Pierpoint nor Wyatt was as comfortable as he would have wished to be. But when Wyatt's reply did materialize it was more helpful than Pierpoint's had been.

"I think I do remember seeing the man of whom you speak, in the corridor."

"When?" intervened Bathurst rapidly.

Wyatt looked up before he replied. The answer dragged. "I really can't remember." Wyatt considered again, but then shook his head with an indication of failure. "I really couldn't say for certain. I think it was either when I came downstairs with Lady Pelham, or when I was on my way back."

"But you said previously that you saw nobody in the corridor." Bathurst came in again relentlessly.

Wyatt shrugged his shoulders with affected nonchalance. "I know I did, and I made that statement to the best of my memory. One can't always remember everything at a given moment. All I can say now is this. I have just a hazy recollection of seeing this man that Sir John Grant has described somewhere along the passage, but I can't remember exactly when, or exactly where, it was."

Loredana struck the table with his hand. "You did see him? Then this mystery is bound up with San Jonquilo! There is a plot against the Republic—against me." He assumed the grand attitude. "I promise you, Mr. Bathurst, that you shall have every assistance from me towards the unravelling of it. Let us find out at the first who it was that played Da Costa's part—that should teach us much."

"I should hate to contradict your Excellency," agreed Anthony Bathurst. He turned to Major Wyatt. "I don't think we need detain you any longer, Major Wyatt."

*　*　*　*　*

Over an hour later, Sir John Grant remembered something more. "It has just come to me, Bathurst," he declared, "that the man with the monocle whom I saw in the general refreshment-room was wearing braided dress trousers. Da Costa, when we saw him afterwards, was not. There have been two Da Costas present here to-night."

"I think you're right, Sir John," returned Mr. Bathurst. "Braided trousers—eh?" He rubbed his hands. "But why double Da Costa?" Grant stared. "Why was *Da Costa* chosen of all people?" repeated Bathurst. "Tell me, Sir John, if I am right in this. Da Costa, I take it, was not Chancellor of San Jonquilo when you held office at Santa Guardina?"

Sir John Grant shook his head. "Quite right, Bathurst. His occupation of the office is comparatively recent. He took over the Chancellorship soon after Sir Beverley Pelham succeeded me."

"Thank you, Sir John. That fact is also helpful to me." Bathurst's hand strayed to his chin. He stood in that attitude for an appreciable time—thinking deeply. Suddenly he turned to the man at his side. "Tell me, Sir John, when the crowd of you heard the dead man's cry and rushed to the scene, who was in front when you reached the communication-doors?"

"Who led the way, do you mean?"

"Exactly."

Grant considered. "I did," he returned eventually, "with the exception of Pierpoint, that is. He had a flying start."

"Any point strike you .as you passed through the doors? Was there anything the least unusual?"

Sir John looked at him wonderingly. "I don't think so. There was no incident or fact connected with us all going through them that I can remember." He broke off, and a curious look entered his eyes. "Stay, though. I'll tell you what I did notice. The door I pushed at seemed to stick for a little while. But you wouldn't call that—"

Bathurst smiled. "You have to push the doors when you go that way and pull them when you come the other. And on this occasion the door stuck—shall we say, Sir John, as though some heavy object was jammed hard up against it—eh? Something on the other side?"

"Yes—that would fit the case, certainly."

"Which was suddenly removed? Yes?"

Grant acquiesced. "Yes."

"Good," responded Mr. Bathurst.

Chapter XII
ANNETTE MORNAY

IT WAS shortly after breakfast on the following morning that Anthony Bathurst was host to a visitor, whom, to say the least, he had not expected. Sir Austin Kemble had already telephoned him from Scotland Yard to the effect that there were so far no new developments. He informed Bathurst that he had instructed Hargreaves to establish immediate communication with the Sûreté in the hope that information might be forthcoming from that quarter which might in time throw the searchlight of truth upon the identity of De Ravenac and at the same time, possibly, expose much of the case that was at present shrouded in darkness. It must be confessed that Bathurst himself was already finessing with certain theories the possibilities of which he found extremely diverting. But, as was always his habit, these theories had been formulated upon the actual data with which the case had already provided him. Let it be said that he was by no means indulging in fancies that had for their basis merely the flights of his own imagination. It was, however, with some little surprise that he listened to Emily, the maid on the housekeeper's staff, when she acquainted him with the fact that a lady was downstairs, and was seeking audience of him.

"Wants me?" he said to the girl, wrinkling his brow. "I can't remember that I have made any appointment for this morning." He walked to the mantelpiece and fished his engagement diary from behind the clock. Bathurst's best friends (that is to say those who were privileged to know him most intimately) would never assert that his living-room was kept anything like so methodically as the way in which his ice-cool brain always functioned.

"In my room," Bathurst was wont to say in moments of introspection, "comfort first, comfort second, and comfort third. Nothing else runs."

Upon this occasion, as he had already anticipated, the diary to which he referred yielded him nothing, and he turned to the maid and repeated the statement that he had made before. "Wants me? Are you sure, Emily?"

"Yes, sir; quite sure, sir. The lady asked for Mr. Anthony Bathurst."

"Young?" inquired that gentleman.

Emily gave the question the benefit of her expert consideration. "Well, sir, that's a question that isn't always easy to answer—and what's more, my step-mother says I'm a poor judge of a woman's age. But certainly not old."

Bathurst permitted himself the luxury of a smile. Things might have been worse, certainly.

"Did you tell her I was in, Emily?" he asked.

"Yes, sir," acknowledged the maid. "I hope that I didn't do wrong in doing so." She seemed to be on the point of adding something, but yielded to a momentary hesitation and repressed it.

Anthony Bathurst took the opportunity to encourage her. "You were about to say, Emily . . . ?" The look that he gave her was an added encouragement. Whenever she was thus favoured, Emily burnt her boats.

"Well, sir, I thought that she seemed troubled and had come to you in the hope that you might be able to help her. That was really why I told her that you were at home. I shouldn't have had the heart to have turned her away."

"Show her up, then, Emily. We'll see what we can do for her."

The girl of Emily's narration had evidently come to the flat on foot, for Bathurst's journey to his window that overlooked the street below showed him no sign of either waiting car or taxi-cab. Turning from the window, he heard Emily back again at his door. He walked across and opened it. The girl outside who had sought his assistance was strikingly beautiful, and Bathurst didn't need to look at her twice to realize this. In figure tall and slim, her dark eyes were like great pools, full of expression, and set off to the best advantage the distinctive modelling of her mouth and chin. Her hair was almost raven-black, and here again this feature was thrown into greater distinction by the ivory pallor of her face. Her clothes were "chic" to the last degree and carried in all of them the hallmark of Paris. "French," thought Anthony Bathurst to himself when he first regarded her. "I have had many clients less attractive than the one Fate has sent me this morning. And very few more so!"

He motioned the girl to one of his big, comfortable chairs and took the opposite one himself. The lady removed her gloves and placed them in her lap.

"I have the honour to address Monsieur Bathurst?" she inquired, with a tilt of her head that bordered upon the provocative.

"I am Anthony Bathurst. I won't comment upon your other suggestion."

The girl stared for a moment and then essayed a smile, but there was an undoubted impression of effort behind it, and it was very plain to Bathurst as he sat and watched her that Emily's diagnosis of the situation was accurate—his visitor was troubled. The fingers of her hands were never still and her lips moved repeatedly in a manner that spoke of an intolerable sorrow.

"My name is Annette Mornay," the girl said simply. "I have come concerning the death last night of André de Ravenac. *The murder of André de Ravenac*." The dark eyes flashed. The mere mention of these last few words was the means of summoning to her, as auxiliaries, every power of Bathurst's intelligence. Much more than she could have ever dreamed. Matters were progressing better for him, too, than he could have legitimately anticipated. But his instincts, alert as always, warned him to run no risks.

"Your information emanates from . . . ?"

"If from no other source, from this morning's paper," she declared.

Bathurst watched her very carefully. There was more than trouble in her mind, he decided—there was also a quality of violent and dangerous emotion, that only needed the essential spark to bring it to the condition of fierce explosion.

"The Press, as far as I have been able to peruse it, is by no means communicative or verbose, Mademoiselle Mornay. You will forgive me, too, if I ask you how you were aware that I was connected with the case."

Annette Mornay flashed him another look of attractive indignation. But her reply was spoken very simply.

"I do not know that you are connected with 'the case', as you describe it. But I have sufficient sense to realize that if you are not now, you very soon will be. That is so, Monsieur Bathurst, *n'est-ce-pas*?"

"Am I permitted to inquire upon what reasoning you base that last statement?"

Annette Mornay shrugged her dainty shoulders with a gesture that was as eloquent as it was charming. "Your journal in which I this morning read of André, your *Daily Bugle*, mentions that the Commissioner of Police, Sir Austin Kemble himself, was a guest at Sir Beverley Pelham's house and naturally appeared upon the scene after André's body had been discovered." She leant forward towards Bathurst with the tears clouding her eyes, and the tips of her fingers of her left hand were pressed convulsively into the arm of the big chair in which she was seated. "And where Sir Austin Kemble is, there also is Monsieur Bathurst. Is that fact not well known? Have we in Paris not read of it?" Her English was almost faultless, carrying only the faintest trace of accent. Bathurst abandoned his entrenchments, for he had no adequate answer to make to the girl's last statement.

"You overwhelm me," he admitted. "Also, if I may be allowed to say so, Mademoiselle wastes no time. How can I assist you?"

"At last we arrive at a question of facts, Monsieur Bathurst. That is what I desired you to say to me. I will tell you in turn what I have come to say to you. I cannot afford to waste any time. If my brain ordered me to doze, my heart would surely disobey." She paused for a moment to control her emotions. "André de Ravenac was my lover and, which is more for a Frenchman, you will understand, has been for many years. Because of that I will do my best to avenge him: listen to me, Monsieur Bathurst, and tell me, please, how it was and why it was that André of all people was invited to Sir Beverley Pelham's *bal masque* last night?" Once again she leant forward towards him, mastered by the eagerness that she found it impossible to conceal.

"I myself have found the question that you have just raised— shall we say—extremely intriguing. Instead of replying to it, I shall be happy to listen to the answer that you can supply to it yourself, Mademoiselle Mornay." Bathurst's eyes held hers as he faced her. There was no trace of hesitation about Annette now. Her confidence in herself bordered upon the superb.

"Lady Pelham invited him," she declared with an air of tragic finality.

"So I presumed," returned Bathurst, "seeing that the lady you have named was his hostess. Would it trouble you to explain yourself with a greater attention to detail?"

Mademoiselle Mornay's eyes held scorn, resentment and a definite measure of contempt. "You know full well what I mean. You are just hiding behind words. A man knows these things before they come to a woman. For one thing, there is always more talk of these things where men are. My sex is not the only one that deals in scandal. Where women merely dabble, you men dig deep. When I say that Lady Pelham invited André de Ravenac, I mean that her husband, Sir Beverley, didn't count! His wishes on the subject were ignored, or, what is more likely than that, never even considered. He is not, as you say, on the map. Yet he is her husband." Annette stopped, breathless.

"Are a husband's desires 'in these things', as you describe them, ever considered?" countered Bathurst.

"Don't play with me, Monsieur Bathurst—I beg of you! I have not come here to be put off with your little personal cynicisms."

"Come to the point, then, Mademoiselle, if you please! Cut out innuendo and give me facts. That is if you seriously desire my help. I gather that you came here because you had news for me—that you intend to tell me something that you regard as important?"

Annette Mornay tossed her head impatiently. "Important to me and I have no doubt very, very important to Lady Pelham— oh, yes—but, alas, no longer important to André de Ravenac." She paused, no doubt to make her next statement the more dramatic, and Bathurst was careful to make no further interruption. "Lady Pelham was in love with André or at least I think that she was."

This was not exactly the piece of information that Bathurst had anticipated, but nevertheless this unexpected interview appeared to him now as though it were about to bear very valuable fruit.

"I suppose that you have some grounds for making that statement, Mademoiselle Mornay? There is scarcely need for me to point out to you its seriousness. You are sure that you are not allowing your imagination or your jealousy to override your intelligence?" It was his desire to be provocative, to induce in Annette Mornay a condition of uncontrolled emotion, out of which state he decided there might yet come more and more of the truth. And success attended his efforts. When her answer came it suggested so much that seemed in the nature of confession that, to him, it also bore the mark of veracity.

"I am jealous—if you like," she conceded. "Or, rather, I was. There is no need to be now. But I am not letting my imagination run away with me as you thought might be the case. I will tell you what I know. Listen. For the last month or so, in fact, ever since Lady Pelham returned home from Santa Guardina, the two of them have been almost inseparable. André has danced attendance upon her. Where he has been, she has been, and vice-versa. After a very little while I suspected how things were. At length I taxed André with it. It made him uncomfortable, but he denied to my face that there was any truth in what I suggested. But his protestations did not satisfy me, and I determined, as you English people say, to keep my eyes open, and perhaps find things out for myself. Twice within the last fortnight André cancelled an appointment that he had previously made with me." She paused as though dubious of passing on to Bathurst the more intimate details of the occasions to which she had just referred. Bathurst brought her to the point.

"What steps did you take, Mademoiselle? For I can see that it is not your nature to remain passive and quiescent in circumstances such as you have described."

"I went to his flat," she declared defiantly, "and upon each of the last two occasions I encountered Lady Pelham coming away. The look on her face, for we women are quick to read and understand these signs, Monsieur Bathurst, told me very plainly that the errand which had brought her there was no ordinary one. I knew it, and she too knew that I knew it."

"Go on," urged Bathurst, for his interest was by now very thoroughly aroused. Wine—be it red Falernian or other vintage, is not the only medium of Truth.

Annette needed no further encouragement and was quickly in her stride again. "I made it my business to see André at once and again unburdened myself of my suspicions. This time I went farther and turned them into downright accusations. He laughed in my face in a way that he had made his own. Told me to mind my own damned business and that those that lived longest would see the most. They were the very words he used," she concluded sorrowfully.

"What happened after that? Tell me everything—please."

"It was the week afterwards that I heard from André that he was going to the ball at Sir Beverley Pelham's. Why? I ask you, Monsieur Bathurst. Why should Lady Pelham invite André there of all people unless she had some vital incentive? It is plain that they were lovers."

"Why do you use the expression 'André of all people'?" Bathurst's question was quiet but insistent.

Annette bit her lip, for she knew now that she had said more than she intended. The action interested him immensely. Seeing that no answer was forthcoming, Bathurst repeated his question more explicitly.

"Why, Mademoiselle Mornay, did you use the phrase 'of all people'?"

"I meant nothing—particularly. All I meant to convey to you was that André de Ravenac was not a member of Lady Pelham's personal circle in the ordinary nature of things. He could not be said to belong to her set."

Bathurst watched her face carefully as she essayed this explanation. "You did not mean, then, by any chance," he suggested, "that De Ravenac's reputation, for example, was sufficient to place him outside the pale as far as Sir Beverley and Lady Pelham were concerned?"

Annette Mornay scouted the idea unceremoniously. "Certainly not, Monsieur Bathurst—as far as I am aware, the reputation of André de Ravenac was equal to the reputation of anybody who was present. But reputation alone is not sufficient to unlock all the social doors. Nothing was farther from my mind than such an idea. No—there was nothing to secure for him his invitation beyond the fact that he had 'an *affaire*' with Lady Pelham. I stick to what I said. For instance, what was there to connect him with the Republic of San Jonquilo?"

"That is another question to which I hope to devote a certain amount of attention in order to discover a satisfactory answer. For it must not be overlooked by any of us who approach the investigation of this strange case that De Ravenac died clutching in his hand a torn piece of silk embroidered with the colours of the Republic that you have just named."

Annette gasped with incredulity, and her hand went impetuously to her throat in an effort to hide her emotion.

"Torn silk, in the San Jonquilo colours? There is no mention of that in this morning's Press, that I remember."

"Yet it is so, Mademoiselle Mornay, I assure you. The Press these days suffers more from dearth of authentic information than from any lack of imaginative power. In fact, the entire affair, as far as can be seen at the present juncture, seems to have what may be called a San Jonquilo significance."

"But that is impossible! André had never been near the Republic."

"Impossible or not," declared Bathurst, "President Loredana is by no means satisfied that he is not the dangerous centre of a pernicious plot aimed at the safety of his Republic. Tell me—was De Ravenac left-handed?"

She shook her head. "No. He was a right-handed man. But why does the President think what you say?" she queried wildly. "I told you that André was in no way connected with San Jonquilo."

Bathurst paid no attention to this last interruption. Instead he proceeded to develop the theory that he had just formulated.

"I may tell you," he added, "that His Excellency the President has publicly proclaimed his intention to bring the murderer of De Ravenac to justice. With that purpose I have every sympathy. So much so, that I have joined forces with him."

A gleam of intense satisfaction flashed into the eyes of Annette. Here was definite promise at last. "It gladdens my heart to hear you say that. For President Loredana will find another ally in me."

She rose with every sign of determination from the chair that she had been occupying. "I rather envy the Republic of San Jonquilo its President," she added. "He sounds something very like a man!"

Chapter XIII
BATHURST AT WORK

Sebastian Loredana lifted the huge white cat that nestled on his knees in sulky complacence and took the card that was proffered to him by his Chancellor, Da Costa, with a gesture of summary impatience. But this gesture of impatience speedily gave way to a much greater feeling of something that was very closely akin to satisfaction. He tapped the card with his finger as he showed it and explained it to Da Costa.

"This young man impresses me," he frankly acknowledged. "He has the quality, or 'knack', as I believe it is called in this accursed country where the sun never shines, of quickly separating the things that matter from those that most obviously don't. He reminds me in some way of myself. I was able to notice that quality from the way in which he conducted his examinations at old Pelham's when he was first called to the dead man. He wasted little time and all that he did seemed to me to be to the point, and I observed very much the same state of affairs when he was inquiring into that rather unpleasant little matter that affected you yourself, Da Costa. Do you remember?"

The Chancellor grunted unintelligibly. But Loredana was used to this, and it made no difference to his eulogy of Anthony Bathurst. He continued in the same strain. "Taking everything into consideration, Da Costa, I am not at all sure that I could have conducted the inquiries better myself. If I had a hundred young men of his calibre in San Jonquilo I would build so that it should lead the world. Tell Mr. Bathurst that I will see him, and come back yourself."

When Bathurst entered the apartment a few moments later with Da Costa at his heels, Loredana was at great pains to put him at his ease immediately and make him feel at home. Sebastian adored the grand gestures.

"You have met my Chancellor before, Mr. Bathurst," he said by way of explanation. "You can speak as freely as you wish in front of him. He is my right-hand man. I do not know what I should do without him. He is as industrious as he is amusing, and as entertaining as he is inefficient."

"As you wish, your Excellency. But going on from where we were when we were last together, I have taken advantage of your offer, and have come to the Hotel Florizel in the hope that you may help me in one or two directions. For I am pretty confident that you can."

"I shall be charmed," bowed Loredana; "but first of all is it permitted for me to inquire of you if you have made any progress?"

"A little, your Excellency, perhaps—but certainly not a lot. And it is with regard to that 'little' that my questions arise. But you shall hear them. In the first place, were you in any way acquainted with the dead man De Ravenac?"

Loredana shook his head. "No, Mr. Bathurst. That pleasure had, alas, been denied to me, and I fear that now Fate will have no chance to repair the omission. 'Twas ever thus!"

"Thank you, your Excellency. I will ask the question, then, in another form. Had you ever heard the name in connection with your country?"

"I think not, Mr. Bathurst. It is just a possibility that Da Costa here could answer that question with more certainty than I. I have known him to remember some things, not many—and I forget when. But we will ask him." He invited his Chancellor to come closer and repeated to him what Bathurst had asked. But to no purpose, for Da Costa also shook his head.

"The name is entirely unfamiliar to me, and if the photographs that have appeared in the Press since the murder are any criterion, I have never set eyes on the man in my life. He is a complete stranger to me." The Chancellor paused for a second and proceeded. "I took the trouble to look for the man's face in the papers particularly. As no doubt you know, Mr. Bathurst, life in a South American Republic is far from a bed of roses, and for some time now San Jonquilo has been no exception to that rule. It has been in a condition of continual ferment. Last year, plot succeeded plot against the Presidency, but happily all failed. Something or other went wrong with one after the other, and I looked at De Ravenac's face when it appeared in the Press to see if he might by chance be one of those who had plotted but who had since assumed another name. But as far as my knowledge goes, it was not so. I can assure you that it was not so."

As he finished speaking, Da Costa took his monocle from his eye and polished it thoughtfully. Bathurst, however, changed the point of his attack.

"I am right, I believe, in stating that Sir John Grant was Sir Beverley Pelham's predecessor as British Minister at Santa Guardina?"

Loredana beamed upon his interrogator. "You are, Mr. Bathurst. Sometimes I thought he was President even and that I myself was a mere figurehead. He was an interfering fool and his conceit is stupendous. In fact, I know only one thing to match it. His ignorance!"

"You are severe, your Excellency. Surely Sir John had—"

"My dear sir, on the contrary. I am kind. The day before he left Santa Guardina I let him empty four bottles of my very best vintage. Severity should be spawned of sterner stuff."

"Sir Beverley's appointment as his successor was gratifying to you, then?"

"Once again, Mr. Bathurst, I would criticize your choice of words. Sir John Grant, Sir Beverley Pelham, Sir Something-Somebody-else—they are all immaterial to me." He shrugged his shoulders with a gesture of disdain. "They may come and they may go—but Loredana goes on for ever. You see—I know something of your English poetry."

"And Lady Pelham?" Bathurst's tone of inquiry was nonchalance itself.

Loredana became at once the perfect cavalier. His white teeth flashed into a smile that showed up his swarthiness of skin more than ever.

"Lady Pelham is an angel," he declared. "San Jonquilo was beautiful before she came to it, but her presence lent it an even greater beauty, and the lily was painted. I, Sebastian Loredana, know what I am talking about. I am a judge of these things. I know none better. More than once I have looked at that old fool Sir Beverley, and instantly all my sympathies have gone out to his charming wife. How it must have galled her to have made my friendship *after* her marriage and to be forced to toy with dreams of the might-have-been. But there—it is not good for one to have everything! She has beauty and charm and youth— she cannot very well expect to have also—Loredana."

"'Twould be an exercise of avarice most certainly, your Excellency. You admired Lady Pelham, then, *immensely*?"

"Mere reciprocity, Mr. Bathurst. The assertion of my natural courtesy. I could hardly do less, could I?"

"Had the lady other admirers?"

"It is possible. 'Lesser breeds without the law.'" Sebastian smiled. "But not from the same cause as I. In that respect I stood alone. That is obvious, is it not?"

"It would surprise you, then, to hear that a story has been brought to me connecting Lady Pelham with the dead man De Ravenac?"

Sebastian's eyes narrowed and he wrinkled his brow into a frown. "Connecting in what way?"

"The statement made to me was that they were lovers."

Loredana stroked his upper lip with his fingers and then slowly shook his head. "They were man and woman, and it is a possibility, I suppose—but no, Mr. Bathurst—I think not. Who was your informant, may I ask?"

"I haven't her permission to divulge her name, so you must excuse me not answering that question."

"It was a lady, then?"

"I told you as much."

Sebastian's lip curled in contempt. "It is an unreliable sex. I shouldn't rely on the information too much if I were you."

"Major Wyatt, your Excellency—ever run against him before?"

Loredana puffed out his cheeks. "Never. Why do you ask me that?"

"The part played by more than one person on the night that De Ravenac was murdered is not yet entirely clear to me. For instance—take your own statement at our last meeting—who was the man who masqueraded as Señor Da Costa? For that reason alone, the antecedents of several of whom I may call the 'more prominent' people interest me considerably."

"You're right, Mr. Bathurst." Loredana looked grave, and there was no doubt in Bathurst's mind that his perturbation was real. "That Da Costa business opened my eyes for me," he stated with some element of despondency. "In fact, it has preyed on my mind ever since. More so, I think, than it has on Miguel's own." He turned to the Chancellor for confirmation.

The old man grinned cynically. "I have enough worries of my own without seeking for others. But at least one thing is evident, Mr. Bathurst. The man who went to Sir Beverley Pelham's early that evening in my name must have known that I was here in the hotel with His Excellency Señor Loredana. That he did so with a sinister intention is clear, I think."

Bathurst nodded agreement. "I think we shall be safe in assuming that."

"Well, then"—a malicious gleam danced in the old man's eyes—"how many people are there who had that definite knowledge of my whereabouts? Find that circle—narrow it down one by one—and you must eventually arrive at the correct solution. Does it not appear to you in that way too?" His tone held a hint of challenge.

"Elementary, my dear Watson," mocked Bathurst.

Da Costa looked surprised, but gave no sign that he understood. Baker Street to him, save, possibly, in connection with Madame Tussaud's, was unknown, and No. 221B had no existence for him whatever. But Loredana had place in another gallery.

"Well, Mr. Bathurst," he cajoled, "would you not like to—what shall we say—develop Miguel's fancy? Don't you find his idea attractive?" A smile lurked round the corners of his mouth as he uttered the invitation. "You must not judge my Chancellor, you know, from his appearance. 'Twould be perhaps excusable, but to do so would be terribly unjust to him. He has quite lucid intervals, I assure you."

Da Costa wagged his head at Loredana's witticism and turned to listen to Anthony Bathurst.

"Tell me, your Excellency, who at Sir Beverley Pelham's knew that Señor Da Costa was going to be at the hotel with you during the early part of the evening?"

Loredana stroked his black hair. "That is not so easy for me to answer. I take it Sir Beverley Pelham himself was aware of it, also, no doubt, Lady Pelham, but beyond that it would be impossible for me to say. What do you think yourself, Da Costa?"

"I know no more than you. How is it possible? I saw that your message was delivered. I had no further interest in the matter." Da Costa shrugged his shoulders as though the discussion of the incident was distasteful to him.

Bathurst seized an opportunity. "How was the message delivered, Señor Da Costa?"

"It was 'phoned to Sir Beverley Pelham's house by His Excellency's secretary, Mr. Twining."

"Twining?" repeated Bathurst. "Wasn't there a Twining at the—?"

Loredana interrupted him.

"Ball? Yes, Mr. Bathurst. I had, I am afraid, forgotten him. My personal secretary, Gerald Twining, is a cousin of Lady Pelham's. It was—er—largely through her very persistent influence that he secured the appointment on my staff." He caressed his chin. "I confess that I find it difficult—very difficult—to refuse the dear creature anything." His eyes met Bathurst's. "That is to say—of course, anything in reason."

"This Gerald Twining, if I remember accurately, was costumed at Lady Pelham's ball as a Turk, wasn't he?"

"Again I couldn't say, Mr. Bathurst. I always endeavour not to waste time over things that hold no interest for me. He had gone out two hours or so before Sir Austin Kemble came here for me, and I didn't see him in his fancy dress at all."

Bathurst relapsed into consideration, to put, after a moment, a further question to Sebastian Loredana.

"Was this Mr. Twining with you at Santa Guardina?"

"Most assuredly."

"And accompanied your party to England?"

Loredana bowed. "Of course." He walked across to the Chancellor with a question in his eyes. "I have no wish to inconvenience Mr. Bathurst, Da Costa—but I fancy that I have an appointment within a very short time from now. Isn't that so?"

"It is, your Excellency. You are expecting Mr. Robin Blaker this afternoon. He wrote and made the appointment with you, if you remember."

Loredana looked at his watch. "What time did he say?"

"Four o'clock, your Excellency. He suggested it. You agreed."

Anthony Bathurst rose. "In the circumstances, then, I will not detain your Excellency any longer. Very many thanks for your kindness and assistance." He paused at the door of the apartment. "This Mr. Gerald Twining who acts as your secretary—is he in at the present moment? I take it that you would have no objection to—"

"You interviewing him?" Loredana was the essence of cordiality. "Not at all, Mr. Bathurst. By all means have a chat with him if you wish it. He should he in—there is much arrears of correspondence at the present moment. He has a room here, above my own suite, and no doubt you will find him in it. Ask him any questions you like. You will find him a very charming young man."

It was by a strange coincidence that both Robin Blaker and Annette Mornay called upon the President of San Jonquilo at three minutes past four that afternoon. For neither knew, of course, that the other was coming, and whereas Loredana expected Blaker, Annette's visit was planned and decided upon by her entirely on the spur of the moment.

CHAPTER XIV
GERALD TWINING'S STORY

AN OFFICIAL of the Hotel Florizel, who somewhat unceremoniously passed Mr. Bathurst on the heavily carpeted stairs, afforded that gentleman, upon courteous request, the information that His Excellency's secretary was within his room. The tap which Anthony Bathurst gave the door was rewarded with an invitation to enter. Gerald Twining, however, did not survey his visitor when he saw who it was with quite as much cordiality as his voice had held when he had issued the invitation. He was a tall, slimmish young man, with dark-brown hair and rather light-blue eyes. Eyes that never rested for very long upon the object which they regarded. His mouth suggested a certain weakness of character, and upon his face there was an expression that bordered very closely on the supercilious. At the precise moment of Bathurst's entrance he wore his plus-fours with an air of negligence that somehow seemed out of place in the affairs of San Jonquilo.

"You'll pardon my intrusion, I'm sure," opened Bathurst, "but I believe that I have the honour of addressing President Loredana's secretary. Am I right?"

Superciliousness gave way to caution. The tall young man regarded him suspiciously. "That is quite right," he affirmed; "my name is Twining. Do we know each other?"

Bathurst smiled. "Hardly that. Although we met on the occasion of Lady Pelham's masked ball. I saw you there, but you probably didn't see me. You went as a guest—I was sent for in another capacity. My name is Anthony Bathurst."

The habitual sense of superiority with which Twining seemed invested momentarily deserted him, for the masked ball at his cousin's was the last thing on earth at that moment to which he desired reference to be made.

"Oh, yes," he admitted jerkily. "That's quite true. I was there, of course, with my brother. I don't know whether you know of it, but we're first cousins, he and I, of Lady Pelham. Still, that's neither here nor there. What is your business with me this afternoon?"

Anthony Bathurst put his cards on the table. "You are aware, doubtless, of several of the circumstances that attended the death of André de Ravenac."

Twining frowned and afterwards nodded. "Naturally. Robin Blaker, my cousin and Josephine's brother, has told me most of the facts connected with the case."

"Good. I need waste no time, then, in preliminaries. I come into the affair through Sir Austin Kemble, the Commissioner of Police, and also at the express wish of President Loredana himself."

At mention of the latter name Twining bit his lip. It was as he had feared, directly Bathurst had proclaimed his name. More than one of Bathurst's previous investigations were known to him, and he very reluctantly prepared himself for the questioning that he felt certain would inevitably follow. But the first query that Bathurst put to him was in the nature of a surprise, and he felt, in consequence, a distinct feeling of relief at the line with which Bathurst opened.

"Mr. Twining"—came Bathurst's question—"take your mind back, if you will, to the day of your cousin's ball."

"Yes; what part of the day, morning or—?"

"That I don't know. But I've just interviewed President Loredana and Señor Da Costa, the Chancellor of San Jonquilo, and I gather from them that you telephoned to Sir Beverley's house at some time or other during the day to the effect that President Loredana and perhaps Da Costa would be unable to arrive at the function until a somewhat later hour than had previously been anticipated. That is so, isn't it?"

Twining thrust his hands deeply into his pockets. "Quite true, Mr. Bathurst. A message was received that morning from the San Jonquilese Embassy informing us that the Spanish Ambassador desired an audience of President Loredana if possible during the early part of that evening. The message was by telephone and I answered it myself." Twining's explanation was ready, fluent, and bore the hallmarks of truth and sincerity. He continued with scarcely any hesitation. "President Loredana agreed to this suggestion when I put it before him, and Señor Da Costa asked me to 'phone the news to Sir Beverley Pelham. I asked for Josephine, my cousin, and told her."

Bathurst pondered over his statement.

"You are quite certain," he said, "that it was Lady Pelham herself who took your telephone message?"

Twining was certainty itself when he replied. "Oh—absolutely! I know Jo's voice all right, don't you fear. It's too distinctive for anybody to make a mistake about it."

"Could you at this stage of the case remember the exact terms of your message?"

"Yes—I think so. I told Jo that Loredana himself wouldn't be along till somewhere about ten, and that Da Costa would do his best to blow along earlier, but that she wasn't to bank on it, and that I myself would be there at the proper time."

"Think carefully, Mr. Twining, please. Do you remember if you told her the reason that was keeping her distinguished guests back."

"I think I mentioned the Embassy appointment to her, but I'm not sure. Is it important?"

"It is rather—or at least it looks like it. Is there anybody else on President Loredana's staff here who had this information besides yourself?"

"There are a couple of girl stenographers. I suppose it's on the cards that they may have known. But really I couldn't say. I didn't tell them, if that's what you mean."

"You, of course, know Señor Da Costa well and intimately?"

"Oh, yes. Very well indeed. I've known him ever since I took up my appointment with the President at Santa Guardina."

"Did you happen to observe him, by chance, or even anybody *resembling* him, at your cousin's ball during the earlier part of the evening?"

Here Twining hesitated noticeably, for perhaps the first time, and Bathurst felt certain that he was concentrating on an effort to avoid agitation. "I'm not quite sure, Mr. Bathurst," he declared at length. "I have just a sort of idea that I saw him descending the staircase that led to the refreshment-rooms shortly before nine o'clock. I couldn't swear to the exact time. Another thing, I only caught sight of his back, so my testimony isn't worth too much, I'm afraid, from your point of view."

The time that Twining had mentioned held for Bathurst an immense measure of significance. He dived therefore for details. "You yourself, Mr. Twining, when you saw this man, were you descending or ascending the stairs?"

The hesitation that affected Gerald Twining now was markedly apparent. He seemed at a loss for words, and his eyes showed a gleam of annoyance.

"I think that I was at the head of the staircase," he conceded at length.

"Alone?"

Twining affected to reflect. "No I don't think I was. I don't know, and I can't remember. After all, the place was crowded like all those crushes are."

But that time, nine o'clock, still appealed to Bathurst. "See anything of De Ravenac about the time you mentioned?" he asked carelessly.

"De Ravenac?" Twining invested his query with a note of surprise. "The guests at the ball were, in nearly every instance, not only in costume, Mr. Bathurst, but also masked. In some cases the masks made identification a matter of impossibility."

Immediately the reply had been made Twining not only realize that he had made a mistake, but was also supremely conscious of the answer's lameness. He looked up to find Bathurst watching him relentlessly.

"I am aware of that, Mr. Twining. But surely it is almost universal knowledge, now, that De Ravenac, when he was murdered, was dressed in the costume of an Arab. I take it that you in common with countless other people know that. So that if I slightly amend the question that I put to you, you may find it easier of answer. Did you see anything of a man dressed as an Arab about the time that you mention—nine o'clock?"

Twining grinned, but the effort was a sickly one. "Well, as a matter of fact I have a sort of hazy recollection that I did."

"Something like your memory of the other man—eh?"

"It was like this. Two or three other fellows and I were assing about—you know what I mean, playing the giddy ox—we're Jo's relations, you know, and I believe I'm right in saying that one of the people whom we held up at the head of the staircase *was* a bloke in some sort of Arab garb."

Bathurst looked grave. "What particular form did your bovine vertigo take, Mr. Twining?"

Twining was unable to separate the raillery in Bathurst's voice from the note of indomitable purpose. He smiled again.

"Oh—er—we were putting up a sort of highwayman stunt. You know the kind of thing I mean—'stand and give the counter-sign' and bilge like that—and the more I come to think of it, the more certain I am that a man dressed as an Arab was one of the merchants whom we held up."

"*We,*" declared Bathurst, stressing the pronoun unmistakably. "Do you mind telling me who the men were who were with you?"

"I shouldn't have thought it important or necessary," replied Twining a little touchily, "but if you must know, they were my brother Nick, and my two cousins Dick and Robin Blaker."

"Lady Pelham's brothers?"

"Exactly," corroborated Mr. Twining. "We were more or less privileged persons, you see."

Almost coincidentally with his last remark a man's voice was audible from somewhere close at hand in the corridor outside. As he heard it, a puzzled look came over Twining's face.

"Pardon me a moment," he said to his visitor, "but I'm dashed if I don't believe that that's Robin outside there now. He may be wanting me for all I know. Excuse me for half a minute, will you?" He dashed towards the door of his room and made a hurried exit.

Bathurst imperturbably awaited his reappearance, and it must be observed that Twining was almost as good as his word and that he hadn't very long to wait. Within the space of three minutes Twining was back.

"I was right," he announced, with a strange jerkiness; "that was Robin all right."

"I anticipated that you were. But you see I already had information. I learned a short time ago that he had an appointment this afternoon with President Loredana. What was it that brought him to the wrong floor?"

"Funny thing—that's just the question that I asked him. Force of habit, according to him, brought him up into my quarters." He laughed and passed his hand across his brow with the action of a man who is either trying to remember something or endeavouring to make up his mind on a certain course of action.

"What's puzzling you, Mr. Twining?" The directness of Bathurst's question seemed to take him a little off his guard.

"Robin had a girl with him. I don't think I was expecting to run into anyone but Robin himself, and when I did it rather took the wind out of my sails. You see, we of the family always look on old Robin as a confirmed misogynist."

Bathurst rose—on the point of departure. "Permit me to thank you, Mr. Twining, for the information that you have given me. Every little helps, you see, when you're on a job of work like this."

Chapter XV
THE FLYING DEATH

Annette Mornay's interview with Loredana had had the effect of clearing her mind considerably, and she could have hugged herself for having had the good sense—nay—the inspiration—to go to him for help. The strong encouragement he had given her and the frankness with which she had rewarded him only caused her to wish fervently that she had been as frank and as candid with Anthony Bathurst as she had been with the President of San Jonquilo. Then she might have enlisted stronger assistance. For Loredana's frame of mind with regard to the slaying of André de Ravenac was such that Annette had been constrained to unburden herself concerning more than one lurid detail of her lover's flamboyant and chequered past.

Loredana, sensing that his attractive visitor was in the mood for confidences, had summarily dismissed Miguel Da Costa, and Annette, fortified by the privacy of the interview and the intensity of her emotion, had withheld no particulars of importance. Knowing De Ravenac as she had done, certain suspicions that had gradually been forming in her mind were now fast becoming certainties, although there still remained much that was impenetrably dark to her. For Loredana's theory of the crime, although startlingly ingenious, did not altogether satisfy her. The amazing nature of the whole thing stupefied her and for a time she moved in a kind of bemused condition that seemed to atrophy all her intelligences.

When she had risen from her chair to terminate the interview, she heard Loredana's promise that De Ravenac's murderer should be found, dazedly, and when she murmured to him that Bathurst was already partly in her confidence, his enthusiastic approval only served to confirm her in the action that she then proposed to herself to take. By the time she had reached her flat in Malgan Avenue, that lay on the outskirts of Maida Vale, she had come to the unerring conclusion that her own life was in the very deadliest peril, and she literally shivered at the realization.

De Ravenac's assassin, if he found her, would show her as much mercy as a tiger would a tender kid. On her way in to the flat she stopped and beckoned to the porter on duty.

"Murrell," she said, "if any callers should chance to come for me this evening—I'm not in—do you understand? I'm not in to anybody. What time do you go off duty, Murrell?"

"The night porter comes on at half past eleven, miss."

Annette made a rapid mental calculation. "That will be all right, I think, Murrell. Promise me now that you won't forget what I've told you."

Murrell touched his peaked cap. "That'll be all right, Miss Mornay. You can rely on me."

"Thanks, Murrell. Take this, will you, and get a taxi for me here as soon as it's really dark. Say about half past nine. It's just possible, Murrell, that I shan't sleep here to-night. I've had an invitation to a friend's. So if I should be missing in the morning don't let anyone get alarmed, because there'll be nothing to worry about."

"Right, miss; and you want a taxi at half past nine? Leave it to me."

Annette pressed a second coin into his hand.

"Thank you, miss."

Without troubling to ring the bell for the lift, Annette raced upstairs to her own apartments. A quick glance round tended to reassure her momentarily, but then a rapid adjustment of her mental faculties was sufficient to tell her that what she had half feared was manifestly absurd. She proceeded immediately to take stock of her entire position from all the angles and points of view of which she could think. First of all, there was the all-important financial one. Going into her bedroom, and, in there, to her private drawer, she discovered that she possessed between nineteen and twenty pounds in actual hard cash. So far so good. That would be enough to enable her to achieve her purpose. Secondly, there was the question of her passport. Happily, too, that was in order, and Annette's spirits rose appreciably in consequence. Thirdly, she was reasonably sure that she had not been followed home by anybody.

Her mind was now thoroughly made up. She would slip away from the flat that night by car as soon as it was dark, sleep in one of the big hotels, from where she would drop a line to Anthony Bathurst, and fly to Paris in the morning. But although her previous panic had to a certain extent subsided, she knew for certain that her fears had reduced her to a bundle of quivering nerves. The slightest noise sent her heart leaping into her mouth, and her tongue was dry with that terrible dryness that only the fugitive and hunted know. When Anthony Bathurst learned the history of De Ravenac, as it stretched back like a dark skein across the pages of the years, and how he had sought at last to enmesh Josephine Pelham, argued Annette to herself, it would surely point out to him beyond reasonable doubt certain facts which now glittered their very truth in front of her, impossible though she found it, at the moment, to fit them all into the story in the proper pattern.

Frightened as she was, Annette yet retained a certain courage that is almost invariably found in the women of her race. The worst hours that she had to endure were those that lay immediately in front. She decided that the best things she could do were to eat and drink, and immediately upon making the decision, began to prepare herself a meal. A few slices from the breast of a fowl taken with a glass of claret added to her strength, and when she received the message from Murrell that she had been expecting, she shook off the cold clutch of horror and stepped into the lift with a heart that was for the time being undeterred. She gave her instructions to the driver rapidly and breathlessly. He was to make for the Luxuriant Hotel and was to drop her outside Paddington Station. She informed him that she would complete the journey herself.

As the door of the car slammed upon her, Annette clutched her suitcase to her, and, for the first time since the fear had tenanted her heart, prayed that she might elude the peril that threatened her. As far as she could tell, from the quick glance that she had thrown to either side, as she left the flat and entered the taxi, there had been none near to observe her going, and as the car crossed Sutherland Avenue, ran smoothly along Warrington Crescent and eventually reached the Harrow Road, she congratulated herself that she had wasted no time in effacing herself from the proximity of Malgan Avenue. She signalled to the driver to drop her in Eastbourne Terrace, and she was out of the car, had paid him and was on her way with a rapidity seldom found in similar conditions amongst the members of her sex.

Entering Paddington Station, she made for the subway at the end of the station that would lead her to Praed Street Underground. As she turned into it, she saw that it seemed entirely deserted, and she raced along it with hope beating high in her breast. But, as the feeling came to her, so also by some strange chance, or occult premonition perhaps, it almost instantaneously departed. The cold air of the subway seemed to strike a chill into her soul, and as she felt this change coming over her, she gave way to such a conflict of racing and bewildered thoughts that she did not hear the stealthy steps that came towards her from behind. She half turned, however, at the sound of a light, mocking cough, and as she did so, she saw the identity of her pursuer. Annette Mornay knew then, without the vestige of a doubt, that her precautions had been taken in vain.

"You!" she gasped. "Here?"

They were the last words that she was destined to speak. She shrank against the wall at her side, for the person behind her, giving a swift glance in the rear, raised a gloved hand, and a knife flung with fierce accuracy found a resting-place in her heart. She collapsed soundlessly and slid down the wall to the ground. The figure behind turned and made swift and noiseless retreat, and when a party of laughing girls found the body two minutes or so later, was back in the car that had followed Annette's—homeward bound.

CHAPTER XVI

THE RETICENCE OF DEAD WOMEN

ANTHONY BATHURST propped his morning paper against his toast-rack and scanned the columns somewhat indolently. As far as he had been informed by Sir Austin Kemble, Inspector Hargreaves had discovered nothing more of importance concerning the murder of De Ravenac, and day by day the columns of the London Press, attracted by the details of a sensational Society divorce suit, had contained less and less of the crime. Recognition, too, had no doubt been paid by them to the diplomatic and social standing of Sir Beverley and Lady Pelham, and the additional fact that the President of San Jonquilo was indirectly associated with the affair whilst a guest of the country had caused the newspapers generally to indulge in less fanciful theorizing than is usually the case. But on the occasion in question Bathurst's nonchalance was destined to be particularly short-lived and to give place to a mixture of feelings that was made up in turn of amazement, anger, incredulity, and finally of fierce and bitter indignation. The column that had translated him into these four conditions was sensational in the extreme. The headings were:

"Murder in Underground Railway Subway. Woman Stabbed to Death at Praed Street. The Orange and Black Again." Anthony Bathurst, noticing the last headline, read the words with avid interest.

A young woman was discovered murdered about half past ten last night in the subway that connects Paddington Station with the station on the Underground Railway known as Praed Street. The circumstances of the crime, as far as can be ascertained from present details, appear to be most extraordinary and to be connected in some way, that is as yet obscure, with the sensational murder of the man De Ravenac at Sir Beverley Pelham's house in Clinton Square. The murdered woman has not only been identified from papers in her possession as Annette Mornay, an acquaintance of the dead man De Ravenac, but also there has been found, a few yards away from her body in the subway, a small piece of black silk embroidered with an orange axe. We understand that Inspector

Hargreaves, who has charge of the Clinton Square murder, is also investigating the circumstances of this second crime, and that Sir Austin Kemble himself, the Commissioner of Police, is giving it the immense benefit of his personal consideration. Up to the time of going to press no arrest had been made in relation to either murder, but we understand that a certain line of inquiry is expected to yield a result before many hours are past.

Bathurst laid the paper quietly on the table and rose to his feet. The lines of his jaw set rigidly and there came a hard look into the grey eyes that was seldom found there. He clenched his fists in the heat of his indignation.

"She came to me for help, poor girl," he muttered, "and for all I know I may have sent her to her death." He lit a cigarette. "But it will be more than a pleasure to me to avenge her murder, and just as Annette Mornay interfered for the sake of the memory of De Ravenac, so will I take a hand on behalf of the memory of Annette."

His reflections were interrupted by the noise of a big car that seemed to him, from the sound, to be pulling up outside the flat. Three quick strides across his room took him to the window, and he was just in time to see Sir Austin Kemble cross the pavement hurriedly and ring the bell. Sir Austin lost no time in valueless description. A glance at Bathurst's face, and a second rapid glance at the newspaper that lay on the table in front of him, told him that Bathurst was already cognizant of the murder of Annette Mornay.

"Well, my boy," he opened, "and what are we to make of this latest development? Nice state of things altogether—isn't it?"

Bathurst took some little time before he replied to the Commissioner's question. When he answered he chose the words of his answer very carefully.

"I know little of this second aspect of the case beyond what the *Morning Message* has told me. But, disinclined as I always am to indulge in reckless prophecy, I nevertheless feel on this occasion that the murderer, whoever he or she may be, has made the one vital and fatal mistake that, thanks no doubt to an all-wise Providence, he almost invariably makes."

The Commissioner took a cigarette from the case that Bathurst offered to him, at the same time criticizing that gentleman's last statement.

"You may be right, of course. Personally I rather doubt it. Seems to me we're up against somebody this time who's as slippery as an eel and as ruthless as a man-eater. This poor girl was murdered in the subway connecting Paddington and Praed Street. Hargreaves is at work on her connections, but so far not a soul has come forward who is able to tell us anything beyond the fact as to how the body was found." Sir Austin shrugged his shoulders in a gesture of despondency. "As for clues"—and the last word contained all the pessimism that he could put into it—"we're just about as well off as we were in the De Ravenac affair. A piece of black silk with an orange axe worked on to it."

"Torn at all?" inquired Bathurst.

"No. Sort of square. Something like the other one."

"Originally found in the dead girl's hand?"

"No. On the ground—I understand. A matter of a few yards away from the body."

"Similar knife to the one used to kill De Ravenac?"

"Yes—very similar—and, like the other knife too, not a fingerprint on it. Manufactured in dozens on the Continent, and the murderer wore gloves in each instance. Now, Bathurst, where's that fatal step about which you were talking so glibly just now? I confess I'd like to take a good look at it."

Bathurst watched a ring of smoke ascend towards the ceiling. The Commissioner was quick to follow up the advantage that it seemed to him he had obtained.

"Guard yourself, my boy, against an optimism that as far as I can see is without foundation. Or else prove me wrong. I shall be extremely pleased if you are able to."

Bathurst accepted Sir Austin's challenge.

"I was speaking comprehensively, sir, and I had nothing in my mind based upon what we may call, at this stage, a particular clue. But, as I think I have told you before, whereas one murderer may move on the impulse of ignorance, another takes a step that is forced upon him by reason of the possession of certain knowledge. I admit, again, that I have but the vaguest impressions of the details attendant upon this second murder. I cannot hope to have any more than that until I see the body and become more familiar with the scene and circumstances of the crime. Admitting all that, however, I am inclined to forecast the opinion that Annette Mornay is one more illustration of the time-honoured fact that dead women, like dead men, have certain limitations with regard to powers of narration. Also I am very interested in that orange axe."

The Commissioner looked at Bathurst as though a new facet of the case had been opened up to him.

Then he nodded some degree of agreement. "You mean that—"

Bathurst finished the remark for him. "Dead women tell no tales, and this is the second axe with which we have been confronted. You see, Sir Austin, to a certain extent I know more than you think I do."

"But you said that all you knew was what the paper—"

"I wasn't referring to that. You will probably be surprised to hear that I had the pleasure of Annette Mornay's acquaintance."

The Commissioner became incredulous. "What? When? How? I had no idea that you knew of her existence even."

"I didn't until the day before yesterday. She called upon me here and actually occupied the same chair in which you are sitting now. In fact, I fancy that she was the last person to occupy it prior to yourself."

The Commissioner found the information the reverse of alluring and fidgeted uneasily in his seat.

"By Jove," he blurted, "this is something for which I hadn't bargained. But what was her object in coming to you? What did she want?"

"Help," replied Bathurst laconically.

"Then she knew that she was in danger?"

Bathurst shook his head slowly—evidently assessing Sir Austin's last contribution. "Don't know. She may have done, but

I don't think that her own danger was at that moment uppermost in her mind. She came to me to help her to find the murderer of De Ravenac—she was no less than his mistress."

Sir Austin caressed his chin reflectively.

"H'm—that opens up possibilities. Did she seem to know anything, Bathurst? Anything, for example, that we don't know?"

"Hinted at an affair between De Ravenac and Lady Pelham."

"Incredible!" expostulated the Commissioner, up in arms in a second. "Ridiculous! More than that—the idea's monstrous. I have known Josephine Pelham on and off ever since she was a girl. Anybody who suggests that she was running an intrigue with a man like De Ravenac is talking through his hat! Or her hat!" he added savagely.

Bathurst regarded the Commissioner curiously. "Possibly you're right, sir. And yet Lady Pelham, if you remember, was individually responsible for the invitation to the ball that was given to the dead man. You are able to recall, no doubt, Sir Beverley Pelham's embarrassment when that particular fact was dragged to light."

"What if she *were* responsible for the invitation?" the Commissioner retorted with distinct heat. "There's nothing guilty or suspicious about that, is there? You'll find that you're on the wrong track, Bathurst, if you think Lady Pelham's mixed up in this business. I've never yet met a woman in whom I have more confidence."

Bathurst proceeded inexorably. "And yet again, Sir Austin, it was Lady Pelham who arranged for the cushions in the colours of the Republic to be conveyed downstairs by Major Wyatt very shortly before she gave the order to Powell that ensured President Loredana's refreshment-room being empty." He tossed the end of his cigarette into the ash-tray. "I confess that I view these actions of Lady Pelham with an immense amount of interest— and also, I must admit, with a certain amount of misgiving."

Sir Austin made as though to reply to the verbal onslaught which he had just endured. For once, however, words failed him. Bathurst rose briskly and buttoned his coat.

"I suggest, sir, that you and I look a little more closely into the matter of the murder of Annette Mornay."

"By all means, my boy," responded Sir Austin, with alacrity. "The very thing that I was just about to suggest myself. I'll make the journey with you. My car's downstairs." He led the way and Anthony Bathurst followed him.

Chapter XVII
THE ORANGE AXE

Inspector Hargreaves listened respectfully to the Commissioner's hotly expressed opinion and put forward a plea of justification. "All that granted, sir," he urged, "the fact remains that the girl had no ticket on her, so that we've no idea as to her intended destination, which won't allow us to follow up your theory. The chauffeur that picked her up at her flat in Malgan Avenue states that she was making for the Luxuriant Hotel, but that he was instructed to drop her outside Paddington Station. The porter at Malgan Avenue is certain that she was running away from something or somebody. He says her manner was strange—that she was undoubtedly upset when she went in earlier in the evening."

"On what does he base that?"

"From what she said to him, Mr. Bathurst, when she went in."

"What did she say?"

Hargreaves ticked four points off on his fingers. "That she was 'in' to nobody! That she wanted a taxi directly it came over dark! That she wasn't intending to come back that night and might be going to sleep at a friend's! That nobody was to be alarmed or to worry if she seemed to be missing the next day! Take the last point on its own face value alone—it's pretty significant."

Bathurst filled his pipe with deliberation. As he pressed the tobacco into the bowl he seemed to be thinking very deeply. "She was frightened all right. There's not a doubt about that," he declared.

Sir Austin nodded his corroboration. "Absolutely. The expression on the poor girl's face and the dreadful stare in her eyes—each told the same tale. There's no mistaking it. I've seen it before—that desperate hunted look. But never quite so plainly as in this instance."

Bathurst held a lighted match to the tobacco and the flame showed the two men with him that the worry of the problem was still written on his face. He drew at the pipe several times before he ventured an opinion on Sir Austin Kemble's statement.

"The human mind is complex, victimized by influences of hate, love, bias, and prejudice, and it's rather foolish perhaps to attempt to theorize on the look that we find on a dead girl's face, but accepting all you say, Sir Austin, I would be inclined even to go a step further." He paused and looked towards the Commissioner as though inviting his comment. "A step further?" queried the latter.

"Yes. There was a strangely horrified expression in Annette's eyes. It struck me when I looked at her just now that there was something there besides terror. Something more."

"How do you mean, Bathurst?"

"It's hard to describe, sir, and it's perhaps even more foolish to attempt the description, but taking a very long shot, the idea came to me that Annette had *recognized* her murderer before he killed her. What have you to say to that, sir?"

"It's feasible, certainly—but it doesn't get us very much farther, if it is so."

"But it may do, sir." Bathurst turned to Hargreaves. "What about her, Inspector? What have you discovered? What acquaintances had she?"

"According to Murrell, that's the porter at the flats in Malgan Avenue, where she lived, she had only one regular caller. That was the man who was murdered the other night—De Ravenac. Apart from him she hardly seemed to know a soul. But she did no work, in the sense of having a regular occupation, although always well supplied with money. Leastways, so Murrell says."

"Was De Ravenac a frequent caller?"

"Very regular. Two or three times every week."

"Couldn't the porter recall *anybody* else as having visited her recently?"

"One young man only. Been there but once, I believe, from what Murrell said."

"When?"

"He wasn't at all sure. But he fancied it was about the beginning of last week."

"Did he describe him?"

"I asked for a description of him," amended Inspector Hargreaves, "but had to remain satisfied with a very general one. Tall, slim, and he thinks with a fair moustache. Murrell thought his age would be about five and twenty, and that he was connected with an insurance company. Anyhow, he only called on Annette once, so I don't reckon he's of much account."

Bathurst frowned and mentally docketed the description. "You can't tell, Hargreaves. You have to snatch at everything that floats by you and then take a damned good look at it. All conversation is so much mental exposure. Through its medium, thoughts, as it were, are dragged to light, and ideas are born that otherwise would have no existence."

The Commissioner nodded vigorously. "Undoubtedly. That's the secret of all successful investigation. Never to take a chance, Hargreaves! I showed Mr. Bathurst the value of that in the first case that he ever looked into for me."

"Now show me something else, Sir Austin," intervened a smiling Bathurst quietly. "Let me have a look at those two pieces of silk, will you? The orange-and-black combination."

At a sign from the Commissioner, Inspector Hargreaves produced the two pieces of silk. Bathurst took them and placed one on each knee. "Exhibit A," explained the Inspector, "is that found in De Ravenac's hand. The unmarked piece was picked up in the subway a few yards from Annette Mornay's body."

"There are many differences here," remarked Bathurst.

"They are dissimilar, certainly," agreed Sir Austin Kemble. "Tell me all the points that you can see that don't tally."

"The first is torn—the second has been cut from something. Look here at this edge where the knife or scissors, whichever was used, has slipped a little."

Sir Austin and Hargreaves bent over the two silken pieces and indicated their agreement. Bathurst continued.

"The first has a stripe in orange. The second has an orange axe—rough—but an axe." Sir Austin frowned at the statement. "And if I'm not mistaken it's very like in shape and general design to the axe on the back of that executioner-chap's costume at Josephine Pelham's ball. I'm hanged if it isn't."

"The man named Martin Pierpoint, you mean," added Bathurst.

"That's the man," said Sir Austin. "Now, what the devil does it all mean? That's what I'd like to know."

"The orange axe appeals to you, then, Sir Austin?" Bathurst's tone was soft as he put the question to the Commissioner. He went on without waiting for a reply. "So it does to me. In fact, I may say that I find it of absorbing interest. But to proceed with those various points of difference that we were discussing. Look here! The first piece of silk is of excellent quality. The second is of much inferior texture. Do you notice that? The orange stripe on the black of De Ravenac's piece has been embroidered with a certain amount of skill. The orange axe on Annette Mornay's piece has, it seems to me, been stitched on to the black almost clumsily—certainly far from skilfully."

He handed up the second piece of silk to Sir Austin. "Look at it for yourself, sir."

The Commissioner took it, and as he did so Hargreaves ranged himself at his side.

"Yes, I see what you mean, Bathurst. I should say, without pretending to be an authority on these things, that the work on this piece is of decidedly inferior quality to that on De Ravenac's piece."

Bathurst hastened to correct him. "There is hardly any work stitched like that on the first piece. The effect has been obtained from a different process altogether. For example, had the designer of the first piece of silk designed the second, I should have expected to find the axe in *appliqué*. See what I mean? On the other hand, of course, the distinction may be intentional. We can't tell, but I can think of at least one reason why this might be so." Bathurst looked up at Sir Austin Kemble to see whether the Commissioner had followed him all the way of his reasoning and had grasped his meaning. But Sir Austin shook his head doubtfully. "Tell me your reason," he ordered.

"If my memory serves me faithfully," remarked Bathurst, "the orange axe that decorated Pierpoint's costume at the ball *was* in *appliqué*. Are you in agreement with that opinion, sir?"

Before the Commissioner could frame his answer, Inspector Hargreaves gave Bathurst the reply that he wanted.

"That is so, Mr. Bathurst. You are quite right in what you say. I was careful to notice that fact myself."

Bathurst returned him a look of gratitude. "Thank you, Inspector. Then you are able to grasp the point at which I was aiming. The distinction may well be a deliberate one. You had better take back these two pieces, Inspector." Bathurst handed Hargreaves the two portions of silk, rose from his chair and paced the room. Suddenly he turned and swung back on to the Inspector.

"Was the murdered girl observed by any railway official, at, say, any of the barriers at Praed Street or Paddington, do you know?"

"No, Mr. Bathurst. By nobody. As far as I have been able to ascertain from inquiries at both Paddington and Praed Street, she neither came to any of the barriers nor bought a ticket at either of the stations."

"Did all the ticket collectors seem absolutely certain of that?"

"As emphatic as they could be in circumstances like these. Not a single one of them was able to remember her."

Bathurst considered the information. "It's quite possible, of course, that, judging by the driver of the taxi that she engaged to take her to the Luxuriant Hotel, she entered Paddington with the intention of crossing at once to Praed Street. She may, for instance, have feared that she was being followed, and was attempting to throw her pursuer off her track. That's certainly a possibility that we must consider. By the way, can any of the officials at either station remember any other person at all suspicious round about the time that she was killed?”

“There is a porter at Praed Street who remembers a tall man in evening dress who dropped his ticket as he was giving it up and who seemed to him to be in a great hurry. This porter states that he watched this tall man cross the bridge that connects Praed Street with the Paddington subway and that he broke into a run as he went across.”

“Probably running to catch a train, I should think,” suggested the Commissioner. “I’ve had to do it myself there before now.”

“The porter said that he was a very distinguished-looking man and that he would be able to recognize him again, should he ever run across him.”

“That’s something, at any rate,” contributed Bathurst. “We aren’t always able to extract an admission of equal value to that. What do you say, Hargreaves?”

The Inspector shrugged his shoulders. “Perhaps not, Mr. Bathurst. All the same, it’s pretty vague, all of it, and doesn’t seem to be of very much use to me. I get vagueness and empty hints everywhere I go on this case.”

Sir Austin attempted to take charge of the situation. “It seems to me,” he asserted with very definite confidence, “that there emerges from the circumstantial evidence of these two cases a distinct significance that has to do with the Republic of San Jonquilo.”

Bathurst regarded him with critical interest. “Go on, Sir Austin,” he said encouragingly. “And what do you deduce from that? Let me see whether I’m going to agree with you.”

Sir Austin was obviously flattered by Bathurst’s words. “I knew that you would come into line with me there, Bathurst,” he declared pompously. “And what I was about to say was this. Let us examine thoroughly all the people in these two cases whom we know to have any connection at all with San Jonquilo. Either now or in the past. Let us make a list of them. When we have done so, that list is bound to contain the murderer of De Ravenac and also the murderer of Annette Mornay. As far as I can see, everything points to a solution coming from that direction."

"I can find no fault with your suggestion, sir," commented Bathurst, "even though I am not prepared at this juncture to travel quite as far as you have gone. Whom shall we include? Remember that the list must be hermetically sealed as it were— that is to say an absolutely complete and comprehensive one. To miss one might mean that we'd missed the one that counted."

Inspector Hargreaves produced his notebook and pencil and waited for Sir Austin Kemble to nominate his members.

"I accept your conditions, Bathurst," said the Commissioner, "and first of all I will put in everybody whom I know to have the slightest connection, even, with the Republic. We will then, you agreeing, of course, delete the impossibilities. I am assuming of course that the murderer was either invited, or alternatively was in attendance without an invitation at Lady Pelham's masked ball."

Bathurst nodded his acquiescence. Sir Austin began his self-imposed task.

"The people who—er—impinge on the two cases—and who have this—er—link with San Jonquilo—are *(a)* President Loredana himself, *(b)* his Chancellor, Señor Miguel Da Costa, *(c)* Sir John Grant."

Bathurst smiled.

"What are you smiling at?" demanded the Commissioner, with a tinge of asperity.

"You are meticulously complete, Sir Austin. You are including names which I never dreamed that you would include. That's all. But go on, please."

"I'm doing the job properly," announced Sir Austin frigidly. "You ought to know, Bathurst, from your experience of me, that it's my habit to do so. Work that is scamped is absolutely useless to me. But I will proceed. *(d)* Sir Beverley Pelham, *(e)* Lady Pelham, *(f)* Powell, the waiter—I think that we may include him as he had charge of the special refreshment-room and, er . . ." Sir Austin paused, and Hargreaves waited with pencil poised over his notebook. "I think that's about all," the Commissioner concluded rather lamely.

"Taking your list, then, as it stands," declared Bathurst, "please delete the impossibilities, as you described them just now."

"We can rule out with absolute safety Loredana, Da Costa, Sir Beverley Pelham and Lady Pelham."

"For what various reasons?"

"The first two because they were not present at the ball when the murder took place. They came along later from the Hotel Florizel—and I know that, Bathurst, because I brought 'em myself. Sir Beverley Pelham, because he was upstairs in the ball-room when De Ravenac was killed, and Lady Pelham because, if you remember, she had gone into the general refreshment-room. That—er—leaves us with Sir John Grant and er—"

"Powell," added Bathurst laconically.

Sir Austin looked somewhat discomfited.

"I would criticize your conclusions just a little," continued Bathurst. "You will forgive me, I'm sure, if I point out that Powell, according to his own story, was unable to find Sir Beverley for some little time after he had gone upstairs with Lady Pelham's message. With regard to Lady Pelham herself, I will reserve for the time being any comments that I may feel disposed to offer. The time is not ripe for them, and therefore they are best left unsaid." Sir Austin grunted evasively. "I would also add to your list, sir, certain other names." Bathurst paused and waited.

"Who are they?" demanded the Commissioner, with some scepticism.

"Consider, sir, the colour scheme. I would include Martin Pierpoint, whose costume was of orange and black. Major Wyatt, who carried down for Lady Pelham cushions that were also in orange and black, and one other."

"One other?" queried Sir Austin. "Whom do you mean?"

"Mr. Gerald Twining, secretary to the President of the Republic of San Jonquilo. I think that exhausts the list of those whom we know to have San Jonquilese associations. But what about those of whom we are ignorant? For example, what about—"

Before he could finish his sentence there came a tap at the door.

CHAPTER XVIII
INFORMATION FROM THE SÛRETÉ

Sir Austin Kemble motioned to the Inspector to attend to the interruption. As Hargreaves crossed the room to go to the door, the Commissioner turned inquiringly to Anthony Bathurst in the hope, doubtless, that he would complete what he had just previously been saying. He translated his look into speech. "You were about to mention . . . ?"

Bathurst shook his head and pointed to the door. "Just a moment, sir, if you don't mind. I am not sure who that is with Hargreaves. I'm not giving—"

As he spoke Hargreaves left the door and came back to them. "Sergeant Gausden, sir. The reply has come through from Paris to the message that you sent, sir."

"From Le Gonidec? Good. Let's have it, Hargreaves." Sir Austin held out his hand and Hargreaves handed the cablegram over to him. The Commissioner glanced at it hurriedly before returning it to the Inspector. "Have this decoded at once, Hargreaves. From one or two of the simpler words in it, with which I am familiar, I am rather inclined to think that we have here a line of very valuable information. Get Gausden to start on it at once."

Hargreaves departed to carry out the Commissioner's instructions. Sir Austin proceeded to take Bathurst into his confidence. "From a certain whisper or so that has reached us concerning the dead man De Ravenac, I made it my business to arrange with Inspector Hargreaves that we should throw out an inquiry regarding De Ravenac's antecedents." He chuckled. "That's where the Yard scores, my boy. Its resources are tremendous. As a result of what we heard we put the usual chit through to Paris. I told Hargreaves to be as explicit as possible, and he sent them a full description and as many details of the case as he had at his command in the hope that De Ravenac might at some period of his career have passed through the hands of the Parisian police authorities." Sir Austin wagged his head. "According to what I saw in the hasty glance that I gave that coded message, the line of inquiry is going to bear fruit."

Bathurst looked at him somewhat curiously. "Very interesting, my dear Sir Austin. I shall be concerned to hear what your friend Monsieur Le Gonidec has to tell you. But before that comes to pass I would like you, if you would be so kind, to retrace your steps just a trifle. It would help me if you did."

"With pleasure, my boy. But how do you mean—retrace my steps?"

"I allude to the remark that you made a moment ago. You made use of the expression 'a certain whisper or so'. I should like to inquire what that whisper was, how old it is, and from where it came?"

"I chose the word carelessly, perhaps. As a matter of fact, the suggestion came to me from Doctor Sugden, the Divisional Surgeon that you remember was called to Sir Beverley Pelham's the night De Ravenac was murdered. He gave a great deal of thought to that strange scar that he discovered on De Ravenac's neck and had a talk with me about it on the following morning. That scar, I may say, puzzled him considerably. Taking this into consideration, then, the dead man's nationality, and also the fact that little or next to nothing is known of him since he came to live in London, Sugden and I agreed that a discreet inquiry of our French friends might not prove to be a waste of time. Hence my gesture towards Le Gonidec." Sir Austin emitted a second chuckle. "We shall see, Bathurst. We shall see, and before very long, my boy."

"I remember Sugden's discovery of the scar. In fact, I've kept the matter alive in my own mind ever since. As Sugden himself said at the time of the discovery, it should prove a valuable link in the chain of *authentic* identification. Which is what we want. Situated as we are, facing so much that is obscure—"

Hargreaves' knock preceded his entrance. He walked straight across to the Commissioner and laid a paper in front of him. "Gausden has done that little job for you, sir, and here is the result."

Sir Austin took the decoded message from Monsieur Le Gonidec of the Sûreté Générale and read it through with intense interest. Bathurst and the Inspector watched him silently. When he had finished, he rubbed his hands and read it aloud to his two companions.

"Listen to this, Bathurst," he commenced. "And you too, Hargreaves. This will serve to throw a very different light upon the two murders. It only shows you how easily you can be led to follow a false trail. I should have thought of this possibility before I banked so confidently on the San Jonquilese association. Listen.

"'From general description of man together with photograph forwarded, it is believed here that André de Ravenac is an alias of a certain Pierre Lamotte. Fingerprints of De Ravenac are without doubt the same as those of Lamotte that we have here. Also, as far as is possible for us to check, from the information you supplied, all anthropometric details of Lamotte that are in our possession coincide. Lamotte's criminal history is as follows. After serving a term of imprisonment in Rouen for counterfeiting, he was convicted at Lyons nine years ago last January for forging, and sentenced to two years' imprisonment. After serving this sentence Lamotte was temporarily lost sight of, but turned up again in Paris in less than a period of twelve months after release. Soon after his appearance in the capital, Paris passed through what may be described as a miniature reign of terror. Nine of its most worthy citizens were murdered by an unknown criminal, who in each instance killed with a dagger through the victim's heart. From the conditions of the assassinations, this criminal was popularly known as "Le Loup de Poignard".

"'From certain evidence which came before the Sûreté immediately following upon the ninth assassination, it was believed that this man Lamotte was the murderer, and steps were taken to effect his arrest. Unfortunately, news of this projected stroke leaked out in the wrong quarter, and when the authorities swooped, Lamotte, who had, no doubt, received warning, had completely vanished. It was believed at the time that the movements and motives of certain officials were not altogether beyond suspicion, and two at least in the Service, one highly placed and one a sergeant, were either punished or reprimanded. Colour is certainly leant to the belief that Lamotte and "the Wolf" were one and the same person, from the indisputable fact that the "dagger" outrages ceased almost simultaneously with the disappearance of Lamotte from Paris. It is almost certain, however, that a gang was operating and that Lamotte had confederates, but only one of these was ever definitely known here, and it was through an action on her part, in connection with a bookseller of the Rue de Saint Merri, that the attention of the police was first directed to Pierre Lamotte. This particular confederate was a young girl named Annette Mornay, and like Lamotte nothing has been heard of her in this country since the affair six years ago.'"

Sir Austin smoothed out the paper and placed it beneath a weight. "By Jove, Bathurst," he declared, "this information gives us not only the whole story but also the key to unlock the solution!"

"With your permission, sir." Bathurst picked up the message from Le Gonidec and re-read it. He was always a believer in the greater value of visual remembrance as compared with aural. When he had finished he folded and handed the paper back to the Commissioner.

"Well?" demanded the latter somewhat impatiently. "What do you think of it yourself? Don't you agree with me?"

"In regard to what—exactly—Sir Austin?"

Sir Austin looked as though he failed to appreciate the finer points of Bathurst's last question. "Why, that this practically clears up the case for us. We have only to follow up De Ravenac's career from the time that he ceased to be Lamotte and we shall surely run across something that will enable us to fill in pretty accurately the remaining links in the chain. There's a man somewhere there whom we shall run across and then put our hands on."

Bathurst thought over what the Commissioner had just said, and both Sir Austin and Inspector Hargreaves wondered what was passing through his mind. There was silence for quite an appreciable period. It was eventually broken by Anthony Bathurst.

"You are prepared, then, Sir Austin, to accept this theory that Le Gonidec has put forward? That André de Ravenac *was* Lamotte—alias 'Le Loup de Poignard'?"

Sir Austin laid the paper flat on the table and stared at Bathurst with some astonishment.

"Theory?" he demanded. "Surely I am justified in regarding it as something very much more than a theory. Take the Bertillon evidence alone. The French system is the last word in efficiency. I would express my position very differently. I tell you, Bathurst, that I have implicit faith in this information from Le Gonidec, and I firmly believe that this man De Ravenac *is* the man whom the French authorities were just too late to arrest six years ago." The Commissioner rapped smartly on the table. "Everything points to it," he concluded with all the signs of emphasis.

"That is the point over which I find myself in complete disagreement." Bathurst's remark, although uttered quietly, had the effect of a bombshell upon Sir Austin Kemble. It was some time before he could find words to express adequately his complete incredulity. Hargreaves, too, appeared to regard Bathurst's opinion as amazingly disconcerting.

"You astonish me! Why do you disagree?" insisted Sir Austin. "You must have infinitely better reasons than I can think of, to make that statement. After all, Bathurst, you must admit that genuine information from a source like the Sûreté is a much more valuable asset than any amount of scientific theorizing, and good, hard, solid facts count in the long run far more than imagination and conjecture. The science of deduction can be—"

"All very true, sir. I've always been ready to admit to you in the past that imagination is a pretty restive filly for anybody to attempt to ride, but, you see, in this particular instance I don't happen to be doing anything of the kind. My disagreement with the line that you have adopted is based on good, hard, solid fact, as you call it, equally as soundly as your own line is itself." Bathurst rose and began to pace the room. "Indeed, I would go farther than that, and say even more so. For the one clear fact to me that emerges bright-eyed and shining, as it were, from Le Gonidec's information is that whoever De Ravenac may have been, there is one person who he certainly was not."

Sir Austin glared, as he saw looming in front of him the imminent destruction that awaited the belief that he had just projected. "And who is that, may I ask?"

Bathurst came back, leant over the table, and tapped Le Gonidec's message with his forefinger. "That gentleman of the Parisian underworld whom you have just named—'Le Loup de Poignard'!"

The Commissioner frowned, and failed at the moment to rid himself of an irritating impression that the famous French Chief of Police was being cavalierly treated. "Let me have your reasons?" he said shortly.

"Surely they are obvious, sir?" replied Bathurst. "De Ravenac and also, mark you, the second victim, Annette Mornay, were each killed in such a manner that, knowing what we do of 'the Wolf's' escapades in Paris, we may well be pardoned if we deduce in the two affairs the presence of that entertaining gentleman himself. You will go as far with me as that, will you not, sir?"

"Yes," conceded Sir Austin somewhat grudgingly.

"And yet, sir, you desire to identify the first *victim* as 'Le Loup de Poignard'." Bathurst shook his head as he continued. "That's the position that I find it impossible to take up," he proceeded. "That is where I must join issue with you. 'The Wolf' liked to *play* merry hell—not to listen to it. My contention is this. In other words, I would much more willingly identify the murderer as 'Le Loup de Poignard' than the murdered."

It was evident from the expression on Inspector Hargreaves' face that he at least was disposed to accept Bathurst's conclusions, and Sir Austin himself prepared to retreat a little, when the full realization of the strength of Bathurst's position came home to him. He was, however, determined to avoid at all costs a retreat that was precipitate. He attempted therefore to compromise.

"What you say is, of course, perfectly feasible as far as it goes. I admit that the circumstances of the two murders certainly point to the possibility that 'the Wolf' may well have been the perpetrator. But, if I may say so, the fact that De Ravenac and Mademoiselle Mornay were killed as they were does not necessarily mean that. After all, killing is not the monopoly of any one man. Let me—er—explain myself more fully. From the information that Le Gonidec has sent us, there is every reason to believe that De Ravenac was Lamotte, who was, and is believed to be, 'Le Loup de Poignard'. Is it not on the cards, then, that more than one member of this man's gang were skilled in the delicate art of murder? The knife, you know, Bathurst, is a weapon beloved of the Latins. I cannot see that we are bound to regard 'the Wolf' himself as being the only gentleman sufficiently adept to administer the *coup de grâce* to an intended victim." The Commissioner paused, preened himself, and then immediately proceeded to amplify his opinion. "No, Bathurst! I respect your point of view, naturally. It has a lot to substantiate it. But all the same, I'm going to stick to my own idea, and I'm moderately optimistic that time will eventually prove me to be in the right."

Bathurst smiled at Sir Austin's obstinacy. "Very well, sir," he declared semi-humorously, "we will agree to differ." He reached for his hat and stick. "With your permission, Sir Austin, I will leave you now to make what I think will prove to be an important call."

"Where?" questioned the Commissioner.

"I am going to investigate the matter of the invitation card of Señor Miguel Da Costa."

"The Chancellor?"

"Of San Jonquilo," returned Mr. Bathurst gravely. "The Republic whose colours are orange and black."

CHAPTER XIX
THE CARD OF DA COSTA

MIGUEL DA COSTA removed his monocle from his eye and proceeded to polish it with almost exaggerated care. For the moment he failed to grasp the significance of Anthony Bathurst's statement. "There were four hundred and seventy-four guests at. Sir Beverley Pelham's on the evening De Ravenac was murdered, and there was the same number of invitation cards in the hands of the chief attendant when they were checked by Inspector Hargreaves. The fact is certain, Señor Da Costa. I made it my business to verify it."

Da Costa finished polishing his monocle, replaced it in its appropriate place and fingered his pointed beard. "Yes," he mumbled. "Yes, I think that I understand. You are counting the dead man De Ravenac in your figure, are you not, Mr. Bathurst?"

Loredana interjected sharply. "Of course, Da Costa. That is very obvious. De Ravenac was a guest and on precisely the same footing, I presume, as everyone else who was present." He called to the great white cat on the rug, which came to him obediently to be fondled. A product of Santa Guardina and as spiteful as sin to those even who fed it, the beast worshipped Loredana as far as worship is possible to a feline, and was rarely happy when away from Sebastian's side.

"I see," muttered Da Costa again. "Yes—I suppose he certainly would be included in the number. Well, Mr. Bathurst, what is your point?"

Bathurst, who had patiently awaited the dawning of the Chancellor's lethargic understanding, proceeded to demonstrate. "I know that we discussed this partly on a previous occasion, but the importance of the matter, Señor, it seems to me now, lies more in the invitation cards themselves. For example, taking the facts simply *as* facts and entirely as we know them, either you, or somebody masquerading as you, entered Sir Beverley Pelham's house and presented a card of invitation which was taken by one of the footmen on duty at the entrance and temporarily retained in the ordinary way. I say 'temporarily' because if it had been left behind the cards would have out-numbered the guests by that one." He paused, and Da Costa took advantage of the opportunity.

"You must believe me when I tell you once again that I did not do that. I was not—"

Bathurst smiled enigmatically.

"We have already discussed that, Señor Da Costa. Please do not think that I am reopening it from the point of view of criticism of you. Look at the question impersonally."

"Don't be a fool, Miguel," snapped Loredana. "Remember, if you can, a small part of one of the many things that I have tried to teach you. If you resemble your mother in most ways, at least you have heard your father's name. Which is no mean distinction in modern San Jonquilo. Please continue, Mr. Bathurst."

The latter gestured his thanks to the President. "The question that arises is this. Was that card the authentic and original invitation card from the host and hostess, or was it a forgery? I am not without hope that you will be able to help me answer that question."

The Chancellor stared as though Bathurst had presented him with an insolvable problem. He fidgeted awkwardly. "How?" he demanded. "How *can* I? I tell you again that I was not the man who attended Sir Beverley Pelham's during the early part of that evening. How, then, is it possible for me to tell you what ticket he gave up at the door? I am neither a detective nor a magician."

Loredana burst into mocking laughter, but Bathurst was more magnanimous.

"I am not asking you to tell me that," he said patiently. "But if I ask you certain questions with regard to your own genuine invitation-card, the answers that you give me should certainly shed some light on the question of the ticket that was delivered up and taken away again by the man whom we will term 'the masquerader'."

Loredana again laughed outright. Bathurst was a man after his own heart. "The word that you use fits well, Mr. Bathurst.

After all, Miguel, there was no need for you to wear fancy-dress. You went exactly as you are—disguised as a Statesman."

The Chancellor, his sensibility dulled by the hammer of experience, endured the satire with stoicism. Bathurst continued with his line of investigation concerning the Chancellor's card of invitation.

"Can you remember, Señor Da Costa, *where* your invitation card was on the evening when you set out for Sir Beverley Pelham's?"

Da Costa frowned. "I don't think I can. Do you mean—?" He thought for a moment, shook his head, and then turned inquiringly to Loredana. "Can your Excellency remember what this gentleman is asking?"

Loredana picked up the white cat, and allowed the animal to climb to his shoulder. "I can, Miguel, very well. Since I came to London from Santa Guardina I have learned to remember all that you forget. My memory is therefore immaculate—a paragon amongst memories. Your invitation card, with mine, and with the others that were sent to the people of my suite, was on the escritoire in my secretary's room. I remember distinctly the fact that Twining brought them in here to me before he left for Sir Beverley Pelham's himself—some time before, it was—during the afternoon."

"And they were in your possession from that moment until the time that you arrived at Sir Beverley's?"

"They were not actually in my hands all the time—obviously. But they were in here somewhere. They must have been. Let me see now. To the best of my memory they were in here on the table."

"Who entered the room during that time? Any idea?"

Loredana reflected. "I don't think I can remember anybody coming in here during that time. Not even Da Costa himself."

Da Costa nodded his head corroboratively. "You are right. I did not come in until I came in to leave for the ball. I was in my own room all the time, dressing, and I came in here when I heard that Sir Austin Kemble had arrived. If you remember, I found him here with you. I think that I was told that you had an appointment that evening, your Excellency, with a representative from the Spanish Embassy. Did that interview take place in this room when the invitation tickets were lying on this table?"

Loredana shook his head. "But it is a strange thing," he stated, "that interview of which you make mention did not, in the end, take place at all. A message came from my Embassy during the morning, fixing it up for me, and when I had made all arrangements and waited here some time, I received a further message to the effect that Señor Alveo found it impossible to come, so that it was cancelled, and when Sir Austin Kemble called here to join me, on my journey to Sir Beverley Pelham's, I was ready and waiting for him, and, to his unutterable delight, in no way oppressed by affairs of State."

"So that we may take it as established that nobody here handled Señor Da Costa's ticket with the exception of your secretary Mr. Gerald Twining?"

"I think that that is indicated without a doubt, Mr. Bathurst." Loredana stopped for a second as though he had just thought of an additional fact. "There is, of course, the time that I myself spent in my own room, dressing. There was a certain interval then. I cannot account for what may have happened in here during that period. But I think that that period of time may be said to be almost negligible." Bathurst rubbed the ridge of his jaw. "This interview from the Spanish Embassy of which we have been speaking—was it in the nature of a surprise to you when you first heard of it?"

"Oh, no, Mr. Bathurst! By no means. I knew that such a thing was bound to take place before I returned to Santa Guardina. In fact, it was one of the chief reasons of my visit to this country. But I had not anticipated it for the evening of Lady Pelham's ball. I had expected it to take place some days later. That part of it was perhaps a little surprising."

"From what you say the matter is important, your Excellency?"

"Vital to the national interest of my country, and affecting not only San Jonquilo but also the adjoining Republic of Braganza,

Mr. Bathurst. Beyond that it is impossible for me to go." Loredana suddenly acquired dignity. "You understand, of course."

"Your Excellency's explanation is ample," announced Bathurst. "I am more than grateful for your courtesy and consideration. The information that you were kind enough to give me upon the first occasion that I came here, supplemented with that which I have been fortunate enough to obtain to-day, has tended to simplify considerably several features of the case that I must confess were puzzling me." Bathurst rose and bowed to Loredana and Da Costa. "I am optimistic enough," he proceeded, "to venture the opinion that a week—shall we say— should bring us very near to the unravelling of our little problem. Good day, your Excellency. Good day, Señor Da Costa."

"Much as I admire confidence, Mr. Bathurst, and still more your own delightful optimism, I cannot say that in this case I am able to share your view." Loredana moved his shoulders with an eloquent gesture, but then took Bathurst's hand and smiled. "I hope that your seven little days will prove me to be wrong. If I am, Da Costa, here, shall pay for a dinner for three."

Anthony Bathurst smilingly accepted the President's view of the situation, but rallied him concerning his last suggestion. "We have a proverb in this country, your Excellency, that two make more agreeable company than the next succeeding number."

Loredana chuckled. "I too," he responded, "have known the truth of that—very many times. The best of them find it hard to leave me alone."

*　*　*　*　*

The journey from the Hotel Florizel to Sir Beverley Pelham's town house was accomplished by Bathurst in a short space of time, and inquiry elicited the fact that the British Minister to Santa Guardina was at home. Sir Beverley seemed to receive the news of Bathurst's arrival with somewhat mixed feelings. He kept the servant, who brought him the information, waiting for an appreciable time before he instructed the man to show Bathurst into his room. From the manner in which Sir Beverley sat there thinking over what his servant had told him, and also from the way in which he slowly paced the room, a shrewd observer would have formed the opinion that Sir Beverley was, if not anxious, at least uncertain as to the best course of conduct for him to pursue when the time came for him to be questioned. Suddenly he rose, and had this same observer continued to watch closely he would have seen Sir Beverley turn suddenly on his heel in his pacing and almost obviously make up his mind. This condition effected, Sir Beverley seated himself at his desk again, and waited patiently for the man who desired to speak to him. Bathurst had not occupied his seat for more than a matter of a few seconds when he detected the mental apprehension of his *vis-à-vis*. But he did not allow this new contingency to turn him from the primary matter that had brought him to the house. He opened exactly as he had all along intended.

"The murder of Mademoiselle Mornay, Sir Beverley, coming so quickly on the heels of that of De Ravenac, has caused the Commissioner of Police a great deal of disturbance. As a result, he is particularly desirous that I should follow up every likely possibility that may be said to centre round the affair that took place here. For there is no doubt that the two crimes are connected."

"I am able, as a public official myself, to sympathize intensely with Sir Austin Kemble in his—at times like this—very unenviable and distasteful position. Command me, therefore, Mr. Bathurst. In what way do you want me to help you?"

Bathurst acknowledged the offer with a gesture of thanks. "At the moment, Sir Beverley, I am looking very closely into that rather amazing story that was told to us on the night of the murder by Quinton—your footman. But no doubt you remember."

Sir Beverley Pelham raised his eyebrows. "Amazing?" he queried.

Bathurst repeated the adjective. "Amazing, sir, because of Señor Da Costa's denial that he was present here when Quinton said he was. Inasmuch as Da Costa's statement that he was at the Hotel Florizel is certainly corroborated independently by the fact that Sir Austin Kemble himself called for him there, Quinton's story becomes, I make bold to say, more remarkable than ever. That is why I chose the word 'amazing'."

"Quinton is an old servant of mine. I have always found him to be eminently reliable," countered Sir Beverley.

"All the better," urged Bathurst. "That is just what I would have you say. If I'd thought he was lying I shouldn't be here now. You have now come to the reason why I should like to see Quinton again and ask him one or two more questions. Have I your permission to do that, Sir Beverley?"

"I see no objection to it. I will send for the man to come up here at once." Sir Beverley Pelham lifted the telephone receiver and pressed a button to give the necessary instructions. Then he folded his arms on the desk in front of him and leaned over in Bathurst's direction. "Tell me," he said quietly, "what are you after?"

"A little matter of an invitation card, Sir Beverley." Bathurst paused, and swiftly considered his position. The mental process that he evolved determined him to take a step that was, situated as he was, very possibly in the nature of a risk. But he went on. "Assuming that Quinton's story is *absolutely* true, the invitation card that was tendered to him by this spurious Da Costa was either the authentic one that came from Lady Pelham, or a forgery. I am about to see whether Quinton can assist me to decide that point. I think it's just possible that he may."

Sir Beverley frowned, and the frown was still in possession of his face when his invitation brought Quinton, the footman, into the room. He partly explained the reason that underlay his summons and signed to Bathurst to proceed with the investigation. Bathurst's manner was calculated to put Quinton at his ease immediately. He began by reiterating the circumstances of Quinton's own previous story, and the man nodded assent as Bathurst touched upon them one by one.

"Quite true, sir. That's exactly how it occurred, sir." Thus he embellished Bathurst's conclusion.

"Now, Quinton," declared the latter, "what I want you to tell me is this. Is it possible for me now to examine the actual invitation tickets that you and your subordinates took from the various guests upon their arrival?"

Quinton looked at Sir Beverley Pelham. It appeared to Bathurst that the servant was waiting for the master to answer the question for him. Bathurst was right in his assumption. Sir Beverley intervened.

"I am very much afraid that what you ask is impossible. Inspector Hargreaves counted them on the night, as you are aware, and Lady Pelham and I both imagined that he had finished with them. We did not anticipate that there was any possibility that they might be required again. As a result, very little care was taken of them, and when the clearing-up work that is inseparable from a function like ours was performed on the following morning, I am very much afraid that the tickets were destroyed. It is unfortunate, I agree, but there it is—one cannot foresee these things. After all, we have a list of all the guests who were present, which is almost as valuable to us as I imagined the cards would have been. As a matter of fact I have already told Inspector Hargreaves what I am telling you, because he has been round here since on a somewhat similar errand to that which has brought you."

Bathurst looked grave at this sudden destruction of his immediate hopes. "I can believe that Hargreaves was intensely disappointed," he declared.

"He certainly seemed so," confirmed Sir Beverley, "but I think he realized that it was just one of those unfortunate things for which no one could be justifiably held to blame. There was just this point, too—if Inspector Hargreaves considered that these cards were as important as they now appear to be, it was his duty to have taken charge of them when he left here on the night of the murder. As he said nothing and did nothing in that direction he must abide by the consequences."

For a moment Bathurst made no reply. He appreciated Sir Beverley's point, and could see that no good purpose would be achieved from a discussion thereon. But just as 'tis said the darkest hour is that which precedes the dawn, succour was at hand from the man standing at his side.

Quinton entered the breach with an air of confidence. "You will pardon me, sir," he said, "but what was your real point with regard to the cards? What was it exactly that you wanted to know?"

Bathurst wasted no time. "I wished to discover by reference to the actual card itself, and to your own memory and knowledge, whether there was any chance of the card used by the man whom we will call the false Da Costa being the same card as that used later by Da Costa himself."

"Then I am able, sir, to answer that question for you." The footman was almost emphatic in his assertion, and Bathurst realized it. "It was the same card."

Sir Beverley Pelham looked surprised, but Quinton, paying no attention to him, went on in explanation. "I am certain it was the same card."

"I am curious," said Bathurst. "How are you certain of what you say?"

"I will tell you, sir," said Quinton eagerly. "When I handled the card on the first occasion, I inadvertently bent the left-hand corner of the card—it's quite easy to do that kind of thing and that wasn't the only occasion it happened during the evening. When I took the card when the gentleman, as I thought, returned, I noticed that the card which he handed to me was bent in exactly the same manner. There was no mistaking it."

"Quinton," interjected Bathurst with genuine admiration, "you're a treasure. In the words of 'the little Corporal' to his incomparable Brigadier, 'I do not know what I should do without you.' And you, Sir Beverley, I must also congratulate."

Quinton beamed in the sunshine of Mr. Bathurst's eulogy, but upon Sir Beverley Pelham it seemed to have the directly opposite effect. He sprang to his feet almost twittering with emotion.

"Before you go, Bathurst," he said, "there is something I particularly want to say to you. It's been on my mind for some time now and I am not going to delay it a moment longer."

CHAPTER XX
SIR BEVERLEY TAKES A RISK

MR. BATHURST relapsed into the chair from which he had just risen. "'In delay'," he quoted, "'there lies no plenty.' I am all attention, Sir Beverley."

Sir Beverley Pelham motioned to Quinton to withdraw. The door had closed upon him for some little time before Sir Beverley found his next words.

"Mr. Bathurst," he opened, "I am in somewhat of a difficulty. I am unaware of the extent to which you are officially connected with Scotland Yard. I use the word 'officially' very deliberately. But you look to me like a gentleman."

"Permit me to apologize for that," murmured Anthony Bathurst. "With regard to the first part of your statement, I can claim no real official connection with Scotland Yard. My acquaintance with the Commissioner, Sir Austin Kemble, is entirely a friendly one. I happened to have the good fortune to solve, some years ago, a little problem down at Seabourne that was giving Sir Austin and Scotland Yard a certain amount of trouble. It has been handed down to history, I believe, as the 'Affair of the Peacock's Eye'. Since that occasion Sir Austin Kemble has done me the honour of inviting my co-operation in two or three cases where he imagined I might be likely to assist him. Similar circumstances have brought me into this case of your own. I trust I have made myself clear."

Sir Beverley Pelham had listened with studied interest to Bathurst's explanation, and from his manner it appeared that it afforded him perhaps a certain amount of pleasure, and certainly a strong sense of relief. "That is very much as I thought," he stated. "That is why I made up my mind a moment or two ago to confide in you concerning a matter that has been a source of great worry to me for two or three days. I take it that what I say to you will be treated by you in the nature of a strict confidence."

Bathurst smiled. "That is, perhaps, asking a great deal of me, Sir Beverley, considering that we are dealing with the case of two murders. But I will respect your wishes, and give you my assurance that what you are about to tell me will remain strictly between us for as long as is humanly possible, remembering my position. I will also promise you that I will on no account impart the information to any third person without first advising you of my intention. I'm afraid that I can't commit myself beyond that."

Sir Beverley Pelham toyed with the ivory paper-knife that lay above the blotting-pad upon the desk in front of him.

"Thank you, Mr. Bathurst," he said at length; "I suppose that that assurance is as much as I can reasonably expect. I will accept the situation on those terms. I sincerely hope and trust, however, that the occasion will not arise for the introduction of a third party to the confidence." He rose and stood by his chair.

"We will hope so, Sir Beverley—at least."

The British Minister to Santa Guardina had certainly aged beyond the natural since the night of the murder of André de Ravenac within his house. His eyes were heavy with anxiety and his tall form seemed more bowed than ever with the weight of his new trouble.

"What I am about to tell you," he declared quietly, "concerns no less a person than Lady Pelham herself." He paused for a moment, and a fire blazed in his eyes that Bathurst had not seen there before. But the flash was short-lived and died down almost as quickly as it had been born. Sir Beverley had learned to control his emotions many years since. Bathurst waited patiently for him to continue.

"Do not think for one minute," he proceeded, "that I am lacking in faith or even lacking in charity towards her. But a man's wife is different from anybody else to him, and because of that I have said nothing to her whatever of what I am going to say to you now. I am, as you know, considerably Lady Pelham's senior"—a flush came to his pale cheeks—"and while I do not wish to hurt or injure her by the effect of mere suspicion even, I am conscious at the same time that I have a duty to myself, and my last desire would be to be misunderstood. The facts are these, Mr. Bathurst. Lady Pelham was, I am sorely afraid, more than an ordinary acquaintance of this wretched man who was murdered here."

Bathurst could see that the confession had cost his host much. "Allow me, Sir Beverley, to interrupt you for just one moment. To do so will, I think, enable you to tell your story more easily, more comfortably, and with less embarrassment. In other words, I am able to put your mind at rest to some little degree. I am already aware of the fact that you have just mentioned."

Sir Beverley Pelham shook his head despondently as he realized the significance of Bathurst's statement. "The news, then, is out already. I feared that it might be so. The idea has haunted me for days. It is a relief, perhaps, for me to know it. I will not ask you from whom you obtained your information."

"You shall know that, Sir Beverley, when you have told me the rest of your story."

"Thank you. Unfortunately for me and for my peace of mind my information comes from a source that is absolutely unimpeachable. My own brother, Lionel. I gather from him that he saw Lady Pelham leave an apartment in Kensington one day last week that he has since discovered to have been in the occupation of De Ravenac. When I consider this, the fact that De Ravenac's invitation to the ball was at the specifically expressed wish of Lady Pelham herself becomes dreadfully significant. I cannot rid myself, try as I may, of the idea that Lady Pelham has not been as frank with me as I could have wished."

Anthony Bathurst nodded his understanding and his sympathy.

"Also, Sir Beverley," he urged, "I think I am right in saying that there are certain other matters not unconnected with the crime that are troubling you?"

"I congratulate you on the quickness and accuracy of your perception. You are right. You are alluding, of course, to the somewhat strange incidents that attended the murder and with which Lady Pelham was certainly partly concerned."

"It is true that one cannot ignore them," assented Bathurst quietly.

The man to whom he spoke swung round on him with something like fierceness. "But all the same, Mr. Bathurst, I believe in my wife. Understand that. I have implicit faith in Lady Pelham's innocence. I think that there is some mystery, some dark secret about it all, that you and I cannot understand and most probably never will understand. Believe me, that were I not thoroughly convinced of Lady Pelham's honour and integrity I should never have confided these matters to you. I ask you for help not for condemnation of her. I think that you can help where the official intelligence would only be calculated to remain utterly dispassionate and entirely insensible to one's feelings, one's reputation, and the—er—sacredness of one's home and one's domestic relations."

Anthony Bathurst realized now more fully the extent of the burden which Sir Beverley was bearing. "My services in the matter are at your disposal. Everything that I can reasonably do for you, I will. Remember also that Sir Austin Kemble is your friend and that all the influences of that friendship, which are not inconsiderable, may be expected to be exerted on your behalf, should a condition of urgency arise."

"I am grateful, Mr. Bathurst, and I rejoice that I took the step that I did."

Bathurst acknowledged the compliment. "Happily, I am much more sanguine than you, sir, that the affair will shortly be unravelled, and things which appear, shall we say, dark and suspicious now, will assume in a little time a much more refreshing shape. As I hinted, nothing that you have told me to-day was new to me. My informant, however, happened to pay very dearly for her information."

Sir Beverley Pelham looked incredulously at the speaker and floundered. "Paid? You mean that bribery entered into—?"

Mr. Bathurst shook his head gravely. "You misunderstand me, Sir Beverley. The source of my information was none other than Annette Mornay." He waited to see the effect of his words upon his companion.

Sir Beverley Pelham gasped and went an ashen pallor.

"Annette Mornay?" he gasped. "The girl who was murdered in the same way as De Ravenac?"

"The same," returned Bathurst. "The fact that she came to me for help and left me to go to her death is one which I confess I find a matter of distinct humiliation. That is the main reason, I think, Sir Beverley, why I shall not rest until I have laid a particularly ruthless murderer by the heels."

A few moments later Sir Beverley Pelham walked to the window of his study and watched the tall figure of his visitor disappear into the distance. He stood in his watching position until Bathurst was lost to sight. Then he returned to his desk and, propping his elbows on it, put his head between his hands.

CHAPTER XXI
TWISTED STRANDS

As was her invariable wont, Josephine Pelham turned in the hour of her anxiety and distress to Wyatt, her one-time lover, and her two brothers, Dick and Robin Blaker. Almost at the same time that found her telephoning to the first-named, Anthony Bathurst was being once again ushered into the presence of Sir Austin Kemble. The Commissioner of Police pushed away the papers that were occupying his attention, and welcomed his visitor effusively. "Well, Bathurst," he declared, "what have you come to tell me this time? I perceive from your demeanour that there are developments of some kind."

Bathurst waved aside the semi-compliment. "There are one or two developments, certainly, Sir Austin, but if you think that I have come to you with a ready-made solution of the De Ravenac murder, I am sorry to sentence you forthwith to disappointment. Quite frankly, I am here to ask your opinion again on more than one aspect of the case. If I appear to go over a portion of the ground again, please forgive me—but I am not satisfied."

The Commissioner commenced to purr. "Command me, my boy. What's troubling you?"

Bathurst negatived the last suggestion with a shake of the head. "It's not that, exactly. But it seems to me, as I begin to collect the various strands of the mystery, that I am dealing with two distinct patterns that have not only a different colour, but are also of a different texture."

Sir Austin Kemble, entirely ignorant of Bathurst's meaning, nodded his head pontifically, in order to show the complete extent of his understanding. Bathurst proceeded to illustrate his point. "You will remember, sir, that the other day the list of 'possibles' that you yourself drew up was in the end reduced to a mere two."

"Quite true. I whittled my list down to Sir John Grant and—er—the man Powell, the fellow that Lady Pelham sent away from Loredana's refreshment-room. But you, Bathurst, were not content, and, if I remember rightly, added several other names to my list."

"Yes. It is about that that I've come to see you. I referred just now to various strands that I stated were of two patterns. Perhaps it would be as well if I gave you greater detail. Let us retrace our steps for a moment, Sir Austin. Let me take your mind back to the incident of the revolver that we discovered in the bowl of claret cup. A revolver that was fitted with a silencer. Tell me—has Hargreaves been able to associate the ownership of that revolver with any of the people whom we know to have been there?"

"Up to last night—no. I saw Hargreaves late last night, and beyond establishing through Le Gonidec the identity of Annette Mornay with the girl who was mixed up with that French murderer he's almost marking time. It's true that he's made another—"

Bathurst intervened. "Well, Sir Austin, I've been giving a considerable amount of attention to that revolver and I've come to the conclusion that once again I am confronted with that *bête noire* of every crime investigator—two absolutely different sets of clues."

Sir Austin nodded again. "I know that. You mean false and true. You've had 'em before in cases, my boy, and there's no reason to believe that you won't have 'em again."

"And that is where I'm inclined to differ from you, Sir Austin. I mean with regard to your words 'false and true'." Bathurst rose and began to stride the room, as was his habit when endeavouring to press home an opinion which he knew very well would be contested. "Let me try to explain. My point is this. I look upon a 'false' clue as a clue which has been deliberately planted by the criminal with the sole idea of leading the investigator astray. The only intention behind it is deception. In the first case that ever came my way, that of the murder in the billiards-room at Considine Manor, the most difficult part of my job was to separate clues of that kind from those that were thoroughly genuine and authentic." Sir Austin nodded. "Somehow, in the case under our notice I don't think that the same conditions altogether apply."

The Commissioner interrupted. "I'm afraid that I don't follow you."

"It's hard to explain, I know. But I can't get away from the idea that the actual murder of De Ravenac did not happen as the murderer had anticipated, and—as I am beginning to believe— had arranged. Then, you see, the position becomes incredibly more difficult. For some of the clues that may well appear to fall into the category that I may describe as 'false', may, if original intentions had materialized, well be entitled to find their real place in the department that we may label 'true'."

Sir Austin fell to considering. "You allude, of course, to the revolver?"

"To that and to other things. Again, was the murder of Annette Mornay part and parcel of the original scheme or *an unlooked-for sequel*? Was the first intention to destroy both De Ravenac and Annette, or *was Annette murdered because she knew what it was that had caused the original plans to miscarry*?" Bathurst turned and shrugged his shoulders.

"I put that forward, Sir Austin, merely as a suggestion that will give you some inkling of my main point."

"I'm very well aware that you were far from satisfied with my list of possibles as it finished, but all the same, Bathurst, I can't get away from one of the names that remained on it. I refer to that of Sir John Grant."

"I'm listening, sir."

"Well, it has struck me since, and forcibly too, that Grant is the man responsible for the story of the mysterious stranger, and, if you remember, that fellow Pierpoint to whom he first made an appeal for corroboration was unable to give it to him."

"Don't overlook the fact that he got it from Wyatt, though, afterwards."

"Yes—but in a half-hearted sort of way, I thought. Wyatt seemed none too sure of his ground, in my opinion. After all, what are Wyatt's qualifications to confirm Grant's story? Wyatt wasn't in the general refreshment-room, and only admitted that he saw this shadowy old man somewhere in the corridor. Which didn't make it a real corroboration of Grant, after all."

"Before you go any farther, Sir Austin, let me point out to you two matters which for the moment appear to have escaped your observation. Firstly, according to the evidence that is above suspicion, you should be able to delete Sir John Grant from your list of possibles and you should have done so when you drew it up. Sir John Grant was in the general refreshment-room when we are told that De Ravenac was murdered. There is the evidence of Pierpoint to that effect and also the evidence of several others. I wondered how it was that that fact had eluded you when you left him in as a starter. Secondly—and mind you, Sir Austin, this is an almost incontestable confirmation of Sir John Grant's story—there is the evidence that has come to us from Quinton, the footman. This man Quinton and his three colleagues are prepared to swear that there was a man who came into the ball earlier than Da Costa and who, we believe, impersonated Da Costa. I found that incident so diverting that I called at Sir Beverley Pelham's and interviewed the admirable Quinton yesterday." The Commissioner murmured something that was inaudible. "My visit proved far from unproductive, Sir Austin." Bathurst stopped his pacing and came to a halt at Sir

Austin's side. Sir Austin looked up at him, and as he did so he saw Anthony Bathurst rub his hands.

"From what Quinton told me, I am able to prove that this man who impersonated Da Costa did so by using Da Costa's original ticket of invitation. Which fact, as Da Costa himself pointed out originally, must inevitably in the end lead us to the truth. Don't you agree?"

It was some moments before Sir Austin Kemble replied. "That fact about Da Costa's card is most vital," he conceded eventually. "But how can Quinton prove what he says? Did you go into that?"

Bathurst explained what the man had told him.

"Appears to be conclusive," admitted the Commissioner; "we're lucky to run up against a servant so observant. As a rule they're thick and heavy. Since the lower classes took to running the country, they've lost most of the little intelligence that they had—or at least it seems so to me."

"Hargreaves is marking time, you say?"

"Just about, Bathurst, and no more. All he's done up to the moment has been to get further news from Paris—from Le Gonidec. About the Wolf chap. I was going to tell you about it just now."

Bathurst showed interest. "What else has he?"

"Well, according to Le Gonidec, in answer to a second inquiry 'chit' that Hargreaves put through to him, every known criminal that was believed to be mixed up with 'Le Loup' at the time of his exploits can be accounted for by the French authorities themselves. They are all either serving sentences or traceable in France in other ways. Not one has been lost sight of entirely. It was a line of inquiry well worth trying."

Bathurst nodded. "I agree. Thank goodness there are other points of attack. It's all right as far as it goes—which isn't a very great distance."

Sir Austin desired information. "What's the next move, Bathurst?"

Bathurst paused at the door.

"Candidly, Sir Austin, I don't know. I incline to a waiting game. Criminals have been known to betray themselves, and I fancy that this affair will prove no exception to the rule."

CHAPTER XXII
JOSEPHINE AND HER BRETHREN

WYATT LISTENED to Josephine Pelham's telephone message and was able to tell both from her voice and her manner that the agitation of which she told him was very real and in no way assumed for the purpose of goading him to a definite course of action. As always, he was ready and willing to place himself at her service with a celerity that should have made her a pleased and proud woman.

"Very well, Jo," he answered immediately, "I'll blow round to you in a couple of shakes. I've one little job I must finish, and as soon as that's over I'll be right along. You said something about Dick and Robin—shall I call in at their place on my way, or would you rather make the necessary arrangements yourself?"

Josephine assured him that she wouldn't—that she would leave it all to him—and accordingly within half an hour all three of the men for whom she had sent out her inquiry were in her presence. Wyatt looked carefully round the room before coming to the point.

"Where's Sir Beverley?" he inquired.

"My husband is out," replied Josephine, with a hopeless sort of smile. "That is one of the reasons that I sent for you to come this afternoon. Because it's partly through him that I have decided to have this talk with you. The cigarettes are on that table, Robin." She indicated the table in question. "Help yourself and pass them round, will you?"

Robin Blaker took advantage of the invitation. "What's the trouble, then, Jo?" he asked, as he handed the silver box to his elder brother.

Josephine's face was white and strained as she answered. "Everything's the trouble, Robin," she blurted desperately. "Things were pretty filthy before all this happened, as you know, and now they seem to have reached their limit."

Wyatt looked straight at her and as usual wasted no time in coming directly to essentials. "Please explain, Jo—everything. Let us know what has occurred. Then perhaps we can look round it and see what can best be done. Whatever happens, we're all in this together."

Josephine tapped the Wilton pile impatiently with her foot. "Sounds delightfully simple and plain sailing and all that. But take it from me, Dan, old boy, it's not going to be anything like as easy as you seem to imagine. I'm not worrying you for nothing." She paused, and for a moment or two the three men watched her, as she seemed to review and weigh whatever it was that was troubling her. Before any of them could interrupt the train of thought that she was following, she had gone on again. "I have come to a decision this last day or two," she stated. "A decision that I ought to have come to before—before things— er—happened. There is no excuse for me for not doing so. I should never have been content to allow myself to remain as much in the dark as I did, and before I tell you of more recent things, I am going to ask certain questions of you. Very, very pointed questions."

Wyatt threw one leg over the other and somewhat ostentatiously blew the smoke of his cigarette towards the ceiling. "Questions about what?" he asked.

Josephine's reply startled them somewhat when it came, not so much for what it was but for the tone which her words held.

"Of course," she went on coldly and dispassionately, "I am eternally grateful for anything that any of you did for me, and don't any of you think otherwise. That goes without saying. But I realize now that I should have had more courage and fought my own battles more by myself. It frightens me now to think that I didn't. I think I am afraid of what's going to happen, and, if you can understand me, even more afraid of what *has* happened."

White-faced, she caught Wyatt by the sleeve. "Tell me, please, what happened here on the night of my masked ball?"

Wyatt attempted to temporize. "Is it necessary for us to resurrect any details, Jo? It was understood between us that as soon as the events had taken place they were to be wiped off the tablets of our memory. That applied to every one of us men. And you, Jo, if you will pardon me pointing out the fact, also agreed with me beforehand to accept the conclusions without seeking to know any facts or asking any questions whatsoever."

"I know that," answered Lady Pelham doggedly. "I know that only too well. I am sorry—very sorry—that I undertook to do what I did on those terms. But I was desperate when I did it. Please don't think me in any way ungrateful or even critical, but the dreadful things that have happened since have put a different complexion on matters altogether. My own past trouble seems to have become infinitesimal. Unless I know more—unless I know everything—I may inadvertently do or say something which may bring disaster to all of us. That's only one of the things that I am afraid of. You must see that." She spoke impulsively and carefully scrutinized the faces of her three companions in order that she could assess the effect of her words and plea upon them.

"After all," she urged in an attempt to strengthen her point of view, "you will only be filling in details for me, won't you? It isn't as though you will be telling me something of which I know absolutely nothing. I'll come to the point at once. Tell me, please, was De Ravenac killed here, as I surmise that he was?"

Now that Lady Pelham had put her doubts into actual cold words the apprehension that each of the three men had felt was tinged with a certain amount of relief. Dick Blaker looked at his brother, who bit his lips and in turn looked towards Major Wyatt. The last-named took upon himself the responsibility of answering Lady Pelham's question. It was his habit to assume responsibility: it had been nearly all his life, and he did not shrink from it on this occasion any more than he had ever done.

"Let us look at your question, Jo, in the right perspective, otherwise certain features of it may become disproportionate. Certain words fit certain situations much more adequately than others. In reply to your query, therefore, and taking it absolutely as you put it, let me say that De Ravenac was dealt with that night in the only possible way that was open to certain men of honour, who had, at the same time, the greater privilege of being friends of you." Wyatt flicked the ash from his cigarette.

Josephine Pelham's fingers were clasped and unclasped alternately as she listened to his reply, and her face worked with the stress of her emotion.

"He was killed, then—because you . . ." She spoke so quietly that her words were almost inaudible.

"He was removed," corrected Wyatt, interrupting her. "Let us say, rather, now that the matter has been dragged to light again, that his foul and poisonous influence was obliterated. The world is a good deal cleaner and sweeter for his annihilation. Personally, I have neither time nor use for vermin—particularly of the human variety. Can't we let the matter end there? What use is there in raking it over again. In any case, please don't ask me for further details."

Josephine made no answer. The fears that had preyed upon her for days were now realized only too forcibly. Wyatt noted her silence and seized the opportunity that it afforded to strengthen his position.

"In any case, I don't know that I can, even. Our arrangements were such that definite knowledge on the part of many of us was completely excluded. That was my idea from the beginning. 'Pon my soul, were it to save my own life even, I don't know now that I could absolutely swear to . . ."

He paused and swung round on Josephine's two brothers. "You can support me in this, you two chaps, can't you?"

Robin and Dick nodded. "It's quite true what Wyatt says," confirmed the former, "you can take our word on that, Jo."

Josephine asked no more questions about De Ravenac for the time being. "Very well, then, if you won't tell me, I suppose that's all there is to it. You heard me say I was frightened," she went on wearily. "I had good reason—oh, ever such good reason—for saying that. What of this poor girl—Annette Mornay? Have you anything to tell me about her?" There was dead silence in the room after the words had left her lips. For Josephine Pelham had put into actual expression the doubt that had been in the mind of each one of them. More than the doubt even—she had dragged out into the relentless light of day the dark suspicion that had been their amazing torment for more hours now than they would have cared to admit. Once again, after what seemed an interminable silence, Wyatt shouldered the burden of reply.

"The murder of the girl Mornay came as a terrible shock to me, and I presume to all of us also. As to how or why it occurred, I know absolutely nothing. You know very well that it was never bargained for, Jo, and I for one was unaware of the girl's existence even."

"After De Ravenac had been—removed?" She seemed to doubt him.

"Of course."

Robin Blaker hastened to corroborate Wyatt's avowal. "Take it from me, we are as ignorant of the circumstances of Annette Mornay's murder as you yourself, Jo. God knows what brought her into it, and why she should have been killed so soon after De Ravenac. Quite frankly, the affair has shaken me up considerably, and I've spent hour after hour trying to piece the two things together so that I might reach a logical conclusion of some kind. But hopelessly. I wish to blazes now I'd never had anything to do with any of it. There's only one consolation, I suppose, and that's the one from which I try to find comfort. We helped you, and you're high and dry in consequence."

"I agree with Robin," supplemented his brother. "I said little when the affair was first mooted, and I haven't said much now. I'm inclined to sit tight, you know. Talking's not my line, but I agree with what Robin has just said."

Josephine turned to the latter. "And I don't know, Robin, that I am as 'high and dry' as you so calmly state. I think that I've been forked out of the frying-pan only to be prodded into the fire. This brings me to something else that I wanted to tell you. My husband suspects." She spoke tonelessly.

"Suspects what?" demanded Wyatt.

"Not what you're thinking of," she answered simply. "But sometimes I think it's even worse than that. The Commandments are not equally attractive. He suspects me—me of all people—of an association with De Ravenac. Think of it, and weep."

"How do you know that?"

She shrugged her shoulders. "How does a woman know these things? From his manner. From certain remarks he has let drop. From certain questions he has put to me. From certain looks in his eyes that I find straying towards me. Oh—from a hundred tiny things which would seem hopelessly trivial to you, no doubt, but which are horribly eloquent to me."

"But how is it possible?"

Josephine wiped the corners of her mouth with the lace square that did duty as her handkerchief. "I imagine that there may be more than one way for him to have found out. Some good-natured friend, bursting with information—or somebody may even have seen me when I went to De Ravenac's flat."

"This is deucedly awkward for all of us," put in Robin. "I thought that we were absolutely safe in that direction. If I had known that earlier, I think it would have made a difference."

"I thought we *were* safe," conceded Josephine. "I told Dan so in the early stages, but it appears that we were not. It only remains for Beverley to confide in somebody—you know very well what he is and how he takes all his decisions from somebody else—for the fat to be in the fire and a good spot of trouble knocking at the door of all of us. In fact, I believe he has done so already." She made the announcement dully, as though she were past caring.

Wyatt looked grave, and his jaw was rigid when he replied to her. "In whom?"

"That man Bathurst, whom Sir Austin Kemble sent for on the night of De Ravenac's removal. See how faithfully I stick to your word," she concluded bitterly.

The faces of the two Blakers equalled Wyatt's in gravity and consternation, and Robin let loose another bombshell to intensify the situation.

"If Beverley has done as you say, it's the worst news I've heard for a long time, and when you hear what I've got to tell you in connection with Bathurst, you'll understand even better what I mean. Bathurst, let me tell you, has been prowling round Loredana and Da Costa. I believe that he's acting with them. Do you realize what that means?"

"I don't think there's so much in that as you might imagine." Wyatt seemed relieved as he spoke. "I fancy, too, that I can throw a little light on that for you. I happened to be downstairs when most of the De Ravenac inquiry was going on, and in the inevitable pow-wow that followed, I heard the President openly declare that he would join forces with Sir Austin Kemble to discover the murderer. The fool seemed to imagine that an assassin's hand was directed against the welfare of his tuppenny-three-farthing republic. I was tempted more than once to tell him that places like that were three a penny on any Saturday night. That is no doubt the consideration that brings Bathurst and him in double harness. So I don't think we need concern ourselves too much over that, Robin," he added reflectively.

But Robin Blaker refused to be satisfied, for he had another card yet to play. "Wait, Wyatt! Have you thought against whom Bathurst will land while he's out hunting with Loredana?"

Wyatt stared, and they looked towards Dick, as though to discover there the answer to Robin's question.

"I can see what you mean, Robin, if Dan can't." Josephine was emphatic in her declamation of understanding. "You mean that he'll meet Gerald."

"I mean a trifle more than that," said Robin, with some sarcasm, "I mean that he's already met him, and God knows what he got out of him. I shouldn't like to trust Gerald's intelligence too strongly, especially if he happened to be in anything like a tight corner. Nor even his loyalty," he added bitterly.

"Do you say that he *has* met Gerald?" queried Wyatt. "Are you sure of this?"

"I am positive. I had an appointment with Sebastian Loredana one afternoon some days ago, and he passed on the news himself. Bathurst had been to him, had had a chin-wag with his inimitable Chancellor, and had gaily asked permission to continue the inquisition with our friend Gerald. Personally, I've been expecting for days for Gerald to let us know what transpired. We're all in this mess together, as you said just now, and I certainly think he ought to have done so. And I'm not alone either—Dick here thinks the same as I do. I had it out with him as soon as I knew."

Wyatt was quick to observe that Lady Pelham's distress was rapidly approaching the stage when it would be difficult to control, and it would have been idle for him to deny that Robin's latest piece of information had undermined his confidence and caused him no small amount of misgiving and perturbation. "I agree with you too, Robin, with regard to Gerald," he declared quietly, "and the natural question that forces itself into my mind is this: Who else of our party has Bathurst seen? If it's not too late the others should be warned against him. There can be no question about that."

"Don't you think it would be advisable for you to have a sort of general conference?" The suggestion came from Josephine.

"An excellent idea, Jo," acknowledged Dick Blaker; "perhaps Wyatt will make the arrangements for one! I would suggest that it be held immediately, or at any rate as quickly as possible. Every day makes our position more precarious." He reached for his hat, and Josephine stood up to say good-bye.

"Be careful," she insisted. "Be careful, whatever you do."

"Trust us to be that. Think what there is at stake." Wyatt gave her this encouragement.

She nodded, and the rush of tears to her eyes as he took her hand in his to say good-bye, worried him for hours afterwards.

* * * * *

As Dick Blaker started his car, Robin turned to Wyatt, seated at the back with him, and determined to ask a question.

"We must warn Nick," he said, "and also Pierpoint. Pierpoint," he repeated, "particularly Pierpoint. Have you thought much about him lately, Wyatt?"

"What do you mean?" demanded the latter.

"Well, he's your friend, and he came into this business at the first through you. I seem, however, to remember two things about him. One—that he didn't seem over-keen, and two—that you hadn't known him anything like as long as you've known the rest of us."

Wyatt eyed him with grim satisfaction. "And you're also remembering that he wore the costume of the orange axe. You've got as far as that. That's your point, isn't it?"

Robin Blaker shook his head.

"As it happens, you're barking up the wrong tree, old man. If you want to know, I was thinking of the murder of Annette Mornay, and of the way he treated your interesting story of 'Le Loup de Poignard'. Remember the incident when we were at Ricardo's?"

Wyatt stared at his companion with amazement.

"What the devil are you driving at?" he exclaimed vehemently.

The car slowed down and Robin opened the door and alighted. "Think it over," he replied to the man whom he left in the car, "and perhaps you'll see things in time as I'm beginning to see them."

CHAPTER XXIII
WYATT TAKES PRECAUTIONS

MARTIN PIERPOINT's dark face, with its lazy eyes, was turned towards Wyatt seated at the head of the table. His glance rested there for a moment, burnt suddenly into the flame of intense interest, and then flickered into the normal again, as he surveyed one by one the features of the four remaining members of the party. Ricardo's seemed much the same as on that night when Wyatt had first broached his "perfect" plan, and although, by definite arrangement, no mention of De Ravenac's death had yet been made by any one of them, there was, nevertheless, a silent understanding amongst them that the real purpose of this evening's reunion would eventually turn out to be not unconnected with the crime at Sir Beverley Pelham's.

To Pierpoint, the affair presented a different aspect from that which it showed to the others, and he wondered as he sat there how long this particular point of view of his would remain his own—for on this especial point a great deal depended. When he was forced to share it, he would be forced also into different action. Little escaped him, however, as he sat in the chair, on the left-hand side of Wyatt, with Nick Twining seated next to him, and although his answers to the scraps of conversation that floated his way were nonchalant and affectedly carefree, at the same time his clever far-seeing intelligence was as keenly alert as ever under his mask of semi-indifference. He knew the time to attack—as many others do. He knew also when the time came to defend, dourly and doggedly. In which knowledge, again, he was not alone. But few possessed his dual power of swift attack and imperturbable defence.

On this evening, he fancied from the atmosphere of the dining-room and from the manner of more than one of his companions the moment would very soon come for him to essay the latter. It was, therefore, with an ice-packed brain that he listened to Wyatt when the coffee was brought in and the latter rose to address the company. As before, the waiters had left their places and the doors of the room had been closed when Wyatt gave the signal for his five companions to bring their respective chairs nearer to the head of the table so that they were all intimately close to him when he started to speak to them. His voice was very quiet and restrained.

"It is not with any sense of desire that I am about to refer to the occasion of our last meeting in this room. At that time, it was, I think, understood by each one of us that whatever was arranged and whatever happened in relation to a certain other evening not very long ago would be relegated, as far as we were concerned, to oblivion. That was so, you fellows, wasn't it?"

The five men that formed the circle around him expressed their agreement in various ways. Wyatt accepted it and went on. His words were very deliberate.

"But unfortunately the affair did not end where we antici-pated that it would, and a second 'influence' has been at work with which I, for one, am entirely unfamiliar." He paused, but the five were silent. "Robin, Dick, and I saw the lady in whose cause we laboured a few days ago at her own request and invita-tion, and when we heard what she had to tell us it was decided by the three of us absolutely unanimously that we must adopt a certain line of action as a whole, and as it were make a united stand that is backed up by a united plan." He paused again to moisten his lips.

"For I regret to say that my confidence in the invulnerabil-ity of the scheme that I outlined to you is considerably less than it was at the time I put it forward. But, as I pointed out before, this has come about through no fault of my own, or, I trust, of any one of us. It is this astonishing sequel to the affair that we staged that has disturbed me—and others—and upset the plans that I made. The plans to which you all agreed, and which were carried out." It was at this moment that the company received their first shock of the evening.

"One moment, Wyatt, if you please." The intervention came from Pierpoint. "One moment before you go any farther. You said just now, 'plans which you made, to which we all agreed, and which we carried out'. I should like to ask you whether you are sure of your ground in regard to the last point?"

Wyatt half turned so that he faced the intervener. A fear that had held possession of his mind for some time now became more real and more distinct to him—a fear, however, that he would have refused to admit to several of those who were with him. "What do you mean?" he questioned; but the question was in the nature of a parry.

Pierpoint stood his ground. "I simply asked you whether you were certain in your own mind that everything on a certain even-ing occurred—shall we say—according to plan? For example, if you wish me to be more explicit—did not the presence of a second weapon, for instance, occasion you some surprise?"

The murmurings of the others that formed the circle demon-strated the extent of their interest in Pierpoint's last question.

But Wyatt was tactician enough to crush immediately any semblance of discussion at this point.

"Oh—I see what you mean, Pierpoint. But we will, I think, leave it at that for the moment. Each one of us here is content to take each of the others on trust. We must. It couldn't be otherwise. That mutual trust was one of the most important foundation stones upon which our original plan was designed and executed. I am perfectly certain that no good purpose would be effected now by any discussion of details, such as weapons, for example, which, after all, now that the job's finished, don't matter a tinker's damn. I am content and I think all of you are content. Surely that's all there is to it." His eyes invited the company for their confirmation. Pierpoint shifted lazily in his chair, perceived Wyatt's policy of evasiveness and shrugged his shoulders with a gesture of indifference.

But before Wyatt could obtain the general approval for which he had so obviously asked, interruption in the form of criticism came from Robin Blaker.

"I have a word or two to say about that. This point of yours with regard to all of us taking one another on trust doesn't appeal to me so forcibly as you seem to think it does. In fact, I should like to ask the opinions of some of the others on that particular point."

Wyatt again sensed danger and again strove to push it away from present contemplation. "Would you mind, Robin," he said, "if you likewise shelved that consideration until I've said a little more? There is another factor in the affair to which I am desirous of calling your attention before I go on to anything else. It is extremely important and touches every one of us here. Do you agree to my suggestion, Robin?"

"Very well, then—as you please. I'll raise it again, though, before we break up to-night."

Wyatt showed his relief. "Do so by all means. That's all right, then. Now, with regard to the factor that I just mentioned. You are doubtless all aware that working on the case are Sir Austin Kemble, the Commissioner of Police, an Inspector of Police named Hargreaves, and a third person whom old Kemble called in in an attempt, or at least so I think, to save his own face. This third person is Anthony Bathurst. Now, Bathurst's no fool, I assure you—very far from it, in fact. I have very good reason for saying this, as a pal of mine knows a certain Colonel Fane who was mixed up with Bathurst when a Major Whittaker was poisoned a year or two ago up in Lancashire somewhere. In addition, Loredana himself is backing Bathurst for all he's worth, and I'm very much afraid that certain of the gentleman's inquisitions may prove to be distinctly pertinent and give at least one or two of us a pretty thin time should he put us through it. By the way, what have you to say about that, Gerald?" Twining flushed as Wyatt turned to him. "It's quite true that a man named Bathurst called upon me," he admitted, "if that's what you mean. I was going to tell you about it to-night, as a matter of fact, but up to the moment I've had no chance. You've been talking for the better part of the time." As he made the admission, Gerald Twining could almost feel the hostility that looked from the faces of several of the others as they turned towards him.

"What did he get out of you?" demanded his cousin Robin sharply, and with distinct aggression.

"Not a great deal, I fancy. I flatter myself that I parried his questions remarkably well."

Wyatt got down to business at once. He probed for the truth.

"Questions? What were they?"

Twining fell to consideration. "Well, in the main they were connected with the appointment that the Spanish Ambassador made with the President of San Jonquilo for the evening of the ball. It struck me that Bathurst had some bee in his bonnet, connecting the real business of the evening—you know what I mean—with San Jonquilo. You can take it from me that there was nothing in any of his questions about that to cause me any trouble in answering."

But neither Wyatt nor Robin Blaker was satisfied to leave the matter here. Their attack became persistent.

"What about the ball itself?" queried the latter. "Didn't he want to know anything about that?"

Gerald Twining now showed signs of discomfort. He hesitated before he answered. "Yes," he replied guardedly, "to the best of my recollection he wanted to know if I'd spotted old Da Costa during the evening."

"What did you say?"

Again Twining was a victim of hesitation. "I think I told him that I had."

"You blithering ass." Robin denounced him fiercely. "What in the name of all that's addle-headed did you say that for?"

Twining's flush deepened. "Why not? I don't see that I did any harm. Sometimes the absolute truth pays better than all your falsehoods and evasions."

"Go on," returned Robin, with mock helplessness. "Let us hear the worst—only get it over quickly, for the love of Mike. Then we may be able to estimate the damage."

"I don't know that there's very much more for me to tell you," responded Twining sullenly. "Oh—I remember—I told him how we were assing about at the head of the staircase when Da—"

"What?" thundered Wyatt. "You told him that?"

Obstinacy began to show in Twining's features. The veins knotted in his forehead. He repeated the words he had used to Robin Blaker. "I don't see that I did any harm. I was quite frank and quite open about all of it. If I hadn't been very likely I *might* have given him cause for suspicion."

Wyatt brushed Twining's attempts at justification to one side. "Please tell me exactly how much you told Bathurst. Then we shall all be better able to judge how we stand."

"'Pon my soul, Wyatt, you're as windy as an old hen. Surely you didn't imagine that you'd get away with the whole job without any questions being asked? Some optimist, aren't you?" Twining, by now, was thoroughly nettled, and the cynical smile that he saw curled round Pierpoint's lips only served to exasperate him all the more. "I told Bathurst that four of us were playing the goat at the top of the staircase—simply that and nothing more. What on earth is there to worry over in regard to that?"

"Did you tell him who the four were?" Robin put the question with emphatic seriousness.

"I did," admitted Twining with calculated coolness. "I gave him the four names. He knew that I knew them. He knew that the unmasking had given it away to me. I should have thought from the frantic way in which your wings are flapping that you would have been damned grateful for the 'alibi'!"

"Alibi—indeed. An alibi would have to be pretty watertight to pass Bathurst," contributed Wyatt. And Dick Blaker nodded agreement.

"Has he been to see you again? Has he come to lap up more?" asked Robin.

"He hasn't! And I don't think for a moment that there's the slightest chance of his coming. I tell you—he was perfectly satisfied. I could tell that from his manner. I'm not such a ruddy fool as you all seem to think I am."

"H'm," muttered Wyatt. "Don't be too sure—though I admit it 'ud be a bit impossible. But there's such a thing, you know, as sitting comfortably on the edge of a volcano. You may enjoy the view of the adjoining country for hours. The upheaval, when it comes, is rather sudden, that's all. Sudden and shattering!" He turned to the others in the terms of a general admonition. "Well, it's pretty evident, you chaps, that we shall have to walk very warily where Bathurst is concerned. It's very obvious from all that we've heard that he's nosing round, and the least little thing may serve to open his eyes to something that it's far more healthy for him not to know. To say nothing of us." His exhortation developed a particular direction. "You, Nick, of all people, had better be specially on your guard. As Gerald's brother he may form the idea that you may conceivably offer a line of least resistance and what he can't get from Gerald he may be able to obtain from you. Or he may try to check up on you. Look out for yourself, that's all. If he turns up, push him off by hook or by crook, and put me wise immediately."

Nick Twining grinned. "Don't worry about me, Wyatt. Leave that to me. It'll be in safe hands. I'll redeem the family reputation—it seems to be under a bit of a cloud."

"That's settled, then," announced Wyatt, apparently more satisfied now that he knew the extent of the leakage. "I shall go home the more comfortable for that piece of knowledge."

"Half a minute. Before you do that," interrupted Robin Blaker, "I should like to finish what I started to say a little while ago. I am sure you remember."

Wyatt was clever enough to check almost instantly the look of annoyance that had begun to show in his face. "Oh, yes—but for the moment I had forgotten. The story of Twining's interview with Bathurst had driven it from my mind. What is the point that you wish to make, Robin?"

It was evident from the eminently business-like way in which Robin accepted the invitation that he desired to unburden his mind of something that seemed definitely serious to him.

"Taking you back to an expression that you used earlier on in the evening, I want to clear the air just a little bit in connection with it. I don't suppose that I am able now to remember the exact words that you used, but as far as I can remember you said something to the effect that we all of us here must be prepared to take the others 'on trust'. It is in relation to that last idea that I join issue with you."

He paused and looked round the company with a strong suggestion of challenge, and each man at whom he looked wondered in which personal direction his accusation would lie when it came. To some of them, cradled and nurtured as they had been, the latent impeachment bordered on the unheard-of, and their eagerness to come to grips with it, when its exact nature should be disclosed, was tinged with a feeling that was entirely unpleasant and distasteful. But none was ready yet to translate either his interest or distaste into words, and Robin Blaker, spurred on by the chilling and ominous silence, proceeded with his statement.

"You referred yourself, Wyatt, some little time ago to what you described as an 'astonishing sequel'. I am well aware that one of the easiest things to do in life is to jump to conclusions, and attribute to what is purely circumstantial evidence a greater value than perhaps it merits, but this 'astonishing sequel' of yours seems to me to require a considerable amount of explanation. Much more, I think, than we are likely to obtain—certainly to-night."

"I think I see to where you're heading." Wyatt spoke in his quietest tone. "But please remember the circumstances and be guided by the utmost discretion. It is plain that you must not be too explicit here."

Robin Blaker waved a deprecating hand. "There is no need for me to be 'explicit', as you call it. There is no necessity at all for me to enter into the slightest details. Even if I wanted to. But it would be incredibly foolish on the part of all of us if we failed to link up the—er—matter which engaged our attention with your astonishing 'sequel', Wyatt. To do so would be deliberately shutting our eyes to facts which to an ordinary person would seem as plain as a pikestaff." In the emotion of his argument he brought his fist on to the table with a crash. "What I want to know is this: Who staged the sequel, and beyond that—*why* was it staged? Also—why was not one of us consulted beforehand? It's desperately unfair that this should have been allowed to happen and so many of us kept in the dark." He looked round again as though demanding by sheer power of personal determination the answers to the series of questions that he had raised.

"You realize very well, I presume, what you are practically saying?" asked Wyatt. "What you say is tantamount to an accusation against one person of being guilty of both—er—incidents."

"If you like to put it like that, baldly and crudely, why, yes! I say that the one hand accomplished both affairs. I should like to hear the opinions of others on the point."

A hush fell on all the members of the party. None responded to the suggestion that had been put forward. Robin Blaker, having travelled so far, went straight forward to the destination that he had all along set out to reach. "I would ask Pierpoint for his observations on the opinions that I have expressed." His words came with cold precision.

The man to whom the challenge had been flung uncoiled himself nonchalantly from the position that he had taken up in his chair.

"I was wondering how long you would be before you crawled from your ambush and came out into the open." He flicked the ash from his cigarette into the tray in front of him. Everyone waited for him to continue, but they were destined to disappointment.

"Well?" demanded Robin. "Don't keep us waiting too long. Or I may be forced to frame, from your disinclination to talk—very reluctantly I admit—a much more definite charge."

Pierpoint smiled carelessly. "Against me?" he inquired, with lazy effrontery.

Robin Blaker pressed home his point. "Against you, most certainly."

Pierpoint's reply surprised him. "It would be a shame for you to keep the company waiting as much as for me to do the same thing. I shall be delighted to answer you if you will only put your indictment into words. I have no doubt that it will prove immensely entertaining."

A dark flush of resentment flooded Robin's face. Pierpoint's reception of his challenge angered him intensely. "Very well, then! Since you ask me, I will. Are you prepared to deny that you used our conspiracy—if I may be pardoned for calling it such—not only to help *us*, but also to further your own ends? Will you gainsay the fact that our activities in connection with a certain man suited your book down to the ground? If you will deny those things on your word of honour, I give you my guarantee that I will accept it and say no more."

The smile never left Martin Pierpoint's lips. "Can't you be more definite?" he asked satirically. "'To further my own ends' is loose, vague, and, to me, distinctly unsatisfying. 'To suit my book' strikes me as ambiguous. I feel sure that, knowing so much, you must be cognizant of even 'the little more'. 'The little more and how much'," he quoted with reflective relish.

"I will even do that," replied Robin fiercely. "I will accuse you to your face of coming in with us to carry out a purely private vendetta," he declared.

Martin Pierpoint's eyes met Blaker's fearlessly but yet mockingly. His smile became a low laugh.

"Since you have put it so nicely, Blaker," he observed, "I will *not* deny it. Shall we—er—return to the subject of how we are going to deal with Mr. Bathurst? Or would you prefer to discuss that little matter of the second weapon?"

CHAPTER XXIV
BATHURST IS FORCED TO DO LIKEWISE

THE THIRD escape that Anthony Bathurst had had within a period of five days was the means of causing him to pull himself up with a jerk and take very careful stock of his position. On the first occasion a matter of four inches or so had served to intervene between him . . . and very sudden death. A big car, with the hood up, that looked to him, from the fleeting glance that he was able to obtain of it, very much like a Packard coupe, had flashed from the Haymarket into Pall Mall without the slightest hint of warning and at a speed that, for the vicinity, was positively sinful. Bathurst had scarcely essayed the crossing of the roadway when the car was on him . . . one shuddering, paralysing second was all that was left to him in which to make up his mind for action, but his finely poised intelligence made full and instant use of it. With the keen anticipation that was alike his flair for, and his heritage from, all ball games, he had flung himself adroitly backwards . . . the tongue of the car had almost licked him . . . its hot breath had scorched him, and he had felt the fan of it on his cheek . . . but that was all. The constable on duty twenty-four yards or so higher up along Pall Mall had come towards him visibly palpitating with a mixture of excitement, concern and indignation. The last-mentioned condition eventually triumphed.

"Ought to be 'ung, drawn and quartered, sir," he cried. "The swine! I've never seen a worse case all the time I've been on this job. People like 'em ought to be strung up. Lucky you 'ad the sense to do what you did. I fair gave you up, I did. I suppose you didn't get his vermilion scarlet ruby number?"

Bathurst had by this time recovered sufficiently to shrug his shoulders. "I'm afraid I was negligent with regard to that, Constable. But you will admit, I think, that the gentleman didn't linger. That is my sole excuse."

The constable grinned at Bathurst's pleasantry. "Good job for 'im."

As Bathurst walked away he heard a second official reference to the crimson Gadarene. This incident had almost passed into the realm of things forgotten when, within forty-eight hours, affair number two came to pass. When it did it revived the first in Bathurst's mind with increased clearness. Returning to his flat at an hour close on midnight, he had found the street deserted. It had been raining steadily since before seven o'clock, and as a result the comforts of home had called to the majority much more persistently and successfully than usual. As Bathurst came to the row of houses that fronted the gardens set in the middle of the square, he heard the "ping" of a bullet unpleasantly close to his ear. . . . Instantly flinging himself down, he crouched low in the cover of convenient railings and listened for another . . . but none came. As far as he could see the place was untenanted save for himself, and the only sounds that reached his listening ears were the soughing of the wind in the tree-tops and the monotonous drip of the rain from the leaves and branches.

After a reasonable time of watching and waiting he emerged from his shelter and covered the distance to his flat swiftly and silently. He had now begun to review the position with some concern, and when the third event staged itself, it made him realize beyond any doubt that if he didn't very soon lay his hands upon the ruthless killer of two people life from his own point of view might be abbreviated very suddenly.

Two days afterwards were sufficient for him to know that his margin of safety had become almost infinitesimal. He had kept within his flat all day, and the two notes that he had scribbled to Sir Austin Kemble he had asked Emily to have delivered for him. But at a quarter past eight in the evening a letter had come for him in an envelope of most resplendent type. It was heavily monogrammed on the back with a florid ostentatiousness, and spoke eloquently of an exotic origin. It was from Sebastian Loredana, asking if it would be convenient for Bathurst to come to the Hotel Florizel to see him at once. Would Mr. Bathurst 'phone his intentions immediately upon receipt of the letter? A matter of ten minutes saw him on the platform of St. James's Park Station. As the train came in he walked in the most natural manner to the edge of the platform. There was a fair crowd for the time of the evening, which fact, he considers, was the main factor in saving his life.

A sudden push in the back, seemingly from nowhere, made him lose his balance and stagger almost helplessly. A desperate attempt to recover his balance was successful only because of unsuspected succour that came to him. A tall man of military carriage and bearing clutched quickly at his shoulder and jerked him back to safety as the incoming train almost scraped his forehead and hair. Subsequent conversation and inquiry elicited the probability that the assailant was a tall, dark-featured man who had been observed by some to push his way aggressively through the press on the platform and range himself almost directly behind Bathurst. It was therefore a carefully calculating mental force that came to the Hotel Florizel to be ushered into the presence of Sebastian Loredana. Da Costa sat at the fire with his thin fingers extended to the comfort of the blaze. Although it was late May it was still cold in the evening, and the Chancellor of San Jonquilo, exiled temporarily from Southern warmth, keenly felt it. Loredana, it seemed, was obviously labouring under a great emotion, and Bathurst's first hurried deduction from the President's manner proved flawless.

"Mr. Bathurst," cried Loredana almost querulously, as he greeted his visitor, "I have sent for you very specially. Therefore, I thank you for coming at once from the bottom of my heart. I ask your aid, and I can assure you that Sebastian Loredana throughout his career has done that of few people." He leaned forward and caught Bathurst by the knee. "But I am afraid," he said simply. "I know that my life is in danger. Every moment I remain in England now is fraught with peril for me."

Bathurst expressed his sympathy and then his interest. "It has been handed down," he remarked, "by a greater than either of us, that flesh is heir to at least a thousand natural shocks. Which is the one that is troubling your Excellency?"

"I will tell you. Let me also say that I am not altogether surprised. Ever since I looked on De Ravenac's dead body and that piece of torn silk in orange and black that was clutched in his hand, I have lived to a certain extent in a state of anxiety and dread expectation. I have not had to wait long, Mr. Bathurst—the night before last I was shot at! Shot at—here in the heart of your great city, London, and the narrowness of my escape still sends me cold to my spine. Another step forward on my part of just an inch or so and San Jonquilo would have been constrained to elect another President."

Bathurst made a rapid calculation and asked for additional detail. When it came it appeared that Loredana's escape had been similar to his own, and they had evidently each missed death from the same agency. Bathurst became practical.

"Suspect anybody, your Excellency? Anybody in particular, that is?"

Sebastian spread out his hands rather helplessly. "That is the strangest part of it all. I can think of nobody. Da Costa here and I have cudgelled our brains—my brains, I should say—to see if we can connect any particular person with these affairs. But we came to what you English call 'a dead end' every time. There is nothing that we can lay our hands on. I have sought in vain to pick out somebody to whom I could pin reasonable suspicion. But I can find nobody, and therefore it would be manifestly unfair for me to make a suggestion even. I wish I could. That is the main reason why I have appealed to you for your assistance."

Bathurst accepted the President's summing up of the situation and nodded his agreement with it. "I respect your Excellency's judgment and I admire your attitude. But is there no one who has appeared in this case—in any part of this case, for example—that can be reasonably said to trace back in some way to San Jonquilo or San Jonquilese associations? Either directly or indirectly?"

Loredana was frank and emphatic in his reply. "There are some whom you know," he admitted, after a moment's pause, "who may be said to fulfil *some* of those conditions. But even so, it is impossible for me to harbour any real suspicion or doubt of any one of them. That is one of the things which I had been discussing with Da Costa before you came. But he and I are in agreement, unusual though such a condition may be. There is no one."

Bathurst decided to add the story of his own recent experiences to that of the President. "What you have told me, your Excellency, of your miraculous escape the other night, holds for me a rather extraordinary interest. For I, too, have been the subject during the past few days of similar ministrations. I rather fancy that the gentleman who annoyed you once has honoured me on no less than three occasions. It is fortunate for us both that his execution has so far failed to attain the same level of efficiency as his ingenuity. But, of course, the near future may remedy this, and it's obvious that you and I can't be too careful."

Loredana looked at him curiously, and as Bathurst reached the end of his sentence Da Costa rose from his chair by the fire and stood in the middle of the hearthrug listening intently.

"Explain yourself a little more, Mr. Bathurst, please."

Bathurst obeyed the President's instruction. "Within the space of five days I have been lucky enough to escape death three times by no more than a hair's-breadth. The first was from a heavy car that bore down on me with precipitate suddenness at the corner of the Haymarket and Pall Mall, the second time I received attentions from what I took to be an air-pistol, which were similar to those that came your way, and the third occasion was as recent as half an hour ago. On my way here this evening I escaped being pushed beneath an Underground train simply and solely because a powerful and quick-witted man happened to be standing immediately at my side and as near almost to the edge of the platform as myself."

Loredana listened to this recital with a face that rapidly whitened. There was no doubt now that his appearance showed signs of a desperate fear that approximated a condition of panic.

"Good heavens! On your way here to-night?" he muttered thickly. "You must have been followed, then, from your flat. Perhaps even now they are but a few—"

"I am afraid," interposed Anthony Bathurst, "that circumstances point very strongly in that direction."

The gravity of his tone seemed to have upon Loredana the effect of the last straw. "They mean getting me, Da Costa," he explained nervously, "that's very evident. They may even have recourse to poison. If I could only lay my finger on the fringes of the plot . . ."

"Your Excellency mentioned poison," announced Bathurst; "that same idea had occurred to me. It is imperative that you take all possible steps to counteract such a contingency."

"You hear that, Da Costa?" cried Loredana apprehensively. "You must see to it almost at once, and you must see, too, that there is no possible chance of whatever you arrange, failing." He turned to Bathurst with an appeal for help showing in his eyes. "What can you suggest, Mr. Bathurst?" he asked.

Bathurst considered Loredana's question thoughtfully, and it was some appreciable time before he ventured to reply to it. "Your Excellency must take extreme care in everything you undertake for the next few days. Let Señor Da Costa be at your side whenever and wherever possible. You must take no unnecessary risks whatever, and I will ask Sir Austin Kemble to look after you with special vigilance as far as he is reasonably able. At the same time I warn you that your own alertness, quick-wittedness and intelligence will be your greatest assets. I advise you, therefore, to use them instantaneously should anything arise to cause you the slightest misgiving or suspicion. Just in the same way as I shall be forced to use mine to protect myself." Bathurst rose, preparatory to departure. "We have at least an advantage now that we did not possess before. We have been warned. You know our English proverb. It is all to the good, and we are, as a result, on our guard."

Loredana nodded doubtfully, and then an idea seemed to come to him. "You mentioned the phrase, Mr. Bathurst, 'for a few days'. Was that deliberate on your part or merely a *façon de parler*?"

Bathurst shook his head in denial. "No, your Excellency, I meant exactly what I said. I don't think that this menace will exist for either you or me for very much longer."

"Why?" demanded Loredana. "What do you think is going to happen, then?"

Bathurst shrugged his shoulders. "For the very good reason, your Excellency, that I hope by the time I have stated that my cunning will have been proved to be greater than the cunning of this criminal against whom I have pitted myself. Let me tell you that I have only two links missing from my chain of solution. Pardon me if I appear egotistical, but I am supremely confident."

Loredana indulged in a half-smile. "Your optimism is truly English, Mr. Bathurst," he declared. "Sir Beverly Pelham has it. His wife possesses it. My secretary Twining often shows evidences of it, while Sir John Grant positively exudes it. It must be, I think, your great national characteristic." He turned and spoke to Da Costa. Da Costa walked over to him. "Do you remember, Da Costa," said the President, "the affair on the Duke of Dorada's yacht, when it rode at anchor in the harbour of Santa Guardina?" Da Costa nodded. "Do you remember the incident of Sir John Grant and the curried prawns?" The two men laughed mirthlessly at the reminiscence.

Bathurst turned away, for the story, as far as he knew, held no interest for him. But as Loredana's opening words reached him, he turned again, and as he did so the two links that he wanted towards the amazing truth were revealed to him.

"I was right, your Excellency," he volunteered, when Loredana had finished his reminiscence of Santa Guardina. "I shall have my man within a week." For he was certain that the two threads for which he had been so patiently waiting were in his hands at last.

Loredana shook his head pessimistically as Bathurst passed through the door.

FORTIFIED BY the knowledge that had just come to him, Anthony Bathurst decided to keep steadily to the main trail and to ignore certain avenues and labyrinthine ways that led from it with attractive temptation until a later and more propitious day presented itself. The first duty that he had in mind was a visit to the Spanish Embassy. He had long toyed with an idea that Twining's telephone call on the day of the murder was no ordinary one and had more bearing on the case than could possibly have been foreseen by an investigator in the early stages. Moreover, the light that had broken in on to him as he had listened to the story of the incident that had taken place at Santa Guardina had only served to make this idea of his even stronger. He would therefore act on it at once, and when he entered Grosvenor Gardens it was with a feeling that success was very near to him. He realized, however, that he must exercise all the best qualities of his courage and intelligence to grasp it and in so doing escape the peril which he knew full well would menace him more and more until the case be finally completed and the criminal brought to justice.

The official that greeted him upon his entrance to the Embassy looked at Mr. Bathurst's card critically and expressed regret that Señor Don Enrique del Monterano was absent. For Señor Don, etc., etc., would have been the very man whom Mr. Bathurst should have had the exquisite felicity of interviewing. There was, so he said, none other who could possibly supply the information that Mr. Bathurst desired—that was a position from which there was no getting away—it was inevitable. But how unfortunate! Sir Austin Kemble? The mention of the Commissioner's name caused the official to lift his eyebrows a trifle, but that was all. He had, of course, every regard for so distinguished a personage as the head of New Scotland Yard, but Mr. Bathurst must see very clearly, if he examined the position closely, that an official's hands were absolutely tied when it came to a question of information of an international character. Mr. Bathurst must remember what great events from little causes spring. He was prostrated to think that refusal on his part must incommode his visitor, but there it was. War itself often hung on a man's word—and sometimes even on a woman's whim. He opened his hands and spread them out in an excess of extenuation. Bathurst debated the issue in his mind and came to a swift decision. He knew the eccentricities of the Latin temperament and with quick assessment acted accordingly. Would Señor Don Enrique del Monterano be available for interview at a later time?

"I cannot say," said the official sorrowfully. "He is, in fact, at the offices of the Consulate-General. It is impossible for me to say when he is likely to return. That is no part of my duty. If I named a time by using my judgment in these matters, I might easily be guilty of a miscalculation and again inconvenience you. It would prostrate me to think—"

Bathurst cut the man summarily. For him a second recital of this point was rapidly approaching the intolerable. He asked a direct question and received a prompt reply.

"In Trinity Square, Mr. Bathurst! E.C.3." Anthony thanked him and took his leave. He departed, nursing the secret hope that his second venture would prove to be more profitable than his first. In this he was not disappointed, for the man whom he sought turned out to be as courteous as he was charming.

"I must apologize for troubling you," opened Anthony, "especially at a place other than your headquarters. But my reason is excessively important. You will, I hope, listen to me, Don Enrique."

Don Enrique smiled graciously and intimated to Mr. Bathurst to proceed. The latter complied, and Don Enrique gave the story his closest attention. When Anthony Bathurst came to the mention of the murder of De Ravenac he intimated that he was not unfamiliar with the more intricate details of the affair. Bathurst took the hint and quickly completed his narrative.

"I have not yet touched, Don Enrique, upon the precise matter which has brought me to see you. But I sincerely hope that when I broach it I shall find that I have not come to you in vain."

Don Enrique bowed gallantly. "I hope that I shall find it in my power to help you. Let me hear your desire."

"I take it that you would be cognizant, Don Enrique, of all official engagements made, for example, on behalf of the Spanish Ambassador or for any of his leading representatives?"

Don Enrique frowned. Things were developing somewhat differently from his anticipations. He began to fear that perhaps he would be unable. . . . "Official engagements—yes—I think that I could assert that." He smiled, and as he did so, wondered if Bathurst understood the reason.

"Good," returned Bathurst. "I think that that answer of yours should pretty well cover what I want to know. Do me the favour, please, of casting your mind back to the day of the murder at Sir Beverley Pelham's. It is just possible, of course, that it will be necessary for you to consult certain records that may be at the Embassy, but on the other hand you may be able to remember without reference the point which I am about to ask you."

Don Enrique caressed his chin. "My memory is good," he admitted softly—"exceedingly good. I think it quite likely that I shall need no reference to documentary evidence of any kind in order to answer your question."

"Better and better," exclaimed Bathurst. "Can you recall whether the Spanish Ambassador, or any one of his representatives, had an official appointment with President Loredana on the day in question?"

"I can answer that question with certainty," replied Don Enrique decisively. "As it happens, I have had personal charge of the matter at issue between my Government and the Republic of San Jonquilo. In some respects I have been the intermediary and acted for Señor Alveo. There was no engagement on the particular day about which you inquire. There was to have been an interview between my chief and President Loredana, but it has been pending ever since the President arrived in England and has not yet taken place. I can give you that information, Mr. Bathurst, with unassailable certainty."

Mr. Bathurst listened to Don Enrique's statement of the facts and drew comfort therefrom. It was as he had desired and suited admirably the theory that he had formed. A further question or two, he considered, would reveal more of the truth.

"So that," he continued, "the statement that the San Jonquilese Embassy telephoned to the President to the effect that they had been informed by *your* Embassy that this suggested appointment was taking place on the night of Sir Beverley Pelham's ball, might conceivably be false?"

Don Enrique inclined his head in corroboration.

"It might undoubtedly be false," he conceded. "The odds, as you say, are certainly on such a condition."

"Yet such a statement has been made," observed Bathurst.

Don Enrique raised his eyebrows. "By whom? By anybody in authority?"

"Yes. I have been informed by no less a person than President Loredana's private secretary, a Mr. Gerald Twining, that he took a telephone message from the San Jonquilese Embassy on the day of the murder, in the terms that I have described."

Don Enrique considered what Bathurst had told him. "It is, of course, in no way my duty to advise you. You know your own business best, and you know also the best means to obtain all that you want to know. That is very cleverly demonstrated, I think, by the fact of your coming here to interview me to-day. But if I were in your place and I accepted this story told by Mr. Twining, I should find the person attached to the San Jonquilese Embassy who was responsible for sending that message. Surely it should not be difficult for you to do that, because your field must be narrowed considerably in consequence. That he had an ulterior motive in doing so is, I should say, perfectly obvious. For I can assure you, Mr. Bathurst, that there isn't the slightest chance of the mistake—shall we call it—having occurred at the Embassy to which I have the honour to be attached. No actual details of this projected interview with President Loredana have yet been arranged."

Anthony acknowledged Don Enrique's expression of opinion with a wave of the hand. "Your advice is eminently sound, sir, and I must thank you for what you have told me. For one very definite fact, at least, emerges therefrom. It is apparent that President Loredana was to be kept at the Hotel Florizel over a certain period of time by deliberate intention. It is equally obvious that President Loredana must not be allowed to arrive at Sir Baverley Pelham's ball until the murder of De Ravenac had been accomplished. For—oh—most vital reasons. Very, very clever indeed," he added softly. "Thank you once again, Don Enrique, for all your courtesy, and good-bye! The next hour or so of my time will be devoted to a consideration of the man connected with San Jonquilo who was responsible for that very significant telephone message."

Don Enrique extended his hand, and Bathurst shook it heartily.

The offices of the San Jonquilese Embassy are situated in Cockspur Street, and Anthony, leaving nothing to chance, repaired there immediately. On this occasion he found the man whom he wanted right away, mentioned Don Enrique's name and explained the position to him. Don Enrique's statement was very soon confirmed and Bathurst able to satisfy himself beyond reasonable doubt that the Spanish Embassy had made no appointment up to the moment with the President of San Jonquilo. Convinced of this, he contented himself with asking one more question. "Was there any chance of a mistake having been made on the day of the murder of De Ravenac and a 'phone message sent in error to Twining at the Hotel Florizel—sent, that is, from the San Jonquilese Embassy?"

The official to whom he put the inquiry saw Mr. Bathurst's point, listened shrewdly, shook his head and promised to investigate the matter for him.

"It would be well," he observed sapiently, "that Mr. Bathurst should have no doubt."

A bell was pressed and at a short interval a clerk reported. The latter heard his senior's request and made a swift exit. Bathurst waited patiently for his appearance, which again was not long delayed.

"No, sir," he announced to his superior. "I have spoken to everybody, sir, who was on the building and who might possibly have been concerned. Not one of them telephoned to Mr. Twining on the day that you mentioned. Everybody is emphatic on the point, sir, so I don't think that there can be any doubt about it." He withdrew at a nod of dismissal from his chief.

"You see, Mr. Bathurst—it is as I thought. Your telephone message did not emanate from here. You can take that as absolutely beyond doubt. I am sorry—but there it is." He shrugged his shoulders in an attempt at commiseration.

"Thank you," said Bathurst. "You have sealed the matter up for me most effectively and for good, too, I should say. You can see, however, that it is only by persistent inquiry and intense perseverance that one is able to reach conclusions of that kind."

CHAPTER XXVI
CONCERNING LINEN

SIR AUSTIN KEMBLE listened attentively to the theory that Bathurst unfolded and more than once looked up at him with a quizzical curiosity. "I will send for Hargreaves as you suggest, certainly," he said at length. "He should be able to accomplish what you want. Anyhow—see him and ask him yourself."

Anthony thanked the Commissioner. "As a machine," proceeded the latter, whilst they waited, "you must admit that the Yard is hard to beat, and all its thousand-and-one cogs move with smooth and swift efficiency. That fact, perhaps, in a way, sometimes spells its undoing. For it becomes essentially material. Matters of psychology, for instance, are pushed into the background of an investigation by the relentless force of mere mechanical routine. Occasionally, however, the latter comes into its own and succeeds where no other activity could. So in this instance. You will probably find that Hargreaves will be able to manage your matter for you quite easily." He paused and listened to the step that sounded outside. "But here he is, I think. Ask him yourself, as I said."

When he heard Bathurst's opening words to the Inspector, Sir Austin Kemble stared amazedly and incredulously. They were as follows: "You have the addresses, Inspector Hargreaves, I don't doubt, of Major Watt and Mr. Martin Pierpoint?"

"I have, Mr. Bathurst, amongst others. Why do you ask?" Hargreaves' face wore a somewhat pained expression, but physical tiredness hardly accounted for it all.

"I am interested in the various laundry establishments that serve the two respective neighbourhoods in which those addresses lie. Could you supply me with a list?"

"That's quite easy, sir. And then, what?"

"Then," returned Bathurst quietly, "I shall probably want you and some of your men to do a little more investigation work."

Hargreaves looked puzzled and sought explanation. "Looking for laundry-marks? I know that it's turned up trumps once or twice, but I'm afraid in this case it's too—"

Sir Austin Kemble interrupted his expression of pessimism. "I know you too well, Bathurst, to imagine for an instant that you are doing work that is unnecessary, but for the life of me I don't see how laundry-marks are going to lead you to the murderer of De Ravenac and Annette Mornay. Take the question of personnel for example. The two men whose names you just mentioned cannot possibly—"

Bathurst intervened with quiet remonstrance. "I think, Sir Austin, that both you and the Inspector here may have misunderstood my intentions. There is no need for my interest in these laundries to stimulate my knowledge of laundry-marks, or even, as you suggest, to lead me to the man we want." He stopped for a second, but continued before Sir Austin or Hargreaves replied. "For the best of reasons—let me tell you. The murderer is known to me now. Please don't think I'm seeking him—or his motives. I am seeking *proof*, and to get that I want the *whole* story of the two crimes. I presume that you would like to hang him?"

If Sir Austin had stared before, he stared now in even greater astonishment, and Hargreaves' face was twisted into a shocked surprise. Bathurst again proceeded.

"Until I obtain that *proof*, my hands, to a certain extent, are tied. I am sure that you, of all people, appreciate that fact, Inspector Hargreaves?"

Hargreaves expressed his opinion vehemently. "For the love of heaven don't make a false step, Mr. Bathurst—you're up against a dangerous man. If he once suspects that you've got him—there's no knowing . . ." He broke off, and a movement of his shoulders served to complete his sentence.

Bathurst's reply was again in the quietest of voices. "I know that what you say is true, Inspector. None better than I. But I must take my risks. That is one of the lessons of life that I learned very early in my career. However, you will be at my side, and I shall probably need your help. This list of laundries, for instance." He smiled expectantly into the Inspector's eyes.

Hargreaves rose, impressed by Bathurst's demeanour. "By three o'clock this afternoon, sir. Will that suit you?"

Bathurst considered for a moment. "Try to kill two birds with one stone, Inspector. Do you mind? To save time now will prove to be of immense value to us later on. Let the list be marked with further information. Let it show the two establishments that, remembering the glory of Solomon, have the privilege of tending the fair whiteness of Wyatt's and Pierpoint's linen. Or shall we go farther and say the white collars of their blameless lives?" He rubbed his hands.

"I'll do my best, sir," said Hargreaves, even more bewildered.

*　　*　　*　　*　　*

Bathurst studied the lists carefully, and Sir Austin Kemble looked over his shoulder. Hargreaves stood at his side intent upon explanation. "The one marked with the asterisk is Wyatt's," he remarked; "the one shown with the dagger against it is Pierpoint's."

"Yet a third dagger in the case?" murmured Anthony critically. "You've done well, Inspector, and you've wasted no time. Another tribute to the machine."

"Thank you, sir," acknowledged the Inspector. "You asked me to put my best foot forward, and I did."

"Tell me this, then—do you think your inquiries are likely to arouse suspicion that will reach either of the two men concerned?"

"Well—it's difficult to stop talk, as you know, sir, probably as well as I do, and there are a number of women on the two staffs—but I made it pretty plain that I wouldn't welcome any."

"H'm—but do you think that's good enough?"

"Frankly, sir, I doubt it. It's those women, you see, Mr. Bathurst."

Bathurst looked at the Commissioner. "Well, sir, you hear what Hargreaves says; we shall have to chance it, I'm afraid. Because now I want something else done."

"Go on," said Sir Austin; "sheep are bigger than lambs, and as I've started I may as well finish! Let's hear what it is you want this time."

Bathurst replied very deliberately. "I want a collar from each of these two laundries. One worn by Major Wyatt and one that has been worn by Mr. Martin Pierpoint. Do you think you can manage that for me, Inspector?"

"If Sir Austin consents," rejoined Hargreaves. "Are they your instructions, sir?"

"Quite so, Hargreaves. Get Mr. Bathurst what he has asked."

"It shall be attended to at once, sir." Hargreaves walked to the door before turning towards Anthony Bathurst with a question. "Any sort of collar, sir?" he inquired.

"I think any collar will suit my purpose, Inspector. But preferably a wing collar—one worn with a dress suit. Mind you tell the laundry people to account to the respective owners for the defections, with a promise that the missing articles are merely temporarily mislaid and will be accounted for next time. After all, a collar missing from the laundry is like income-tax, the rate collector, and wrong 'phone numbers—we all get 'em."

"They don't *lose* my collars at laundries," corrected Sir Austin scathingly, "they bite 'em to pieces. They swing on the stud-holes and get gouging machines to dissect portions so that I can never wear them more than twice. They massacre them with merciless malevolence. They tear great—"

Bathurst put a quiet closure to "Kemble on Laundries and Linen Destruction". "Give me a ring, Hargreaves, when you've 'clicked', and I'll come over." He rose. "By the way, Inspector, it might interest you to know that your fears for my safety are not altogether unfounded. There have been no less than four attempts on my life since last Tuesday. The fourth took place early this afternoon. It was rather clumsy—the vicious lorry trailer that I'm strongly of the opinion was intended for me ran on to the pavement and its victim was a plate-glass window. Shattered glass and shattered hopes! Ah, well—they are teaching me to keep my 'eyes skinned', as our cousins say, and my feet nimble. Don't worry, Sir Austin, I bear a charmed life; and don't forget to ring me, Hargreaves, when you've collared those collars." He sauntered away as Sir Austin shook his head pensively.

CHAPTER XXVII
THE TWO WING COLLARS

MR. BATHURST examined the two dress collars that Inspector Hargreaves held out to him with a strong degree of curiosity.

"There you are, sir," exclaimed the Inspector. "One of Major Wyatt's and one of Pierpoint's. Each of the special kind you wanted. And I've made arrangements on the lines that you suggested about them having been mislaid for the time being. They've both got the laundry marks on, sir," he added with some eagerness. "Wyatt's is E two hundred and nine and Pierpoint's is DAR eighty-six. So they ought to give you what you want."

Bathurst shook his head. "Thank you, Hargreaves; but the laundry marks themselves don't interest me a scrap."

At this admission Sir Austin Kemble looked up and listened keenly for what was to follow. He knew his Bathurst. The latter made his position plain.

"The two features about which I am concerned in regard to these collars are: one, the names of the hosiers who supplied them to the buyers, and two, the sizes."

Hargreaves' face gave play to a puzzled grimace. "But they're different sizes, sir," he began to argue; "they're almost bound to be. Not only do they belong to, but they've actually been worn by, two different men."

Bathurst smiled at the Inspector's eagerness to justify his statement. "When you say that, Hargreaves, in relation to my point regarding 'size', you allude to the size of the wearer's neck. That, however, was not my meaning. My reference was to the size of the collar itself—in height. Or depth if you prefer it."

Sir Austin's look of concentrated attention became almost a glare. "What on earth do you mean, Bathurst? What the blazes has the height of a man's collar to do with running a murderer to earth?"

Anthony smiled easily. "I imagine that in the case under our notice, Sir Austin, it will be found to possess a very significant relation to the crime when I have visited the two hosiers from whom these two collars were purchased. I shall know then whether my theory is a sound one. I purpose making those two visits my next moves. Believe me, I haven't given our friend the Inspector the trouble of obtaining these two collars out of mere curiosity. Till then we must possess our immortal souls in patience. It's an exercise that in these days of immoderate haste is sadly underrated."

The first hosier's establishment which Mr. Bathurst entered happened to be that which ministered to the sartorial requirements of Major Wyatt. He explained the position, produced Sir Austin Kemble's documentary support and very quickly convinced the proprietor of the gravity attaching to the matter, and of the necessity for the two conditions of confidence and secrecy. The hosier was willing to give him certain information for which he asked.

"I have had the privilege of supplying Major Wyatt with what we call 'men's wear' for several years. He is, I may say to you, sir, numbered amongst my very best customers. As to collars—that is to say dress collars—we have had them specially made for him, together with his shirts, for quite a considerable period now."

"That is the condition that I hoped and expected to find when I came," responded Bathurst readily. "What was the size of the collar that you ordinarily supplied to Major Wyatt?"

The man turned and motioned to an inquisitive-looking assistant behind the counter. "Turn up the last order that we supplied to Major Wyatt, Greenaway. I think you'll find it somewhere about the week before Christmas. It included, if I remember aright, shirts, collars, gloves, ties, and socks."

Greenaway handled various books and papers. Within a few minutes he came forward with the required information. "Here you are, sir," said the proprietor of the establishment, turning to the indicated page; "this should give us what you want to know. Let me see, now—here we are—December seventeenth—Major D. O. Wyatt—fifty-six Clanricarde Gardens—shirts, socks, collars, yes—here we are—one dozen 'Altitude' collars, two by sixteen and a half. That's right, sir—I remember now, that's Major Wyatt's usual, two inch by sixteen and a half inch."

Bathurst nodded. The particulars were in accordance with those on the collar that Hargreaves had obtained from the laundry.

"Perhaps you can answer one more question?" he added cordially. "Can you tell me if Major Wyatt by any chance has purchased a collar here within—say—the last month, that was less than two inches in height?"

The man rubbed his chin. "I don't know about that," he said reflectively. "I might be able to—it depends. Greenaway!"

The industrious assistant came forward again, and his employer put the question to him as Bathurst had just presented it. To Bathurst's delight Greenaway's reply came readily and emphatically. "Yes, Mr. Bradley," he exclaimed, "that is so. Now you mention it, I remember that I served Major Wyatt a week or two ago with one dress collar of his ordinary type, but which was only one and a half inches in height—he specially asked that it should be that size."

"I am most distinctly your debtor, Mr. Greenaway," declared Bathurst; "you have told me exactly what I wanted to know."

As he left the establishment he dwelt upon the slow development of his idea. The links were beginning to connect—masks a shade larger and collars a shade smaller!

Pierpoint's hosier had premises in Gracechurch Street—a considerable distance away. Bathurst signalled to a passing taxi, which crawled to the kerb, waited for him, and then put him down at his destination surprisingly quickly. Within this second shop Bathurst wasted no time on finesse. He explained his position and his business there with an economy of words, and the proprietor listened to the explanation with an air of extreme concern.

"We serve Mr. Martin Pierpoint, certainly," he admitted, "although he's only a comparatively recent customer. I remember the name only too well—because we had trouble over the first order that we supplied to him. There was a question, I think, of the colour of a soft collar, and Mr. Pierpoint's a rather 'difficult' customer. Sometimes the shades of these collars are so very fine that it takes an expert to—"

He broke off abruptly and seemed to be considering very carefully a point that had evidently just occurred to him. "By the way, sir," he stated after a moment's thinking, "it isn't so very long ago, as it happens, that Mr. Pierpoint was in this shop. About a couple of weeks, I should say—no more. Came in all of a hurry he did too."

Bathurst seized the opportunity that Fate appeared to be offering to him. "It's just on the cards that that visit of his to which you refer may clear up the very matter that is troubling me. Could you remember if Mr. Pierpoint made a purchase on that occasion?"

"Ten to one he did, coming in so quickly, although I only passed the time of day with him as I walked through the shop. But the assistant who attended to him would be able to settle that question for you without any trouble. I'll call him. Marsden!"

"Yes, sir."

"That gentleman you were serving about a fortnight ago who made that remark to me about only bookmakers being able to afford luxuries—can you recall him?"

"Very well, sir. I've served him two or three times within the past month or so."

"That's the style! What did you serve him with on this last occasion? Can you remember that?" Bathurst waited eagerly for the man's reply. If the answer came as he anticipated it would, his theory was proved sound beyond the vestige of a doubt.

The man Marsden answered slowly, but nevertheless with decision. "Several articles, sir. I think I can recollect most of them if you give me just a moment for thinking. . . . Gloves, a dress bow—butterfly shape, half a dozen collars—an extra collar, smaller than the others—I don't think there was anything else. But if it's of great importance I can refer to my—"

"Don't trouble," interposed Bathurst; "I assure you there is no need. I am confident that the information which you have given me will enable me to solve my little problem most effectively. Very many thanks."

Upon his return to his flat, Emily found him in a much more jubilant mood than usual.

"You know most things, Emily," he sallied. "What do you do, as a rule, before you cook a hare?"

The girl looked puzzled but responded to the unusual question to the best of her natural ability. "Well, sir, it depends. If I were going to roast it, I should first of all skin it, then draw it, and then truss it. After that you should brush the hare all over with nice warm butter—"

Bathurst, listening gravely, interrupted her. "I'll tell you something more important than all that, Emily. Something that you've left out."

"What, sir?"

"Catch it."

An indignant Emily, closing the door of his room, could still hear him chuckling as she descended the stairs, and when she related the incident a few minutes later, her confidant was in full agreement with her that Mr. Bathurst wanted a deal of understanding. "But there," she said, "so do most men, until you're married to one of 'em—and then you don't trouble to try."

Chapter XXVIII
FINAL PLANS

Sir Austin Kemble sat at ease in the big revolving chair that almost filled his room at New Scotland Yard and listened to his henchman, Anthony Bathurst, with the gravest attention. Inspector Hargreaves looked more mystified than anything else, but the experience that he had had of Bathurst already was sufficient to cause him to consider carefully the statements that he heard. On the present occasion Bathurst's account of the incident of the collars was the chief cause of his mystification, and Sir Austin himself harkened to it and wondered at the same time why so trivial a matter should occasion, within Bathurst, such a condition of mental elation. When Bathurst had finished his recital, Sir Austin for a time sat silent, content to tap with his penholder the edge of the desk in front of him. Eventually he broke his silence.

"This is all very well, Bathurst, as far as it goes. The question is, how far *does* it go? Too far or not far enough? That's what's worrying me."

"I think it will be found to go all the way, sir." It was impossible to miss the tone of confidence that Bathurst's words held. He continued with considerably more eagerness than it was his habit to show. "You see, sir, it really amounts to this. If Mahomet can't go to the mountain, well, then, the mountain must come to Mahomet. Don't you remember the way in which we forced out the truth when we investigated the murder of Julius Maitland in the case of the 'Five Red Fingers'? In what other way could we have been certain of a solution?"

Sir Austin hummed and hawed. "I remember on that occasion you prevailed upon me to take a risk," he conceded, "although I'm willing to admit that in the end it turned up trumps. But I certainly don't see how you're going to set to work in the present affair."

Bathurst embarked upon explanation. "I do not think, sir," he said deliberately, "that I've ever been opposed to so cunning a criminal as in the present instance. I know that I'm speaking from my own limited experience, but there it is. I'm convinced that he must be forced into the open. It's absolutely the only way by which we shall get him. Once I've got him in the open, I hope by a certain means which I shall employ to make him betray himself. All the same, I'm very well aware that it's going to be exceedingly difficult to bring off. If my plan succeeds—that is to say if the mountain can be induced to come to Mahomet—we shall land our lean-jawed pike high and dry. If it fails, if the mountain won't budge and stays firm, well—Mahomet won't be any worse off. It will simply mean that I shall have to try something else. Possibly a spot of faith." He laughed. "Now do you see, sir?"

The Commissioner dwelt on Bathurst's words with every appearance of burdensome responsibility. "How do you propose to act? I shall certainly have to know that. Let me hear your ideas in the rough."

Bathurst smiled across at Hargreaves when he heard Sir Austin's invitation, and the Inspector realized that once again this enterprising young man was about to obtain his own way.

"This is my idea, sir, 'in the rough', as you put it." Bathurst's mood changed suddenly. "On my way here to-day I called at the Hotel Florizel and had a word with President Loredana. He was alone as it happened—Da Costa had gone to a tea-fight, love-feast, or something—playing the skeleton perhaps—and I gave our friend Sebastian some inkling of my plans and what I wanted. He's quite game and willing to help us in every way possible. At my suggestion he will place his own room at the Florizel, together with his secretary, at our disposal for the evening of the day after to-morrow. That, I think, will be our best time. We shall hold there, with your consent, sir, something in the nature of a conference. You will naturally be in full charge of the business, with my support, and I want you to invite—in your own name—a number of people who have been connected in one or two particular ways with the two murders."

A frown appeared on the Commissioner's brow. "Before I agree to this I must know who it is that you wish invited. Are you including Sir Beverley and Lady Pelham, for example? I mention those names because I think to act without them would be, to say the least, indiscreet and injudicious. Also, I feel, a trifle discourteous."

"I agree. There are also Sir John Grant, the previous Ambassador, you remember, at Santa Guardina, our two gentlemen who suddenly changed their sizes in collars, and the three other people whose names you have here." Bathurst handed the Commissioner a slip of paper containing the necessary particulars.

Sir Austin read the information and frowned heavily. "Why these three, Bathurst?" he demanded.

"They were in close attendance upon De Ravenac a few moments before he died. They are three young gentlemen who interest me tremendously, and I shouldn't like any one of them to be deprived of the pleasure with which I am sure our conference will provide him. Having helped on the *lever de rideau*, they ought to be given a show when it's rung down."

The Commissioner still showed signs of being unconvinced. He stroked his back hair. "There's another thing. What are the terms of the invitation to be? Tell me that."

"I was coming to that, sir. I want every one of these people to know that the mystery of the two murders has been solved—that the whole plot is known to you with one important exception— and that directly the truth of that exception be forthcoming, an arrest is imminent."

"Rather optimistic, aren't you?" hinted the Commissioner dryly.

"Perhaps I am, sir. All the same, I am confident that the mountain, serene and secure in his altitude of presumed inaccessibility, will come to Mahomet. Or in other words, sir, that the invitation will 'fetch him'. It's surprising how vain and conceited most criminals are, and I'm fairly certain that the one under our present notice is a trifle more conceited than most."

Sir Austin played with the tips of his fingers all the time that Bathurst was speaking. "Very well, Bathurst," he at length conceded, "I'll fall in with what you want. I only hope that it will come off, as you evidently think it will. We'll leave it at this, then—the evening of the day after to-morrow in the President's room at the Hotel Florizel. What time shall we say?"

"Neither too early nor too late. Make it about dinner-time," responded Bathurst. "Suppose we do the thing properly and say seven-fifteen or seven-thirty?"

The Commissioner nodded and turned in his chair. "See to it, Hargreaves, for me, will you? Here are the full particulars that you will require." Sir Austin wrote down the list of names for the Inspector's attention. This accomplished, he fired his last shot. "Supposing one of them refuses? Supposing one of these ca' canny mountains evinces no desire to meet Mr. Mahomet? What are you going to do about it then, Bathurst?" The Commissioner's questions, however, were met with a smile.

"Even then, sir," replied Anthony, "we shall have a name beneath the refusal, shan't we? From which we may be able to draw our own conclusions. That's so, isn't it? At Philippi, then."

* * * * *

Martin Pierpoint crushed his letter of invitation from Sir Austin Kemble between his two hands and tossed it with a smothered curse into the open grate. Swift as ever to realize a situation that spelt difficulty, danger, or failure to him, the inner meaning of the Commissioner's communication had been revealed to him immediately he had received it. The thought that all his carefully laid plans were coming to naught mortified him beyond measure and entered as iron into his soul.

His face was savage with the conflict of thought. Rising from his seat, he advanced to the grate into which he had just thrown the letter, and looked with brooding eyes at the crushed ball of white paper lying there. Was there even now a way out for him? He was sharp enough to realize that the chief factor in the game, as it was to be played now, was the element of time. Had he time to avert the menace which threatened? The appointment at the Hotel Florizel was fixed for the evening of the morrow, which allowed him, roughly, a day and a half. If he were going to act at all, he must act therefore almost at once. To leave it till the morrow itself would be to court inevitable disaster. That fact established in his mind, his brain cast round in a search for ways and means. If only he were more sure of certain details—if only he could dispel that gnawing doubt that had haunted him now for more days than he cared to remember.

One mistake on his part, at this stage of operations, he knew meant the end of everything. Could he by the exercise of the most meticulous care move without making that mistake? Could he outwit this Bathurst whose entry into the case had meant so much to him? After some very careful consideration and deep thinking, he came to the conclusion that he could—by taking the one great risk of the *coup de grâce*—by striking the blow that would end matters for good and all.

Taking three steps of the staircase at a bound, he made for his bedroom and opened the door of the wardrobe. The suit that he took from its hanger was unknown to his friends in London for the simple reason that Pierpoint wore it for special duty only. He walked to the big mirror and surveyed himself therein. A few deft touches here and there would assist materially. The closer he could get without betraying his identity, the more chance he would have of effecting the "master-stroke". Yes! It was all or nothing now, he determined—a fight to a finish. Stepping stealthily from the bedroom, he closed the door gently behind him, and swiftly and noiselessly slipped down the full staircase till he came to the big door that opened on to the street. For a moment he paused there, but, shaking his head quickly, made up his mind. "Now, Mr. Bathurst," he muttered softly to himself, "we shall see within the next few hours who's the better man—you or I. You should have thought twice before you measured swords with 'Le Loup de Poignard'." He closed the door, crossed the road in front of him, and slid silently into a telephone call-box.

Chapter XXIX

VERY NEAR TO THE CURTAIN

ANTHONY BATHURST turned quickly in his armchair and listened intently, every sense keyed to the highest pitch of which it was capable. He could hear nothing now, although he could have sworn that there had been a soft-sounding step outside his door. His hand went to his pocket, but before it reached its full destination the bell of his telephone rang sharply and insistently. Bathurst looked round and then unhooked the receiver, but was careful to face the door as he did so. It was Hargreaves at the other end of the line. Bathurst recognized his voice immediately.

"Yes . . . Bathurst speaking. . . . What is it, Inspector?"

"Sorry to trouble you, Mr. Bathurst, but the Chief's been away all day to-day on that poisoned-chocolates case—down in the country somewhere. But half an hour or so ago he 'phoned through a message to you."

"To me?" Bathurst registered surprise. "Why didn't he 'phone me here? He usually does when he wants me particularly."

"Couldn't say, sir. I expect I should have asked him, but I didn't take it myself; one of the chaps here took it. Anyhow, the main point is that Sir Austin wants you to meet him at Annette Mornay's flat in Maida Vale this evening. He'll be there, he says, as soon on nine o'clock as he can make it."

Bathurst's mouth was twisted and he was a second or two before he replied. "What's the big idea, Hargreaves?"

"Couldn't say that either, sir. Sir Austin gave nothing much away on the 'phone. I gave the flat in Malgan Avenue the once-over directly following the murder. Put a small-tooth comb through it—to no purpose. But according to what I hear to-day from the fellow that Sir Austin got on to, somebody's 'squeaked', and the 'squeak' is—'have another look at what Annette left behind and then come in out of the rain'. I think that about sums it up, sir," concluded Hargreaves.

"I'm sorry, Inspector, but I don't agree with you."

"How do you mean?"

"I think there's a lot more in it than appears on the surface. Still—I'll go. I think this may be the move for which I've been waiting. I'll keep the appointment at a quarter to nine. At any rate, I shan't go into it with my eyes shut, shall I? But I'd like you to cover me, Hargreaves, if you wouldn't mind."

The Inspector whistled.

"That's easy, sir, if you're thinking that way. I'll send a couple of men down with you—or better still, perhaps, come along myself with a couple."

"No—that would spoil matters—either plan would. It's a thousand to one that our man would take cover again. He's a wily bird, you know. I want him in the open, and if I go, as I fancy he is suggesting and arranging I should, I shall get him there. Let me see, now. Eight forty-five—give me—say—till a quarter past nine—that's half an hour. If I haven't communicated with you by nine-fifteen, in some way or other, come to Annette's flat, hell for leather. O.K.?"

"Right you are, Mr. Bathurst. Say nine-fifteen, then. If I haven't tidings of you by then I'll be right along. I shall know then, I expect, if Sir Austin will be there or not. If not—he's bound to come along with me, I should think. Good-bye."

Bathurst hung up the receiver, and, thinking hard, went back to his chair. He knew full well, now that Hargreaves had rung off—and without the smallest shadow of a doubt, too— that the last stages of the struggle were at hand. For some time he had been anticipating them, and now they had drawn very near. He took his revolver from the right-hand pocket of his coat and examined it thoroughly so that everything about it might be in order. The more he looked at the case the more he felt certain that the last conflict would be fought out on lines of "no quarter". The hand that had taken the lives of De Ravenac and Annette Mornay would not scruple to take a third to save its skin. In fact, the more he thought over it, Bathurst felt certain that this was what his enemy intended to do, but at the same time he felt confident that given an equal break he would be able to checkmate him. He looked at his wrist-watch. The time showed as half past six—he wasn't due at Annette Mornay's flat for over two hours. Rising and unhooking the telephone receiver again, he was about to ask for a number when an idea came to him, causing him to hesitate. Explaining himself to the operator by means of an apology, he replaced the receiver and returned once again to his seat in the armchair. If the murderer of De Ravenac and his mistress were the person he was convinced it was, Bathurst felt that that item of knowledge on his own part was certain to give him an initial advantage, for psychological appreciation of the complexity of the human mind means much to the criminal investigator. If he had not been able to dissociate successfully the two main strands of the crime he would still have been groping in the dark, which fact alone would have then invested his antagonist with an even greater power than Bathurst believed him to possess.

He determined to go along to Malgan Avenue in his own car, and it was on the stroke of eight-thirty that he unlocked the door of the garage that housed the primrose-wheeled Crossley and prepared for his short journey to the outskirts of Maida Vale. To have the Crossley handy, he decided, might in certain circumstances prove a valuable asset, and the sight of it might also tell the time of day to Hargreaves, hot-foot and desperate, if the luck went against him, and the worst came to the worst.

As the powerful car slid smoothly on to the crown of the road and turned into the main way, a dark, furtive figure crept from a coign of vantage near and jumped with a hurriedly uttered instruction into a waiting taxi. The two vehicles sped towards the flat in Malgan Avenue . . . and each carried a passenger swayed by a dominating purpose. As the powerful Crossley purred round a corner into Malgan Avenue itself, its pursuer slowed down and stopped at the turn, and the man who had requisitioned it alighted. From a convenient position near a pillar-box he watched Bathurst pull up the Crossley, descend from the driving-seat, and walk across the pavement to the block of flats that confronted him.

He saw Bathurst look up as though in the act of scanning the windows and then, after a short interval, enter. No sooner had Bathurst effected entrance than the silent watcher turned quickly and ran silently but with incredible swiftness to the back of the block of flats. When he came to the spot that he wanted he measured the wall before him with his eyes and leapt with rapid agility towards the top of it. A few quick movements and he had gained the summit of the wall. From here he looked anxiously in the direction of the long line of living-rooms.

In the particular flat under his notice, every room was in darkness and over it all there seemed to hang an air of dark and brooding horror. Since Annette had left it, to walk to her death, only Hargreaves and his men had come to it, to turn it over and to question Murrell the porter . . . until to-night. But to-night would see the last act of this sinister business and Annette would be avenged . . . perhaps, that is . . . unless, of course, things went wrong and this interloper Bathurst held the ace . . . little Annette whom he had only seen once since that night in Paris when . . . A light stabbed through the patch of darkness in the room that he watched and a tall figure shadowed its silhouette across the window. The watcher on the wall dropped quietly over the side into the space below and crept stealthily towards the light.

CHAPTER XXX
THE "WOLF" AND THE DOOR

As BATHURST left the Crossley by the kerb and walked to the entrance to the flats, Murrell, the porter on duty, saw him as he approached and came forward to meet him. To Bathurst's surprise it seemed almost as though the man whom he saw advancing was expecting him. "Sir Austin Kemble?" queried the porter.

Bathurst mastered his surprise and shook his head.

"Not quite," he answered, with one of his irresistible smiles; "my name's Bathurst. Anthony Bathurst, to give it to you in full. There's my card if you care to have a look at it."

Murrell took the card and examined it a little doubtfully. "I was expecting Sir Austin Kemble himself, sir. He 'phoned through about five o'clock this afternoon that he would be coming along here this evening. He never mentioned anything about anybody else. I don't quite know where I stand, you see. I have to watch my step. Inspector Hargreaves left me certain instructions—very strict they were—and I've been careful ever since I got them not to make a mistake about them. You see, in your case, sir—"

"When did you last see the Inspector?" questioned Bathurst.

"Oh—some days ago, now, sir."

"Well, you'll find it all right; you can see from my card who I am and whom I represent. Give an eye to my car, will you? It's just possible that Hargreaves may be along in about half an hour's time. He'll give me a character, and vouch for my good intentions."

"Well, sir, if you say it's all right, I suppose it is all right. Anyhow, you look honest, so I'll trust you. What is it you want to see? Miss Mornay's rooms?"

"You've hit it in one. Take me up to them, will you?"

"They're all locked up, sir, as I expect you know. Just a moment and I'll get hold of the keys."

Without waiting for the lift, Bathurst followed Murrell up the stairs until the latter stopped before the apartments that had been the ill-fated Annette Mornay's. The porter found the right key and unlocked the door of the living-room. Hargreaves' many and varied attentions were visible to the trained eye, but beyond the effect of them the room was very much as Annette had left it when she had recognized the red sign of danger and resolved on her policy of flight. Bathurst felt on the wall, found the switch, and flooded the room with light.

"Leave me up here till Inspector Hargreaves comes along. If I want you again, I'll ring for you. I'm just going to have a look round." He walked to the windows that looked out on to the rear of the block of buildings.

"Right-o, sir. I'll leave you the keys of the room. I shall be knocking about downstairs somewhere, till half past eleven— that's the time the night-porter comes on duty." Murrell closed the door and retired.

No sooner had he done so than Bathurst proceeded to make a rapid inspection of the premises. The room in which he found himself communicated with a kitchenette on one side and a fair-sized bedroom on the other. Satisfying himself that each was unoccupied, he locked the door of each room, and went to the main entrance door to listen. His watch told him that it was now thirteen minutes to nine—his self-instituted host was already two minutes late. As he listened he caught the sound of a step below—a step that seemingly shuffled over the ground rather than hit it. He caught his breath, and turning instantly, he snapped out the light, took up the strategical position by the wall which would place him behind the door when it opened, and let his fingers close over the butt of his revolver where it lay in his right-hand pocket.

He heard the shuffling step come on slowly but surely . . . ascending the stairs one by one. It was by far the slowest ascent to which Anthony Bathurst had ever listened. The tension of the moment brought reminiscence back to him on swift wings. The eerie wait in the dark grounds at Considine Manor when they took the "Spider" in that little problem of the murder in the billiards-room . . . the long-drawn-out vigil on the stairs outside the shop-parlour of Stefanopoulos, the crook at Amsterdam, when the "Peacock's Eye" came home to roost . . . the midnight assignation in the pavilion near the tennis courts at Swallowcliffe Hall when Major Whittaker stood at bay against the devilries of the Silver Troika . . . the stealthy crawl down the garden to the spot outside the library at Assynton Lodge in Berkshire when the mystery of the twenty-two black pearls of Lorraine was . . .

The man who had ascended the stairs stopped outside the door of Annette Mornay's living-room and tried the handle softly. Bathurst could hear him breathing as it yielded and the door opened to admit him. He stood on the threshold, silent . . . listening, menacing. Then he turned with a lithe movement and in a voice that was strangely familiar, yet in more than one way just as unfamiliar, exclaimed to the man who awaited him, "I beg of you, my dear Bathurst, this is positively distressing to me. Please take up a more comfortable position to receive me. For I can see now that you must have perceived to some extent, at least, the object of my invitation." He laughed softly and went on. "I would suggest, O excellent Bathurst, a little light, and subsequently, that you come away from the discomfort of the wall. The idea of so astute a person as yourself having gone to the wall, I confess, intrigues me."

Bathurst pressed down the switch with the fingers of his left hand and darted into the middle of the room. Prepared as he was to encounter the murderer of De Ravenac and Annette Mornay, he nevertheless gave way to a certain measure of amazement when he saw the figure that confronted him. The man was attired in the height of evening dress. His opera hat was tilted on his head in the grand manner, a monocle was in his left eye, he wore a grey pointed beard and over his right arm was folded a magnificent black opera cloak. It was the figure of Miguel Da Costa, Chancellor to the Republic of San Jonquilo. The muscles of Bathurst's right arm and hand clenched in his pocket.

"Don't move," he murmured pleasantly, "for if you do I'm afraid that I can't hold myself responsible for the consequences. I have you covered, you see, from the right-hand pocket of my coat."

"Singular that you should say that," came the reply with equal nonchalance, "for I have you covered from beneath my cloak. We must put it down to the long fingers of coincidence."

"I was afraid you had," returned Bathurst, "when I saw your cloak move as I put the light on after you entered. The movement was very slight, it is true, but just enough to assist me towards a better understanding of your intentions."

"Really—I must be more careful next time. But I am not as young as I was, and there were more stairs than I am accustomed to travel. I could scarcely call attention to myself by using the lift. Shall we—er—for the present—call it a stalemate?"

"In what way?" demanded Bathurst. "Like you, and like everybody, I too have a birthday every year."

"Let me put it like this. If you would care to dispense with that lethal weapon that you are clutching so affectionately and toss it on the table there, I should be positively delighted to follow so admirably pacific an example."

Bathurst hesitated for one second before he accepted the suggestion. The decision to which he ultimately came, at the end of that second, was destined to prove his undoing. "I'll take you at your word," he agreed. He tossed his revolver on to the table and the man opposite to him followed suit.

"Shall we now discuss our little differences?"

Bathurst shook his head, and as he did so, contrived to glance at his wrist-watch. It still wanted a minute to nine, which meant that he must hold his opponent in play for at least another sixteen minutes before help in the shape of Hargreaves could come to him.

It was typical of the mentality of his opponent that this latter realized instinctively the direction of the thought that was passing through his mind. The man smiled, but the smile held a quality of implacable hatred from which Bathurst recoiled. He had made a mistake and at that moment he knew it. He had been well aware of the risk when he came, and had been quite ready to take it in order that he might draw the man from his cover and gets to grips with him. But he knew now that he should never have surrendered his revolver. There can be no rules when the warfare lies close to the jungle. To have been bluffed as easily as he had been, when he could have . . .

"I'll seat myself, if you don't mind, my dear Bathurst—after all, why shouldn't one be comfortable? At the risk of being monotonous, I will repeat that I'm not so young as I once was. Oh, no, have no fear, not near the table—believe me, those revolvers are perfectly safe from me. On the contrary, I will take this chair here by the window. Would it be troubling you too much if I asked you to close the door? Much as I appreciate this country and all it stands for, I have always abominated its climate in general and a damned draught in particular."

"Really? Touching the question of your years, I should have said, had I been asked, that your age approximated my own." As he spoke, Bathurst backed towards the door, keeping a watchful eye on the speaker all the time. He pushed the door to behind him, and simultaneously a clock somewhere away in the distance could be heard striking nine. The sounds struck on the night air as clearly as the notes of a bell.

"Nine o'clock," exclaimed the man on the chair by the window, ignoring the pointed nature of Bathurst's last remark. "How time flies! Well—we have the best part of the evening in front of us, and when I tell you that the adjoining flat is empty, it will enable you, I'm sure, to appreciate the inherent possibilities of the situation even better."

Bathurst stood still, with his back against the door, every nerve tingling, and the knowledge that his life depended upon a thread, the alertness of his intelligence, and that came home to him at that pulsing moment with overwhelming force. The man whom he watched carelessly shifted the black cloak from his right arm to his left, and as he did so something came to life within Bathurst's brain and told him that the vital moment of acute peril had come for him. As the man moved to shift his cloak, his right arm and hand were bent swiftly back towards his shoulder, and a knife shimmered through the air straight for Anthony Bathurst's heart. "Le Loup de Poignard" had spoken!

Chapter XXXI
INCH BY INCH

BUT THE exquisite understanding of that rare and precious second sent Bathurst swerving towards his own right, and the knife buried itself in the muscles of his swaying left shoulder and pinned him, almost helpless, to the door. He had but one chance now—one chance in a million—and he knew it. As the "Wolf" had bluffed him, so he, at his last gasp almost, must try to bluff the "Wolf". If he could but deceive this adversary into thinking that the knife had gone home, and that yet one more victim was added to the list, there might perhaps be time for Hargreaves to come to save him. The pain in his shoulder was intense, but he retained sufficient consciousness for his head to loll unsteadily on his shoulder, and for his body to sag, droopingly and life-lessly. Even as he did so, Bathurst, with eyes half closed, heard and felt the "Wolf" approach him closely, and then heard his own doom pronounced. His enemy commenced to speak.

"I repeat myself yet again. Despite your opinion to the contrary, I know of a certainty now that my youth has gone. My aim is not as true as it was. Nevertheless, dear friend, there will be no more birthdays for you. What a blessing I brought my revolver with me as well. It may interest you, my dear Bathurst, in your self-imposed capacity as a student of crime, and give a certain colour to your last moments on earth, to know that you will be the first person I have ever sent to the flames of Hell by means of a revolver. I have always cherished a remarkable affection for the knife—which until to-night never failed me."

Bathurst resisted the overpowering impulse to pull the knife from his shoulder, for he could now see that his enemy held one of the revolvers in his left hand—in fact, it was almost at Bathurst's heart. But he knew beyond the tiniest particle of a doubt that the slightest movement on his part would be fatal to him . . . that the "Wolf" would fire. . . . If he remained absolutely still and lifeless he had yet a fractional part of his one chance left to him . . . the chance that the "Wolf" would despise him now and rule him out as even a possible antagonist. That the "Wolf" would throw caution to the winds in the fullness of his contempt . . . that he would come one step . . . no . . . two steps nearer . . . that would be the distance. . . . Only two little steps! Two steps would do it. Could he entice him that distance nearer? Bathurst threw out his last effort. He sighed, his head rolled forward helplessly, and his whole body seemed to shrivel almost as it simulated utter and complete collapse.

His enemy moved, and curled his finger lovingly round the trigger of the revolver. He came just a trifle nearer. Like all artists, he took his time to effect his master-stroke. Haste in such conditions would have been both inartistic and indecent. "I regret the necessity, my dear Bathurst, but I fear that I must bid you adieu. Open your eyes for the last time and watch for the bullet that is going to—"

Bathurst struck! His right hand, with its muscles of steel, caught the "Wolf's" flickering wrist and bent it upwards as by a lightning-stroke. The revolver shot rang out clear and loud and the smoke curled round and about the room; but the bullet had found its billet in the plaster of the ceiling high above the two men's heads.

"Curse you!" snarled the "Wolf". "But there are five more chambers, and one will be—"

But he had breath for no more spoken effort. With his other hand he clawed and tore wickedly at the vice-like grip that held him. Realizing this to be ineffective, he strove to find Bathurst's throat, but his arm was too short and that other rigid, steel-like arm between him and his objective proved an impassable barrier. Every movement now gave Bathurst a spasm of exquisite pain, and the wound in his shoulder bled profusely and began to stain the white panelling of the door. The sweat stood out in glistening beads on the "Wolf's" forehead as the relentless pressure on his wrist and arm increased. His veins swelled large and blue and his dark, murderous eyes never left Bathurst's face. But the eyes into which *he* looked were mocking and merciless, and the "Wolf" read the message that burned therein with unerring accuracy.

With a sudden swooping movement he forced Bathurst's hand down, and the revolver wavered for a millionth part of a sickening second in front of Anthony's throat. But gradually Anthony forced it away again . . . inch by inch . . . and inch by inch the "Wolf's" arm gave way . . . and . . . bent . . . and curved, and the hand that had threatened Anthony now pointed towards the wall on its own left and on Anthony's right. It was extended there for but a second. For now the "Wolf's" power of resistance was weakening . . . growing less and less . . . and gradually . . . bit by bit . . . his wrist was forced back . . . and his arm bent back . . . like the hand of a clock moving the wrong way . . . very slowly . . . but very surely . . . until the barrel of the revolver was pointing at his own temple . . . backwards. His tongue was dry with fear . . . his strength had gone, this enemy at whom he had mocked had mastered him most marvellously. . . . He thought of Annette . . . God. . . . His hand, fingers, and arm were useless now . . . he was unable to feel even the trigger . . . his whole hand was numbed with the merciless and paralysing strength that Bathurst had exerted.

As the "Wolf" thought these things, and his brain pageanted them one by one before him, with a movement of amazing swiftness Anthony shifted his grasp from wrist to hand . . . from hand to fingers, from fingers . . . to that one once-wicked finger that was now almost dead of its venom—but yet still curled round the trigger. The "Wolf" knew all that that swift movement meant. Hatred and craven fear burnt in his eyes. Bathurst's despotic and triumphant finger crooked and did its work. . . . There was a flash and a second shot rang out through the room and the murderer of many sank in a huddled heap on the floor at Anthony Bathurst's feet. Anthony pulled the knife from the door and his own shoulder . . . winced at the pain, swayed giddily, and fell beside him.

* * * * *

Martin Pierpoint beat Hargreaves to the room by a short head only—entering by the window—whereas the Inspector with his two men used the more usual entrance of the door.

Bathurst came back to consciousness as Hargreaves lifted him and propped him in a chair.

"There's your murderer, Hargreaves," he said weakly, pointing to the floor. "It was touch and go—but I bested him at the end. I'm afraid he's plugged a hole in my shoulder, though."

"Never mind, sir. We'll soon see to that for you. A doctor will be up here in a brace of shakes." He walked across to the body. "Da Costa!" he exclaimed. "Da Costa, of all people! Great Scott— and I ruled him out from the very beginning! Well—well—you never know."

"I think not," murmured Bathurst from his chair. "A splendid impersonation of Da Costa, I grant you, but when you remove the wig, beard, and monocle you'll find that it's Sebastian Loredana."

"That's as right as you'll ever be," contributed Pierpoint somewhat sorrowfully—"but when I first ran across him he was known as 'Le Loup de Poignard'."

"And how the devil do you know that, may I ask?" demanded Hargreaves in astonishment.

"Only too well," replied Martin Pierpoint. "It may interest you to know that this is the second time that he's slipped through my fingers, and each time at the very last moment. You see—I happen to be Sergeant Perpignan, late of the Sûreté Générale in Paris."

Chapter XXXII
MR. BATHURST UNFOLDS THE CONSPIRACY

ANTHONY BATHURST lay at full length on the big Chesterfield—his head supported by two cushions. Sir Austin Kemble, excessively solicitous, sat at his side. Major Wyatt and Sergeant Perpignan faced him. There was no need now for the proposed conference at the Hotel Florizel, which, had it taken place, would have been a week old at this date. Bathurst gestured towards the whisky and the cigars.

"I have told you before, sir," he said, addressing the Commissioner, "that the main difficulty in many of the cases that fall into an investigator's lap is for him to be able to separate successfully 'faked' clues from those that are authentic. In the case that we have just concluded, the starting point was even more difficult than that, because—putting it absolutely literally, we had two sets of 'true' clues. Major Wyatt and Sergeant Perpignan will bear me out in that statement a little later on. They will see what I mean when they listen to my suggestions as to how the murder was intended to have been carried out in the original instance."

"Interrupting you a moment, Bathurst," intervened Wyatt—"not murder, if you please. The justice that was to have been executed upon De Ravenac was many degrees removed from 'murder' as I understand it."

"We will not quarrel over that. You have your point of view, doubtless, just as I have mine."

Sir Austin frowned heavily. "Quite so—Bathurst. Quite so. Society can only tolerate one law—and I am not here to-day to discuss metaphysics."

"With your permission, then, sir," continued Anthony, "I will first sketch the rough plan of the 'intended' killing, as I named it just now. What was behind it all in the first instance, Major Wyatt—blackmail?"

"It was," contended Wyatt shortly and sturdily. "De Ravenac had certain rather delicate letters—Lady Pelham has told me since that she believes a maid had stolen them from her and he had bought them off the girl. Very likely she was one of his agents, for the blackmail game was one of his most lucrative modes of living."

"Letters written by Lady Pelham, I presume?"

Wyatt was silent.

"Your silence is sufficient answer. I will not dig any deeper into what, after all, is a personal matter."

Wyatt bowed his acceptance of the position.

"I will resume. You and your friends 'arranged' the murder that was to have been, and I think it was on the fines that I will indicate. Correct me where I stray, will you?" Wyatt looked a little amused, but nodded his agreement. "The farther I went into the case, the more I came up against what I will call 'circumstances of conspiracy'. I will detail them to you as they occurred to me. There were (*a*) the incident of De Ravenac being stopped on the stairs by the Blaker-Twining combination; (*b*) the descent of Lady Pelham with a certain 'footman' who was carrying cushions to the San Jonquilo refreshment-room; (*c*) the sending away of the waiter, Powell, from that room on a trivial errand; (*d*) the delay in that same Powell finding Sir Beverley; and (*e*) the almost universal evidence that no possible murderer was seen by *anybody who mattered, at the time that mattered, near the place that mattered*. But although there was this definite evidence of a conspiracy, which seemed on the face of it to involve Lady Pelham herself and her six musketeers— nevertheless each one of them had a perfectly watertight alibi for the time when the murder had been committed. The two Blakers and the two Twinings were upstairs, Lady Pelham and the 'Headsman' were in the general refreshment-room, and the helpful and sympathetic 'footman' who conveyed the cushions was on the other side of the panelled doors. His statement to this effect was supported by at least a dozen people who saw him when the first rush was made to the scene of the crime. You will observe, Sir Austin, that even in its embryonic stage it presented a pretty little problem."

Sir Austin nodded twice and rose to replenish his glass. Wyatt and Perpignan made no comment—yet. Bathurst smiled across at them and proceeded.

"I began to cast round to see if I could find one strand labelled 'possible' protruding from this skein of seeming impossibilities. After hours, and even days, of unproductive thinking, I turned my attention very strongly to the murdered man's death-scream. It had interested me from the first. After a time it began to fascinate me. Why did the murderer put the revolver in the claret cup, a revolver fitted with a silencer, mind you, to use the knife and risk the cry? Also, Doctor Sugden gave it as his carefully considered opinion, when he examined the body, that death was to all intents and purposes instantaneous. Yet the man cried out! Mark that! Know anything about Good Friday, Major Wyatt?"

Wyatt's face expressed amazement at the sudden deviation. Failing to understand, he answered cynically: "Oh, yes! I believe that salt fish and a certain appalling type of bun are—"

Bathurst waved him off protestingly. "I'm afraid that you misunderstand me. My point was simply this. Good Friday is the most sacred day of the Christian calendar, and for many centuries it has been believed and taught that the Crucifixion which it commemorates took place on a Friday—as we call the sixth day of our week. But most authorities that count agree that Our Lord was crucified in the Year A.D. thirty, to employ the terms of our modern notation. The period was that of the Passover, which is always held on the fifteenth day of the month of Nisan, which in that year, governed of course by the New Moon of March, commenced on the twenty-third of March. The fifteenth day of Nisan therefore fell on the sixth of April—a Thursday as it happens. Now, as the Crucifixion, we are told, happened on the 'eve of the Passover', this brings us to Wednesday, April the fifth. Or, in other words, Good 'Friday' was a 'Wednesday', and the term, as we have come to use it, a complete misnomer in the sense that our Friday of commemoration never was a Friday. So, gentlemen, the death-cry of Monsieur André de Ravenac never was a death-cry. The cry that everybody heard was the cry of our friend the 'footman'—*after the murder*, and when he gave vent to it, as had been previously arranged, Martin Pierpoint, or Sergeant Perpignan, as I will call him, was almost as much in the dark as anybody. But greatly to his own surprise. For something had happened—"

"Major Wyatt, you mean, Bathurst," corrected Sir Austin. "Wyatt was the man who cried out. You forget that Perpignan was the 'Headsman'."

The correction left Bathurst unperturbed. "I think not, sir, as you will hear when I outline the general scheme."

Wyatt and Perpignan exchanged significant glances, and then the latter's dark eyes flickered back to the quiet man on the settee. He had already started again.

"The cry therefore did *not* clock the time as everybody imagined that it did—so exeunt the alibis, one and all. Having arrived as far as this crucial point, I began to move. To progress in the following fashion! I had been able to observe one or two most significant pieces of evidence which, in the added light of my now growing theory, began to assume much greater proportions of importance. Firstly, there was the extraordinary fact that you, Sergeant Perpignan, although claiming to have been in the general refreshment-room when the monocled man was there, couldn't recall even having seen him there. Despite the fact that I had unimpeachable evidence that you and he had met there almost face to face. That struck me as being distinctly remarkable, but when Wyatt, the man who was supposed to have been in the corridor during that time, admitted having seen him, I came to the conclusion that that fact taken into conjunction with the other was even more remarkable still. 'Where had Wyatt seen him?' I asked myself, and almost immediately I found myself contemplating something odd. Something that appeared, on the face of it, as strangely illogical."

Sir Austin nodded. "I think I begin to see."

"So did I, sir. The light was gradually breaking through. I found myself now giving great attention to the various costume details of both the 'Headsman' and the 'footman'. Each had black shoes, black hose, and black knee-breeches! Exactly! The only difference that I could remember was in the footman's coat and the 'Headsman's' black doublet and skull-cap—not forgetting his orange axe." Mr. Bathurst smiled whimsically. "Their masks were large enough to hide their faces—each was of a height—the hair in each case was much the same colour and parted in the same way—and one could become the other by the mere exchange of coat for doublet and skull-cap—if in each case, mark you, the white collar required for the role of footman was low enough to be completely hidden by the black doublet buttoned high up to the neck." He turned his head towards the two men whom he arraigned so relentlessly. "Am I right, gentlemen?"

Wyatt laughed, but the laugh was mirthless. "You are. But you amaze me all the same."

"Inquiries at certain collar-supplying establishments in the city of London amply confirmed this opinion. Both you, Major Wyatt, and you, Sergeant Perpignan, had worn collars on the night of the murder which were an unusual size for you and small enough to fulfil that highly important purpose for which they were required." Bathurst paused again and took a sip of water from his glass. "Now this was the manner of the murder to be. Lady Pelham, I take it, acting under instructions from you, fixed a time and place with De Ravenac for the purchase of her letters. You know the time, and the venue was the special room that was being reserved for Loredana. Wyatt, as footman, accompanied her downstairs. They were followed by our friend here, Perpignan, costumed as the 'Headsman'. The four others were to let De Ravenac through at the appointed time—*but nobody else*! Hence the 'holding up' business at the head of the staircase.

"Arrived downstairs, Lady Pelham gets rid of Powell, on an errand that she knows will take him some little time. Wyatt and Pierpoint change costumes—coats and hat that is—in the special room, which is now empty. This operation was performed in a few seconds. Wyatt, *now the 'Headsman'*, establishes his unshakable alibi by entering the general refreshment-room and by making himself obvious to a number of people. De Ravenac was to enter the other room, beyond the panelled doors, where Pierpoint was to shoot him—silently—and, this accomplished, obtain Lady Pelham's letters. Pierpoint was then to come through the doors, give the 'death-cry', be seen by Wyatt, and—more—*be vouched for by him and others as being nowhere near the scene of the murder* which Pierpoint, most intimate to the cry, would indicate and impose on the minds of the crowd by pointing dramatically to the doors and beyond. The second alibi would thus be established. Wyatt, being ready, and equipped with anticipation begotten of knowledge, was at the general-room door first. He and Pierpoint led the way through the two doors and had passed between them, well in advance of all the others.

"Now, Sir John Grant, when I taxed him, remembered that when *he* reached the doors at the head of the crowd—they *stuck*. Of course they did!" Bathurst rubbed his hands in the pleasure that his elucidation of this point had given him. "Shall I tell you why they stuck—Sir Austin? Because Wyatt's foot and body made them. While Wyatt, after tossing the clothes to Pierpoint, held the doors, which only opened by a push *towards* him, Pierpoint, close to the body, effected in a second or so the change of jacket again, and, lo and behold, they were back in their original parts."

"But why?" demanded the Commissioner explosively. "For the life of me I can't see why the change was necessary. Why run the risk and take the trouble. Each had a cast-iron alibi—or so it seems to me."

Bathurst smiled at the collaborators. "For a long time that puzzled and worried me too, sir. But at last I 'arrived'. We now come to the matter of the 'Orange Axe', which had its place in the scheme of arrangements in the same way as every other detail had. It had two parts to play. It had to establish suspicion and complication *because Lady Pelham must never know the name of De Ravenac's murderer*."

Chapter XXXIII
THE ORANGE AXE AGAIN

"The point is this, you see, Sir Austin. It was necessary that very strong suspicion should be directed against our friend the 'Headsman', which suspicion would fly harmlessly from its object by reason of the 'Headsman's' irrefutable alibi. Think of the torn piece of orange-and-black silk that was found clutched in the dead man's hand. Think of the 'Headsman' being discovered kneeling by the body. The man that was bound to be suspected was the man whom it would be impossible *for anybody to prove guilty*. The man who wore the colours of San Jonquilo! The colours in De Ravenac's hand! The coincidence would be far too strong all round to be missed. Also, they must get back to their original parts in time for the enquiry that they knew must follow, and when that came to be able to say, semi-truthfully, 'I was elsewhere when the man was killed.' The chief instigator of the plot, however, who was, I think, Major Wyatt, reckoned without two contingencies."

"Three—if I include you," muttered Wyatt.

Anthony shook his head disclaimingly at the indirect compliment. "The contingencies to which I refer were these. Pierpoint, his friend and ally, was, unbeknown to him, something more than either, and joined the cast in the hope of bringing to fruition an overwhelming desire of some years' standing."

"I'll tell you," put in Perpignan, "if Mr. Bathurst here will allow me. I've been wanting to, for some time, and this appears to be a convenient moment. My failure to arrest 'Le Loup de Poignard' in Paris six years ago placed me under a nasty cloud and eventually resulted in my dismissal from the Sûreté. Over there, we never knew who he actually was, but the fact that André de Ravenac was one of his chief lieutenants was pretty well established. De Ravenac's real name was Pierre Lamotte, and I took the affair so much to heart that I swore that I wouldn't rest until I had snared the 'Wolf' if it took me twenty years of my life to do it. My one chance was De Ravenac, and I had been on his heels for years hoping against hope that he would ultimately lead me to the 'Wolf' himself.

"When he came to London I followed him, met Major Wyatt here, and cultivated his friendship. Judge of my astonishment when I was roped into his conspiracy, as you have described it. But I determined to go through with it, up to a point, in the hope that I might be able to force some of the truth at least from De Ravenac and enough perhaps to put me on to the track of that greater criminal whom I so badly wanted.

"On the night of Sir Beverley Pelham's masked ball I waited for De Ravenac in the empty room that had been reserved for Loredana. Directly he entered he would have felt the point of my revolver in his ribs. But I waited and waited . . . he didn't come . . . and when I went into the corridor I found him lying there dead, with that knife through his heart. For a moment I was undecided . . . amazed . . . spellbound . . . sickened almost with a fear that was a shuddering dread of the unknown. Then I came to my senses and made up my mind that the best thing I could do was to play the part that had been assigned to me by the conspiracy. But I knew with an unassailable conviction from the manner of De Ravenac's death that the 'Wolf' was at hand once again . . . and very near to me at that . . . and my heart leapt in the expectation that my dream might at last come true. My problem was—who was he? . . . It still remained . . . just as it had been all those years before.

"When Mr. Bathurst showed his hand at the end and Sir Austin here invited us to the unmasking of the murderer, I knew that my last chance of getting my man off my own bat was to forestall Bathurst . . . to get him to pull the chestnut from the fire for me . . . and then slip in and pouch the chestnut from between his fingers. I tried and failed, as you know. But Mr. Bathurst may take this satisfaction to his comfort. Had he failed in that last desperate fight with the master-criminal, his murderer would never have got away scot-free. I, Marcel Perpignan, would have seen to that. I watched the last stages of the struggle from a kneeling position on the window-sill outside the flat and dared not interfere for fear of bringing disaster to the wrong man. Now

I can go back to Paris—still a failure, with my time and money wasted." Perpignan spoke with bitterness and shrugged his shoulders disconsolately.

"Hardly wasted," remarked Bathurst sympathetically. "You have, for instance, the knowledge that the 'Wolf' will kill no more. In his way the man was a genius, and for quite a long time deceived me completely. When you realize that he fled from Paris six years ago to South America and in that time became President of San Jonquilo you are able to perceive some of the man's strength of personality and dynamic force. I am told that the stroke of arms that put him at the head of the conquering political party in San Jonquilo was as daringly audacious as it was brilliantly intelligent. But De Ravenac recognized him when he landed in England and was mad enough to let Loredana know—that's the only name by which I know him.

"De Ravenac probably commenced blackmail in that direction too, which move sealed his fate completely and absolutely. *For Loredana already hated him beyond measure.* For De Ravenac had taken Annette Mornay and her affections from the 'Wolf' six years previously. Loredana laid his plans, which, like the others, were based on a solid foundation of an absolutely perfect alibi. He 'fixed' a diplomatic interview which would keep him from the ball at Lady Pelham's until a late hour of the evening, made up as Da Costa, walked over from the Hotel Florizel, which is a comparatively short distance away, followed his man downstairs when he saw him leave the ballroom to meet Lady Pelham, and killed him in his own sweet way. That accomplished, he strolled home, for you, Sir Austin, to call for him as he had arranged. That was very clever, for he counted on your evidence sealing his alibi."

"One moment, Bathurst." Sir Austin interposed a question. "Why did he impersonate Da Costa, of all people? I don't quite understand his idea in that."

"For two reasons, I think, sir. One—he knew Da Costa intimately and also every trick of his manner and appearance, and two—the vitally important one that he could use Da Costa's genuine ticket of invitation while Da Costa was in his room dressing. He must have his entrance and exit to Sir Beverley's absolutely unquestioned."

"How did he kill De Ravenac?" queried Wyatt. "I'd like to know that, for he certainly wasted no time over it."

"It is impossible for me to supply full details of every tiling—you must realize that. I can only suggest certain likely chains of events. I should say that he carefully watched De Ravenac leave the ballroom when Lady Pelham sent her message, followed him downstairs and kept behind him until the latter passed through the panelled doors. At that moment Perpignan was in the special-room and Wyatt in the general. Then, slipping through the connecting-doors himself, he probably made a certain sound or called a name that attracted the man's attention. De Ravenac turned . . . and died. By the time the body was discovered the murderer was on his way back to his hotel."

"What eventually put you on to Loredana?" asked Perpignan; "it was a long time before I even suspected him."

Bathurst, pale under the strain of his recital, shifted himself a little higher on his couch. "I'm afraid I take little honours there, as I was hopelessly dense for quite as long as you say you were. But I think, in the first place, two incidents hammered the fact into my brain that something unexpected had transpired and that the original plan of the murder had in some way miscarried. The first was our discovery, Sir Austin, of the revolver at the bottom of the claret cup. The second, which came appreciably later, was the murder of the girl Annette Mornay. It was manifestly evident to me that she was killed because she possessed *knowledge* that was highly dangerous to the *murderer*. With whom therefore could I link her up? That was my problem, and I began to reason it out on these lines:

"The man who, in all probability, had upset the Wyatt conspiracy was the spurious Da Costa. There was evidence that the 'Headsman' had shown surprise at seeing him in the general refreshment-room. Who was he? Sir John Grant had told me on the night of the murder that he had worn braided trousers. Sir Beverley Pelham, Loredana and Grant himself had worn braided trousers. That fact I had noticed."

He broke off and looked quizzically at Sir Austin. "You see, I began by the inclusion of Grant even—the man who had supplied me with a great deal of the most vital information. In the meantime, however, I had had a stroke of luck. Annette Mornay had come to me for help. I dangled Loredana in front of her purposely, and quite legitimately, as another possible ally, who would assist her to avenge her lover. She went to him as I hoped that she would. Judge of her consternation and horror when she met him. I think that they recognized each other, but neither gave the slightest sign to that effect. When Annette left she was faced with a terrifying problem, but before she could escape very far, the 'Wolf', her old compatriot, and, I think, former lover, had struck, and her lips were sealed for ever. It was a clever move on his part to bring in the orange-and-black silk again. He hoisted you that time, Major Wyatt, with your own petard!

"I then turned my attention to the question of Da Costa's invitation ticket, and when I learned that the only persons who could be said to have had reasonable access to it were the President, Da Costa himself, and his secretary, Gerald Twining, I commenced to realize that the accumulation of evidence was beginning to point very forcibly in one direction. Culminating confirmation of my theory came rather strangely and also rather suddenly. Can you guess how?"

The Commissioner and the other two listeners shook their heads at Bathurst's question.

"Well, I was in the 'Florizel' one day, and I happened to turn my head carelessly towards the two gentlemen of San Jonquilo. They were standing close together, and their bodies, in a certain attitude and position, were extraordinarily similar. I realized how a beard and a monocle would go a long way towards transforming one of them to the other. When the attempts on my life started and information came from Loredana that he was being favoured with like attentions, I felt pretty confident that my little problem was uncomfortably close to solution. You know how I dragged him from his cover—it was a near thing while it lasted, but there you are. . . ."

Bathurst reached to the table for his glass, and the Commissioner pushed it towards him.

"A thoroughly interesting case, Sir Austin, and perhaps, taking into consideration moral values, the unluckiest person of the affair has been the Sergeant here. I am sorry that he failed to attain his object. Such devotion to a cause deserved success."

"Thank you, Mr. Bathurst," replied the Sergeant. "In this life, however, it's been proved to me, on innumerable occasions, that neither merit nor hard work leads a man to the top, of a certainty. He's got to have something else besides. You English have a saying that 'there's always room at the top'. That's true—but I've noticed that there's much more room down below, and many an inferior man reaches a position of eminence and gives orders to his superiors, while a first-class man lingers in the ruck. The luck hasn't run my way—that's all. If it had . . ." He shrugged his shoulders fatalistically and rose from his chair. Wyatt rose with him.

Sir Austin Kemble's cough was well-timed and of just the right strength. About to give an order, he remembered just in time the most objectionable philosophy that Perpignan had advanced, and checked himself hastily.

"I don't want to worry you now, Bathurst," he said instead; "you're tired. I'll pop in and see you again some time to-morrow evening. That suit you all right?"

Anthony smiled acquiescence. "Come to dinner, Sir Austin. Emily will show you what a splendid cook she is. Only *don't* expert either jugged or roast hare."

Sir Austin stared at the injunction. "As it happens, I'm no lover of hare, Bathurst—either—"

"It's rather a sore point these days, with Emily, too," observed Mr. Bathurst.

THE END